With Me
a novel

GABBIE S. DURAN

Copyright © 2014 by Gabbie S. Duran
Editing by Edee M. Fallon, Mad Spark Editing
Cover art by Melissa Gill at MGBookcovers
Interior book design and formatting by JT Formatting

Printed in the United States of America
First Edition: February 2014
Library of Congress Cataloging-in-Publication Data

www.facebook.com/authorgabbiesduran

Duran, Gabbie S.
  With Me/Gabbie S. Duran – 1st ed
    ISBN-13: 978-0615956060
    ISBN-10: 0615956068

1. With Me—Fiction   2. Fiction—Romance
3. Fiction—Contemporary Romance

*To everyone who serves, or who have served,
and to the families that stay behind to wait;
thank you for your service.*

Chapter 1

Kasey

"ARE YOU SURE your parents are okay with me being here?" Joseph asks for the second time, the hesitation clear in his voice.

"Of course," I lie to him, giving him a reassuring smile.

Truthfully, my parents don't know he's here, but neither are they, which is the reason why he's here now. Actually, it's not the true reason. He's here because I'm cooking dinner for him tonight. This is the last night before he leaves for boot camp. I've been planning it for a month now, since the day I discovered I wasn't going to be able to go with my parents to their annual bible retreat.

They've gone every year since I was born, but it's the first year I'm unable to go due to work. I couldn't get the weekend off since a co-worker is on maternity leave, which for me was a sign from God. It gave me the opportunity to cook dinner for Joseph. I know I should feel guilty for not going, but

I don't. I'd much rather be here with him right now. Joseph looks nervous, but I can't blame him. He knows I'm not allowed to have boys over without my parents present.

"Now, I'll ask again. Do you want pop or water?" I ask him holding up one of each in my hands, trying to change the subject.

He looks over in my direction and smiles before saying, "Pop would be great, thank you. I really doubt I'm going to get to drink one for the next three months," he answers, making me smile.

I head to the table, taking a seat as I place his soda in front of him. As I'm about to start saying grace he picks up his fork and starts digging into his meal. We always say grace in my house, but I assume by the way that he is looking up at me, confused, they don't at his house.

I give him a forced smile and he goes back to eating. I bow my head and say a quick prayer, hoping he doesn't take notice. When done, I grab my own fork and join Joseph in eating.

When dinner is done, with Joseph's help, I wash up the dishes.

Joseph walks into the living room, forcing me to follow, and I'm already growing disappointed that he already wants to leave. He abruptly turns to face me, making me crash into his chest. He catches me as I sway, his eyes already bearing down at me. "Thanks for dinner, Kasey. It really means a lot to me."

Not wanting him to leave so soon, I abruptly say, "You don't have to leave yet. Do you want to stay a little longer and keep talking?" I wait, nervously biting my lip, hoping he'll say yes.

My stomach is in knots as I wait the few seconds for his answer. He nervously looks around the room, as if he's expecting my parents to randomly surprise us with their presence.

"Sure."

I release the breath I was holding and walk over to the couch, taking a seat. When he joins me, I begin to grow anxious. I don't know how to act around him. Running my sweating palms on my jeans, I begin to bite on my lip, hoping that he doesn't notice how nervous I really am at this moment.

"So what do you plan on doing this summer?" he asks, as he leans back on the couch, as I begin to relax.

With a shrug of my shoulders, I answer him. "Work, until I start college here in Savannah. I plan on cutting back my hours once I start school, though," I reply, already feeling the blush on my cheeks as I catch myself rambling on.

I've always felt nervous around Joseph, no matter how comfortable he tries to make me feel. It's the reaction I've had since the first day I laid eyes on him. I was only eleven and instantly became infatuated with the new boy next door. It was also the day he caught me spying on him. With a simple wave I was hooked. That day I became the shyest ninny in the world, even more so when he came over to say hi.

Being that my parents are extremely religious, I was never allowed to date. So as the days went by, my schoolgirl crush for Joseph only increased, never to become anything more. Knowing I never had a chance didn't stop me from dreaming, but left me to watch as he dated every other girl that threw herself at him, and it hurt.

However, he never did ignore me. His excuse being: I was the girl next door, it was his obligation to look out for me. I didn't know whether to take it as a compliment or as an insult. Either way, I accepted it.

Hating the awkward silence in the room, I begin to talk, "So, are you nervous about boot camp?"

He considers the question for a moment before answering, "A little. I hate not knowing what to expect. I mean, they've told me what to expect, but it's not the same as experiencing it."

"What time do you leave in the morning?" I quietly ask.

"Early. My recruiter said he'd pick me up around five a.m. I have to be on the plane by eight."

Raising my eyebrows at him, I say, "Wow, that's really early."

He shrugs his shoulders. "I guess I better get used to it. I hear we have to wake up before the sun comes up and you don't go to sleep until it's down," he says, chuckling at the same time.

I don't know how he can find it so amusing. If it were I in his situation, I would be frightened, I think to myself.

"Well, I better go. It's getting really late and I know I shouldn't keep you up. You've done enough for me already," he says as he stands up, forcing me to do the same.

I hate that he seems in such a hurry to leave, but it's probably because he already has other plans. I feel disappointed he's leaving. I almost want to blame myself for being so boring. It's probably the reason why he wants to leave.

As I lead him to the door, distracted by my self-pity, I crash into his chest, causing me to look up at him. I'm so embarrassed by my awkwardness, that my body becomes paralyzed to the spot as our eyes meet. My stomach feels like it contains a hundred different butterflies flying around in it.

I'm trying to swallow the nervous lump now lodged in my throat as I anxiously hold my breath, waiting for something to happen. His eyes grow dark and he slowly lowers his head down towards mine; our lips gently meeting as he kisses me.

I am surprised by this kiss. I've never been kissed before,

so I don't know what to expect, or even know what to do. With my hands already on his chest, I wrap my fingers into his shirt, needing to hold onto something to prevent my body from falling to the ground. My legs are on the verge of collapsing from feeling weak.

The warmth of his lips leaves me both scared and apprehensive. What if I'm doing it wrong? I've seen plenty of people kiss before at school and it never looked like this.

His lips are gentle and soft against mine. I suddenly feel his tongue gently nudge against my lips, wanting entrance. Opening up for him, his tongue meets mine and with my hands still gripping at his shirt, I pull him closer.

Closing my eyes, I let the sensation of our touch take over, our tongues gliding slowly against each other. I feel his hands come up to cradle my head in his palms, tilting my head so he can take and demand more of my mouth. I can taste him completely. This, the way he's kissing me, is the way I've seen people kiss and now I know why they do it so often. I can already tell I'm addicted to it.

Slowly I match his movements inside my mouth. I'm praying I'm doing them right.

I feel him slowly pull away, making me whimper at the loss. Why did he stop? I must have done something wrong. I didn't want to disappoint him.

Slowly opening my eyes, I can see him breathing as heavy as I am. Our chests are rising and falling, trying to catch our breaths, as he rests his forehead against mine. My heart is racing from the passion rising in me. I can barely keep my breathing under control.

"I've waited so long to be able to do that," he declares, his eyes intensely staring down at me.

My body is still humming from our kiss and I'm weaker

than before. I'm still speechless as I pull him back down to return to kissing him. He returns the kiss, this time much more fiercely. When I feel him pull back, severing our kiss, I whimper from the loss.

"I better leave now, Kasey, before I end up doing something I'm going to regret," he quietly growls, as he tries to push my body away. I don't let him, keeping a firm grip on his shirt to hold him in place.

"Please don't leave. Not now," I whisper to him, practically begging.

I don't know why I want him to stay, but deep down inside I know that I don't want him to leave. Not tonight.

"Are you sure, Kasey? I won't be able to control myself if you don't let me leave right now," he says, his voice sounding hesitant and restrained. Almost as if he fears I'd tell him otherwise.

I nod my head to answer his question. I grab for his hand and start to pull him towards my bedroom, already comprehending what I want from him. I need to know that he'll be mine, even if it's only for one night.

The second we enter my bedroom he wraps his arms around my waist, pulling me up against his body. My feet are now dangling off the ground and I can only hold on to him as he walks us backwards towards my bed. I feel my legs hit the edge, our bodies descending onto the bed as he comes down with me.

As he breaks our kiss, his lips slowly start trailing down my neck. His kisses leave a heated trail behind and I tilt my head, giving him better access to tantalize me. I feel his hand slowly starting to tease its way up my stomach, grazing my skin with his palm. It's scorching a trail to match the heat of his lips along the way. My body feels like it's on fire from his touch.

Wanting to feel more of his body, my hands start to explore him; loving the way his body feels against my palms. His skin feels smooth and warm and I crave to feel it against my own.

I frantically start to yank his shirt off and he does the same with mine, ridding us of the barriers. Our chests meet and the warmth of his body above mine makes me lose all control.

Slamming his lips onto mine, my hands start roaming up and down his back. The feeling of his warm skin against my hands is amazing and I want to feel more. I lower my hands and feeling brave, I skim them across his ass. I feel him chuckle against my mouth and I know I shouldn't have done it. Quickly, I lift my hands away, as if they were burned.

"I'm sorry, Kasey. I didn't mean to laugh at you. I like that you did it, that's all." His deep voice, whispering into my ear, causes a shiver to travel through me, all the way down to my toes.

He goes back to kissing his way down my neck. If my body didn't already feel like it was on fire, I'm pretty sure I would have turned beet red from his comment. Before I even have time to feel ashamed of what I did, his hand reaches under my back and I feel the clasp of my bra being undone. He pulls my bra completely off me and tosses it aside, leaving me naked from the waist up.

With the light of the streetlamp outside my window, I watch as his eyes roam up and down my body. The hunger evident in his eyes should frighten me, but I feel the same way as him

The excitement rebuilds within me when he lowers his mouth down to one of my breasts. The feel of his lips lightly brushing my nipple, teases me, until I feel him take it into his mouth sucking it softly, causing a moan to escape from my lips. When his mouth starts sucking harder, I'm forced to grab for his head, afraid he might stop.

He moves his mouth to the other, my back arching up, thrusting myself at him. My fingers are now digging into his ruffled hair, gripping it for dear life. The noises that are coming from me are surprising myself, but I can't control them.

When he stops, he brings his head up to look down at me, before his hands reach for the button of my jeans to undo them. Still intensely peering down at me, his hooded eyes are strongly focused on my own, as if he's waiting for me to stop him. But I don't. I can't.

He lifts his body completely away and uses both hands to pull my jeans off, taking my panties with them. I'm already barefoot, preferring to not wear shoes while in the house, so my pants easily slip off.

Laying there, staring back at him, I take him in. His body is long and lean. His hair looking disheveled from my hands, and his eyes are dark with hunger as he stands tall peering back at me. His lips are turned up in a sensual smile. Slowly, he unbuttons his jeans, his eyes never leaving mine. I would have preferred to do it myself, but right now I'm not sure I would be able to. I lie there, taking in every inch of his body as he removes the last of his clothing. When he's done, I catch one quick glimpse of his erection standing long and tall. My eyes go wide when I see how big he is. I'm left a little scared.

Gradually, he makes his way back to the bed, and I slowly scoot up so I'm in the middle. He climbs back on top of me, my legs opening to allow his body to come down on mine. My hands start feeling every inch of his naked body, with my fingertips grazing his skin. It's when I feel something hard nudge against my thigh that I grow frightened again. But I'm soon distracted as he starts kissing me, making all of my fear quickly disappear. It's replaced with desire. Our kiss grows passionate and I start to feel an ache between my legs.

The teasing of his hand as it skims my skin intensifies the desire that I'm still unfamiliar with. His hand finds it's way under my back and down under my ass; forcing me to lift up to him. At the same time I feel something nudge at the opening between my legs, as if demanding entrance, but just as quickly I feel him enter me in one quick thrust.

I let out a loud scream as I feel myself being stretched completely. A slight burn quickly follows. My hands reach for his shoulders to hold onto him, my nails digging into the skin from the pain I'm feeling at this moment. My face meets the crook of his neck as I try to catch my breath, hoping it will subside soon.

I feel his body grow rigid and tense. "Oh shit, Kasey. I'm sorry. I should have been gentler with you. I forgot this is your first time," I hear him whisper into my ear as he lies above me, his warm breath against my skin.

When he attempts to shift himself, I stop him, holding him tight. "Please, don't move," I plead to him, scared if he moves the pain will only increase. This is nothing like the ache I felt earlier.

Still rigid above me, I can feel his warm breath on my neck. I lay there not knowing what to do next. "Kasey, let me know when I can move. I don't want to hurt you again," he desperately pleads into the hollow of my neck, his voice sounding strained.

Squeezing my eyes shut, I lay underneath him, waiting for the pain to subside. It only takes a couple of seconds for the pain to slowly disappear. I still feel full from having him inside me, but when I try moving my hips a little, it starts to feel better.

I hear Joseph groan, as if he's in pain as well. "Did I hurt you, Joseph? I'm sorry," I apologetically whisper to him.

He chuckles against my neck, before kissing my skin, sending a shiver down my body. "It's not pain I'm in, Kasey. Unless you call torturing me when you wiggle like that, pain. Then yes, I am," he says, almost laughing.

Confused why he'd find the situation amusing, I lift my hips up to test how I feel, but I soon discover that he must have lost his patience. He starts to slowly thrust inside of me, sending a wave of pleasure up my body, building it more and more as he continues.

My legs voluntarily wrap around his waist, wanting to feel closer to him; more than we already are. Eventually I find a rhythm that matches his, making the desire inside me build higher and higher. It increases with each minute that goes by and eventually I begin to grow frightened by it.

"Joseph, you have to stop. I think something is wrong," I tell him.

He obeys, coming to a complete stop above me, his worried eyes looking down at me. "What's wrong, Kasey? Am I hurting you?" he fearfully asks, his eyes looking frantic at this point.

"No, it's not pain I feel, but something else. I can't explain it," I whisper to him, unsure of what more I can explain. I feel him let out a gush of air that he was clearly holding in.

"Kasey, I think I was going to make you finish," he explains with a satisfied smile spreading across his face. It only confuses me more. "I don't understand," I confusedly respond, but when he kisses me, I completely forget what I was trying to explain as our tongues slowly glide against one another. His hips start to resume their rocking. "Just let go, Kasey. It will feel good, I promise."

I still don't understand his meaning, but the feeling soon builds as he returns to kissing me, making me close my eyes. Within minutes my body grows tight and I just let go. I feel as if I'm exploding from inside, but just as quickly being lifted off the ground and ascending into the clouds. The sensation continues for what feels like minutes.

My eyes are still closed, but I can feel Joseph's body grow tight over me. His thrusting becoming faster before he yells out my name as he tries to muffle it against my neck. I feel him thrust one last time against my core before his body comes to a stop above mine. I open my eyes and I'm looking into dark eyes that are staring back down at me.

We're both breathing heavy, almost gasping for air. My heart feels like I've just run a marathon. He brings his lips to mine, kissing me gently. His hand wipes away my sweat filled hair that is on my forehead, pushing it back before he says, "That was amazing, Kasey. It's never felt that way before with anybody."

Instead of being satisfied with his words, they pierce my heart. I know I'm not his first; I'm most likely not going to be his last. The words hurt, even though he was trying to tell me how special it was. I simply force myself to swallow the lump of disappointment I feel deep down inside and turn my face away.

I'm still disappointed when he asks, "Did I say something wrong?"

The only thing I can say is, "No." Hating the way his words make me feel.

Rolling himself off my body, he pulls me with him, draping me across his chest. Wrapping me in his arms, he tightens his hold on me and I feel comforted and safe. He buries his face into my hair, leaving my face to find a spot on his shoulder. Within minutes I feel his breathing begin to calm. By the shallow rise and fall of his chest, I know he's fallen asleep. His earlier words keep repeating in my head, as if they are mocking me, and there is nothing I can do about them.

We eventually make love one more time. Joseph claimed he couldn't leave without saying goodbye, but when we began to kiss, it grew passionate, resulting in our lovemaking. I know I shouldn't have given in, but since my body already had a taste of the pleasure he'd given me, I couldn't resist taking it once more. He was as gentle as the first time and just as generous in bringing me pleasure. But deep down inside, my heart was aching the whole time.

When I finally wake up, the sun is shining through my window, gleaming into my eyes. I am alone in bed. The scent of Joseph is still on my sheets, along with the memory of our night together; a memory I will treasure forever.

Chapter 2

Joseph

Five Years Later...

"MAN, IT'S ABOUT time you were finally able to get back here to visit. It feels like it's been forever since I've seen you," my best friend Mark says to me as we walk down the aisles of the Farmers Market he's brought me to.

"It's only been a year since we've seen each other," I remind him, but it does feel like a long time since I've seen him last. I guess it's expected when you are away overseas. The days seem longer and you start to miss the people you care about the most when you're in the desert surrounded by other Marines in the same boat.

Military life *can* suck sometimes, but it's the only life I know.

"So what's new in your life? The last couple of times we've talked it's been quick, so we haven't been able to catch up. You still with that girl you hooked up with a couple of years ago in Vegas?" he skeptically asks, looking as if he really doesn't care what the answer will be regardless.

"Her name is Elizabeth and yes, we're still together."

Apparently not expecting that particular answer, his eyes go wide. "Oh. Really? When you brought her along on the last visit, I was pretty sure she would've dumped your ass. Especially after the little tantrum she threw when you mentioned you were considering re-enlisting. I thought for sure the minute you signed the papers she would've been a goner," he announces, making me remember how pissed Elizabeth was when I told her. He's right; she almost did leave, but changed her mind when I told her there was no changing my decision.

It had been a year and a half ago, when I had gone to visit Mark, before shipping out to Afghanistan. I wanted to make sure I visited with Mark and Ashley one final time. Elizabeth wasn't too happy with the idea of me leaving her behind, so I brought her along with me. I thought she'd be excited about meeting them, but apparently I was wrong, considering the way she acted the entire trip.

The thought causes me to grimace. "She's gotten over it," I answer him, lying through my teeth. "Actually, it's a good thing you've brought her up. I've been meaning to ask you something, but I thought I should ask in person," I say to him, watching as his face grows worried. "I finally popped the question to Elizabeth and we're getting married. I was wondering if you'd be my best man?" I nervously ask him.

He abruptly stops walking. The shock of my question is clear on his face. His mouth hangs open while he continues to stand and stare at me. This expression isn't a good one. It's the one he gives when he thinks someone has lost their mind and I'm pretty sure that's what he's thinking of me right now.

Over the past five years I've known Mark, I've seen that

look plenty of times. He's my best friend, having met him the first day I shipped out to boot camp. We were lined up next to each other through the gruesomeness of processing, before finally being put on a bus that would lead us to the next three months of hell.

Being placed in the same platoon, stationed at the same base when we were done, and even placed doing the same job, you would have thought we were related and they were trying to keep us together. Some people have even mistaken us for actual brothers several times because we also looked alike, but being that I didn't have any actual siblings, he was the closest thing I had to one. So I was glad to call him my best friend.

The difference between us today is Mark is no longer in the military. Not by choice, but by force when he was medically discharged from an injury two years ago. He took it happily though. By then he had found Ashley and wanted to marry her and start a family right way. I, on the other hand, had re-enlisted when my four years were up, giving me a ticket straight overseas. I still kept in touch when I was able to, which was harder now than I would want it to be.

Looking back at Mark, waiting for his answer, he asks, "Are you sure she's the one dude? Like the one you can't live without?" His questions make me doubt my own decision to get married.

Pondering his questions, I silently answer to myself, no she isn't the one I couldn't live without. That girl I left behind long ago and I've haven't seen her since, but by the time I realized it, it was too late to do anything about it. She was gone.

Shrugging my shoulders at him, I reply, "I don't know what difference it makes. We've been together for a while and I actually love her." Although I say the words, right now I'm not feeling as if I do. I blame him for making me doubt myself.

It has to be the reason why I feel this way.

"Plus, I think it's time I grow up and settle down. I see you and Ashley and I want that. Since Elizabeth has been riding my ass about our relationship, I figured I'd pop the question," I answer around the lump that's somehow formed in my throat.

That was one of the issues with Elizabeth. In this last year I've been gone, every time we spoke, she wouldn't hesitate to ask if there would ever be a serious future for us. With every phone call or video chat, she made me realize it was time I grew up and settled down, so I made the decision and I asked her to marry me when I finally got back.

With a curt nod, Mark begins to walking, leaving me to follow. "I don't know, man. Don't you think you're rushing into this?" he skeptically asks. "When you first met her, it was rocky from the beginning. I don't understand how you'd want to marry someone who you spend most of your time arguing with? Plus, you haven't been together that long," he argues, speaking his case.

If his intention was to make me feel like shit about the whole situation, he accomplished it, but I can't blame him for having his hesitations about Elizabeth. She didn't really make such a good impression the last time he'd seen her.

Chuckling at his honesty, while shaking my head, I respond, "We've been together for almost two years now. I think having a long distance relationship with her is the reason why it's so rocky. It was hard on her to only see me through a video screen. Since she's still going to school in Vegas, she couldn't move in with me when I got back. Can you blame the girl for wanting to get a college degree?" I feel the need to defend her.

He purses his lips and stays silent, giving me the opportunity to continue.

"I think once she's graduated and we can move in together, things will be better. She isn't all that bad once you *really* get to know her. You'll see."

Mark considers my response, shrugging his shoulder as he keeps walking. "Alright man, whatever makes you happy. I'm here for you no matter what," he utters.

Giving him a stern nod, we continue walking though the small crowd that is slowly starting to dispense. Mark picked me up only a couple of hours ago from the airport. I got back almost a week ago, being forced to take almost a month of leave, I already knew I wanted to come visit with Mark in Wisconsin. It's where he now lived with his wife. So here I am.

"Why are we here again?" I ask Mark, looking around confused why we'd even be in a Farmers Market of all places. It seems kind of out of place for Mark.

"Ever since Ashley found out she was pregnant she been trying to eat healthier for the baby. She prefers organic shit right now and since the market is close to the house, she makes me come here. Happy wife, happy life," he says giving me a mischievous smile. "You better remember that since you plan on taking the plunge," he says in more of a mumbling rant than a statement.

Skeptically raising my eyebrow, I keep walking a couple of steps as Mark goes over to a booth with vegetables lining the tables. As he starts looking through what look like squash, my eyes wander to a booth that is selling handmade jewelry. Deciding I should pick something out for Elizabeth, I head in that direction.

I start walking over to the booth, but I'm soon hit by something in the legs. When I look down, I see a little girl looking at me with a frightened face, as if she's worried she's done something wrong. She's staring up at me with the brightest blue eyes a little girl can have. She's small, only coming to below my waist, with a set of loose curls that flow down her back.

"Whoa there, little girl," I say to her as I continue to stare into her wide blue eyes, causing me to think about a set of blue eyes that still haunt me to this day; the memory of a girl I still miss. I see the little girl's eyes avert to something on the ground, drawing my eyes down too. I bend down into a crouch to pick up what she's dropped for her. It's a small bottle filled with juice and when I take a closer look, it makes me smile.

"Cherry apple cider. Sounds like an interesting flavor. Is it any good?" I curiously ask her as I tilt my head, waiting for a response.

"My mommy always tells me I shouldn't speak to strangers," she declares, lifting her chin and squaring her shoulders, trying to make herself look bigger.

I simply chuckle, handing the small bottle to her. Her little hands reach out to take it from me, grasping it against her chest. "Thank you," she says, clutching the bottle tightly.

"Well, your mommy is right, you shouldn't speak to strangers," I tell her with a smile to try to calm her.

I'm still crouched down. I don't want to frighten her any further, so I stay down to be able to look her directly in the eyes. The shock must have already worn off because she smiles back; the sweetest smile I've ever seen.

Knowing I really shouldn't be encouraging her any further to speak to strangers, I still have to ask, "*Where is your mommy?*" I do it more for reassurance she isn't wandering around alone.

She looks past me and I take a quick glance over my shoulder at her line of view, seeing several people visiting the booths lined along the walkway.

I turn my head back towards her when she answers.

"She's at her booth. She let me go get my drink, but I'm supposed to go straight there and back, not stopping to talk to strangers. I already know I've disobeyed her by speaking with you," she says as her lips go into a flat line and her shoulders slump forward.

As I'm about to stand up, I hear someone shout behind me, "Josephina, didn't I tell you not to speak to strangers," the voice coming out in a scorn, my mind instantly recognizing it. It's the same voice I grew up listening to; the one I miss so much. It's the voice that belongs to the memories that haunt me in my dreams almost every night when I fall asleep, keeping me from wanting to wake up. Sleep is the only way I can hold onto those memories.

I want to see with my own eyes if it's really her, so I force myself to stand, turning my body to look in the direction of the woman's voice. When I see her, it only confirms what I believed as she walks in my direction. It's Kasey. The same Kasey I left behind so many years ago, a regret I still have to this day.

She doesn't notice me immediately, going directly to the little girl standing in front of me. When she does, her body freezes in place. She grows rigid, her eyes going wide in shock when she sees my face.

It matches how I feel as we stand there staring at each other. Fully taking her in, I notice not much has changed, but she does look more mature.

I feel as though my heart has dropped into the pit of my stomach as I say, "Hello, Kasey," my eyes narrowing down at her.

I should feel excited to see her, but for some odd reason

it's the opposite. I feel confused and full of questions. She quickly tugs the little girl to her side, protectively wrapping her arm around her. I can see the little girl wince from the action. It looks as if Kasey is trying to guard her from me as I look down at both of them.

"Mommy, you know this man?" the little girl enthusiastically asks, looking up to Kasey, waiting for an answer. It makes me look at her as well, as I wait for her response. In the corner of my eye I can see the little girl looking back and forth between the two of us, confused and curious at the same time.

"Joseph, what are you doing here?" she asks, sounding fearful; her voice breaking with every word, as she keeps her eyes still locked onto mine.

The little girl suddenly grows excited. "Your name is Joseph? That sounds like my name. My name is Josephina. Doesn't his name sound like mine, mommy?" Her eyes are wide with excitement as she looks back up to Kasey, waiting for a response.

Taking in the declaration, it occurs to me that we do have similar names. Thinking it's only a coincidence, I look down at her, fully taking the little girl in. Of course she's small, but finally analyzing her, I realize she must be at least four or five years old.

"Yes, sweetheart, it sounds like your name," she calmly states through clenched teeth. The animosity is clear in her eyes as they glare back at me; her body still rigid.

Kasey breaks our eye contact, lowering her body so she's looking directly into Josephina's now. "Go back to the booth and wait there with Alley. I'll be there in a moment."

I hear a grumble come from the little girl, but when Kasey stands up she nudges her in the direction of the booths behind us, not giving her a choice to stay. The little girl takes a couple of steps before turning around to look back at us. "Since *technically* you knew this man mommy, he wasn't a stranger, so I'm not in trouble right?" she tries clarifying to her mother, but Kasey disagrees. "He was still considered a stranger being you don't know him. Now go wait with Alley like I ordered and we'll discuss your punishment when we get home," Kasey announces, pointing her finger in the direction of the booths.

The little girl's face quickly grows disappointed before saying, "I know what that means. I'll be in timeout when I get home for sure," she grumbles as she turns and walks in the direction that Kasey pointed her to.

I hear Mark laughing behind me. "She's a smart little girl," he says, surprising me.

Kasey glares at him, her silent reprimand of his comment scaring even myself. Mark clears his throat, looking off into another direction, giving me a chance to take a couple steps closer to Kasey. She tries to step away, but I gently grab onto her arm to keep her from moving. I see her suck in her breath and I can practically see her pupils dilating from fear. *Why?*

Thinking she's afraid of me, I try to reassure her. "Kasey, please. You know I would never hurt you," I tell her, feeling her body quickly relax. Not completely though, but enough to let me know that she still trusts me.

"I'm surprised to see you again, Joseph, that's all," she answers, trying to sound calm, but her voice is portraying her deception, and by the way her eyes keep averting towards the direction of where she sent the little girl, I know something is wrong.

"I won't lie. I'm surprised to see you as well. I never thought I would see you again," I tell her, tilting my head down at her blue eyes, losing myself in them.

Her face grows saddened. "I didn't think I'd ever see you

21

again either," she says, her voice matching the sorrow in her face. Her expression is telling me she feels torn and broken over her words. Making me wonder… *Why is she reacting this way?*

Remembering the reason why I didn't want her to run, I ask, "Is there something you need to tell me, Kasey?" My eyes narrow down at her, demanding an answer.

Her eyes grow wider, her body returning to its tense state, but she stays silent for a couple of seconds, as if refusing to answer. Almost at a whisper, for only her and I to hear, she replies. "I don't want to talk about it here," she says, looking in Mark's direction, as if he's the reason she didn't want to answer. I look back at Mark confused, wondering if she knows him. However, from seeing the same confusion on his face at seeing Kasey, I'm pretty sure they don't know each other.

Looking back at her, I try again. "Why did you leave, Kasey?"

Her face turns stunned. "You *left* me first, if I recall. I waited for you, and you never came," she utters.

"What do you mean I never came? I did go back and you were already gone."

"I wrote to you, waiting for you to come to me and you never did," she declares.

"Wait, I'm confused. When did you write?" I ask her, now more confused than before. Searching my mind, I know I never got any letters from her.

"Man, this is one interesting conversation." Mark's sarcastic tone rings out, making Kasey and I look in his direction. I shoot him with a glare and when his eyes go wide, I know I've made my point. He simply lifts his shoulder, a typical response from Mark.

"Look, I have to get back to my daughter," she says, trying to tug her arm from my hand. I tighten my grip enough to hold onto her, refusing to let go.

"No, Kasey. I'm pretty sure we need to talk," I repeat.

She shakes her head at me. "Not here," she says again. .

"Then where? Because we *are* going to talk. I need to know why you left."

"I didn't have a choice, Joseph," she insists, sounding bitter. "I was forced to leave."

Taken aback by her answer, I keep trying to comprehend what she means. It isn't what I was told when I went back looking for her. "I did go back, Kasey. Your parents told me you left for college out of state, but they wouldn't tell me where," I try explaining.

She snickers. "Of course they would say that," she disappointingly grumbles.

"Then where did you go?" I ask her.

She looks in Mark's direction, looking hesitant as to whether to reply, but finally looks back at me as she answers. "I had to leave because of what happened the night before you left. I was left with no choice," she whispers, so only I can hear.

"You keep saying you didn't have a choice, but you're still not making any sense, Kasey. Why wouldn't you have a choice?" I ask her, forcing myself to try and understand.

Her silence makes me think, it occurs to me, the realization hitting me like a ton of bricks as I remember back to that night. The fear has dropped into the pit of my stomach as I take in the only explanation that would force her to leave.

Looking back in the direction of where the little girl left, I ask, "How old is she, Kasey?" I force myself to ask around the shock taking over my body.

She looks hesitant to answer, but then does, "She turned

four in March." Her eyes grow glassy from the tears building up.

Taking in her answer, I quickly do the math in my head, confirming what I was thinking; Josephina is my daughter.

I feel Kasey try to yank her arm from my grip, but I continue holding onto her, refusing to let her go. "Why didn't you tell me?" I growl at her, no longer being able to control the anger coursing inside of me. I want answers and I want them now.

She frantically looks around. "I already told you. I'm not talking about it here," she says, as she finally manages to free her arm from my grip. She tries to walk around me, but I keep her planted to the spot when I lift my arm out to block her way.

"If not now, then when? Because whether you want to or not, Kasey, *we are* going to talk about this. I had a right to know."

She looks in the direction of the street, taking her lip in between her teeth, nervously chewing on it for a moment before facing me once more. "See that park?" she says, pointing her chin in the direction across the street. I look to see a park. "I always take Josephina to it after I've packed up, usually around two. You can meet us there."

Knowing I have no other choice by the look on her face, I simply nod my head in agreement, lowering my arm to let her walk away. I watch her stroll away without another word, blending into the small crowd until she steps into a tented booth.

"Care to explain who that was, or what just happened?" I hear Mark say at my side, breaking through the many scenarios traveling through my mind. I watch Kasey disappear into a tent as I answer, "That was the old neighbor from Savannah I told you about. And I'm pretty sure that little girl is my daughter," I say in disbelief, still trying to absorb the shock of the situation.

My heart feels like it's dropped into the pit of my stomach as I say it and it's making me feel like shit. The problem is, I don't know who's to blame.

Mark only whistles before saying, "I sure hope Elizabeth likes kids."

Chapter 3

Kasey

THE TIME FOR me to start packing up my items came faster than I wanted. Some days it seems like the day drags on. Others, like today, can go by faster than I wish them to go. Today was one of those days I felt like I wanted time to completely stop.

I wasn't ready to face Joseph yet. I wasn't prepared to explain Josephina to him anymore. That time had disappeared long ago when I had desperately waited for him to show up. Of course, I had just as many questions as he had for me, but my questions had long been pushed away. I'd faced the reality that I might never see him again, forcing myself to realize he would never come looking for me; choosing to believe he never wanted anything to do with us.

At least, that is what I told myself.

I had given up on Joseph. Given up the notion that he would show up like some knight in shining armor to rescue

Josephina and I; it never happened

Forcing myself to return my focus on packing, I let out a sigh, wishing again that time would slow down. Normally I would want to hurry to put everything away, excited to finally be done with the day so I can take Josephina to the park, but today was the opposite because I know Joseph will be there waiting. At least, I think he will be.

Giving myself the excuse that I'm taking my time so I don't misplace anything, I make sure everything is packed and ready to go for next week. I slow my pace a little, only because I'm dreading seeing Joseph again.

Even as I keep packing, I keep wondering to myself... *What is he doing here? Was he purposely looking for us?* Shaking the second thought from my mind, I have to tell myself that he wasn't. If he had chosen to look for us, he would have done it a long time ago. He should have done it when Josephina and I really needed him, when I had begged him to come to us.

"Mommy, hurry. You're taking too long," Josephina whines up at me as she tugs on the hem of my shirt. "I really want to go play now."

Sighing, I know that I've already made her wait longer than I should, so I quickly start to pack the last of the items into the container in front of me. Taking the box back to my small SUV, I lock it up and grab a hold of Josephina's tiny hand, leading her straight towards the park.

I've been bringing her to this park since she was a toddler; when I first started selling my soaps at the local Farmers Market. I didn't have a choice but to bring her with me every Saturday. I didn't know anyone at that time being that it was only Josephina and I back then. I moved to Madison in hopes of providing a better future for the both of us.

The closer we get to the park, the more my stomach is beginning to turn. The nerves are starting to build up with every step I take, knowing Joseph will be there waiting for us.

The sight of him sitting at a picnic table, his head hung low facing the ground and his elbows resting on his knees, tugs at my heart. I can see the stress rolling off him as he runs one hand back and forth across his nearly bald head. That was the first change I noticed about Joseph. Growing up he always had a full head of hair. Now he had it cut so short all over, it practically looked like he was bald. It made him look more masculine, instead of the young boy I remembered.

Even with the distance between us, I can tell he's concentrating hard, making his body look tense and worried. Seeing him like that, knowing the reason why, hurts me just as badly. I never meant for him to find out this way, but I never thought he'd come back into our lives.

Josephina sees him, excitedly shouting, "Look mommy, it's your friend," before letting go of my hand and bolting straight for Joseph.

He must have heard her because his head snaps up and when he spots her running towards him, his face lights up, smiling. It's the kind of smile that could light up a dark cloudy day.

Walking faster to catch up to them, I can already hear Josephina asking the many questions that I knew she would; her curious little mind always wanting answers. She had begun asking me questions when we returned to my booth, but I kept telling her I couldn't answer them at the moment, earning me a very disappointed scowl. She knew I was purposely avoiding her questions.

It isn't that I didn't want her to know the truth; I just didn't know *how* to tell her. Up until now she's been told she didn't have a dad, like every other child does, *because she was special*. I know it wasn't the answer she deserved, but it was the only answer that I could ever give her. I didn't know what had happened with Joseph. Even now, I still don't know. And I accepted that.

The first question I hear come from her mouth is, "How do you know my mommy?" The moment she finishes saying it, I grow worried about his answer; leaving me fixed to the spot I'm standing in, hoping that he doesn't say more than necessary.

"Your mommy used to live next door to me when we were little," he answers, his voice sounding soft and gentle as he speaks to her.

Josephina's eyes light up. "You grew up on a farm too?" she says, the excitement clear in her voice as she asks the question, surprising Joseph.

Josephina has never known the truth of where I *really* grew up. The only place she knew of was the place she was born, which happens to be a farm. So of course it would be the place she would envision that I grew up as well. Knowing I need to stop her curiosity before Joseph can reveal the truth, I say, "Josephina, I don't think it's very polite to bombard Joseph with questions."

She's about to say something, but I purse my lips and narrow my eyes straight at her in a warning not to challenge me. She stays quiet for a couple of seconds before asking, "Mommy, can I go play now?"

"Yes, sweetheart, but you know the rules. Stay where you can always see me, okay?" I remind her.

She smiles as she nods her head and runs off towards the play area without looking back, too excited to play. Smiling to myself, I watch her start to climb the jungle gym. When I know she's safely playing, I quickly avert my eyes back to Joseph, remembering that he's still there.

I see him intensely watching her. His stare focused straight at her as she moves around with the other children. He doesn't take his eyes off her at all; the admiration on his face is astonishing.

Standing there, I wait for him to face me. When he does, I explain her earlier comment, trying to clear his confusion. "Sorry, Josephina thinks I grew up on a farm my whole life. It's the only thing she knows about me," I tell him.

Joseph's somber face is staring back at me. "I don't know what to say to you, Kasey. I'm so angry right now, but at the same time, I'm more hurt and confused than anything else. In my head I keep repeating what you said earlier, without being able to understand a word of it. What do you mean you were forced to leave, when I was told that you chose to leave? It's as if you were trying to punish me by not telling me I had a daughter, or that you were even pregnant. Was that your intention the whole time?"

"You think that I *chose* to keep her from you?"

"What other explanation can there be, Kasey? I came back after boot camp and you were already gone. *I came back looking for you*. Your parents told me you left for college out of state. So the way I see it, you had already made your decision by leaving. You made the decision to keep her from me," he says, his voice laced with anger.

Just as mad, I take a deep breath to try to calm myself before I respond. "*I didn't choose* to leave, Joseph. My parents forced me to when they found out I was pregnant. I didn't have a choice," I tell him, my mind going back to the awful memory of when my parents confronted me.

It happened one night as I came home from work. That

day I had worked a double shift when someone had called in sick. I didn't want to at first, but I wanted the extra money, so I stayed. Later regretting it as the day grew and I began to feel sicker.

"Kasey, your father and I would like to speak to you," I hear my mother say as I walk into the house from work.

Quickly closing my eyes, I take a deep breath to help fight off the nauseating feeling that has been following me around all day. I don't know what is going on with me lately. I think I might be getting sick, or have the same flu as the other girl at work, because I feel like throwing up again.

Walking in the direction of the kitchen, I see my father walk in from the back porch. Both of my parents look angry. The panic inside of me rising as I walk my way towards them. Did they find out I had Joseph over the weekend they were gone?

Apprehensively, I take a seat in one of the chairs at our dining room table, my father taking a seat across from me. My mother stops her pacing before she begins speaking.

"Young lady, is there something you'd like to tell us?" she asks, the infuriation in her tone further worrying me as she stares into my eyes, waiting for my answer; an answer I can't give her. I shake my head at her, still trying to fight off the nausea that is rising in the pit of my stomach.

Rapidly walking straight up to me, she slaps me on the face. "Don't lie to me!" she shouts.

Bringing my hand up to my stinging face, I look over at my father and his face is expressionless. "Look at me," my mother growls, as she tightly grasps my chin in her hand forcing me to look at her.

"Tell us who the father is!" she shouts down at me, mak-

ing me wince both from the pain of her gasp and tone she's using.

I'm confused and full of fear now as I sit there, my face still burning. "I don't know what you're talking about," I frightfully say to her, which is the truth.

She shoves my face away. "You can't pull off that innocent act anymore, Kasey. You thought we wouldn't notice you being pregnant? All you've been doing is throwing up every morning, sleeping at all hours of the day, and when you aren't throwing up, you're eating everything in sight. I've noticed you haven't had your period recently. Did you really think I wouldn't notice?"

Taking in her last sentence, I realize she's right. I haven't had my period, but I've neglected to notice because of how sick I've been feeling. It never occurred to me that I could be pregnant.

"So I'm going to ask you again. Who. Is. The. Father?" she growls.

I don't know what to say. I'm too scared to tell her anything in fear of the consequence.

"I don't know," I rapidly whisper to her, swallowing the pit of fear from her reaction.

I see her hand come at me, and I don't fight her as she slaps me again. "You slut!"

"That's enough, Caroline," my father demands, his voice low, but stern. "Kasey, we've decided to send you to my sister's farm up in Wisconsin. We've already bought you a bus ticket. That is, unless the father of the baby takes responsibility for you and takes you in. But regardless, you're not staying under this roof. We don't condone sinners is this house. So, we'll give you one last chance to speak up about who the father is," he grimly discloses.

I close my eyes and wonder whether I should speak up about Joseph being the father. Even if I did tell them, would they believe me? He isn't here anymore to stand by my side as I tell them. What am I supposed to do? I sit there silent for a couple of seconds, finally shaking my head to answer. The guilt drops to the pit of my stomach knowing that I am lying to them.

"Then it's done. You're going up north with your aunt. Remember that this is your mistake, Kasey, so you now have to live with the consequences."

Joseph's voice jolts me from my memory. "Why didn't you go to my parents for help?"

"I wanted to, but I couldn't. I was too scared of what they'd think of me, or that they wouldn't believe me," I reply, remembering my thoughts from just moments ago. "I didn't know I was pregnant, but my mother noticed right away. She knew before I did, because I was so sick all the time and all I wanted to do was sleep when I wasn't working."

His brow furrows as he asks, "You said you tried writing to me, when?"

"Several times, actually. The first letter I left in your parent's mailbox the night before I was scheduled to leave, hoping they'd get it to you somehow. I didn't leave any details, only that I was moving up here to Wisconsin with my aunt. Then again when I was seven months pregnant, knowing you'd be done with boot camp, hoping it would get to you in time before I delivered. I waited everyday, up until the day I delivered for you to show up, but you never came. The last time I wrote to you was right after Josephina was born. To notify you about Josephina, but it came back a couple months later stamped: *return to sender*. I pretty much gave up after that."

I didn't cry the day my parents confronted me. I couldn't. The fear had taken over. It wasn't until the day I received the returned letter that the tears came. Until then I had stayed strong, waiting for him to rescue me, waiting for my knight in shining armor. Instead, that day I learned Joseph was never coming for us, and there was nothing I could do but move forward with my baby.

I don't know if it's the pain of remembering everything, or knowing that Joseph never knew. Regardless, it's all caught up to me, and the tears are uncontrollably falling down my face. They keep coming like a broken dam.

Desperately needing them to stop, I quickly wipe them away, not wanting Joseph to see my weakness, but it's too late. He stands up from the bench and engulfs me in his arms. I hate that I look weak in front of him. I never wanted him to see me this way, but now that I'm back in his arms, I can't help but feel loved and secure. They remind me of the only night we were together. Even then I knew it wasn't love, but I still wished it had been.

"Why didn't you try calling my parents house, asking where I was?" I hear his deep voice rumble into my ear that is pressed against his chest.

Sniffling up the tears in order to answer him, I respond a little broken up, "I couldn't, we didn't have a phone where I lived. It's why I tried writing to you."

I hear him sigh, his chest taking in a deep breath as he holds me.

"I came back for you after boot camp. I thought about you every day during those three months, Kasey. The day I got back, I came looking for you, but you were already gone. I believed your parents when they told me you had changed your mind and went to a college out of state. I was pissed you had left, but I thought that it was probably for the best. A couple of months later, when my parents passed away, I briefly came home. But you were still gone. I haven't been back since then. I should've tried harder to look for you, but I didn't, and I'm sorry for that. It's something I'll regret for the rest of my life," he explains, his sorrowful words making me continue to sniffle.

"I'm sorry about your parents, Joseph," I mumble, not knowing what else to say.

I hear a piercing scream from the jungle gym and I recognize it immediately as Josephina's. Shoving Joseph away, I start running towards the playground without hesitation, needing to get to her. When I reach her, she is on the ground gripping her knee. Tears are streaming down her cheeks, matching the ones I just had.

Bending down, I look at her knee and see she's scraped it pretty badly. I know she doesn't usually cry unless it's something serious. Wiping her hair away from her forehead, I give her a kiss. "I think it's time we head home, sweetheart. I think we've both had enough of the park today," I tell her, knowing it's best we both leave now.

As I'm about to scoop her up in my arms, I feel Joseph next to me. "Let me," he says already reaching down to do it for me. As he cradles her up against his body, I take in how tiny she looks next to him. He stands there, waiting for me to move. Snapping into action, I stand up and lead them towards my car.

Josephina's cries have now turned to a sniffle, her tiny arms wrapped around Joseph's neck holding onto him. Every couple of steps I quickly glance at them and see him looking down at Josephina, returning the smile that is on her face. The sight warms my heart, knowing she's enjoying being held by

Joseph. It's as if she knows it's her dad holding her.

When we finally reach my SUV, I open Josephina's door so Joseph can place her inside. The entire time, he's telling her everything is going to be fine in a calming voice. He buckles her in and when he pulls back, I see her face looks worried, almost panicked.

She keeps her eyes focused on Joseph. "You're not coming home with us?" she asks him. She's desperately looking at me with her begging blue eyes, twisting at my heart. As much as I try to be stern with her, it's near impossible to deny her request when she looks at me that way.

Joseph stares at me with the same look. It's at that moment I realize he's where she's gotten it from; they look so alike with their matching expression. Hating to feel like the evil villain of the day, I'm forced to ask him, "Would you like to come over for dinner?" hoping I don't regret my decision if he refuses, but he doesn't, when he answers, "If you don't mind, I would love to come over."

Josephina starts clapping, cheerfully squealing, and obviously happy that he's agreed. With Joseph climbing into the passenger seat, I climb into the driver's side and make my way to my house. Actually it's not really a house; it's more like a small sized warehouse. I started renting it a couple of years ago, needing a workspace for my business. I pull up into my driveway and out of the corner of my eye, I can see Joseph peering through the windshield looking at the building. His face doesn't conceal his disappointment.

"You live here?" he asks, sounding shocked and curious.

The look on his face angers me. He's making me resent inviting him over at all. "Yes, I live here. It's not a house, but I needed space for my studio, so this worked out great. The rent is really cheap, but what really matters is that I'm able to put a roof over our heads," I sternly inform him, ignoring the anguished look on his face as I begin to climb out of my car.

I'm already unbuckling a sleeping Josephina from her booster seat when Joseph is quickly at my side. "She's completely out. Here, let me carry her," he offers, already reaching in to pick her up, making me step back to give him better access.

She's usually asleep by the time we arrive home on Saturdays, the poor thing. I usually get her up around five a.m., since I have to be set up and ready to start selling by six a.m., but she has never once complained. She's been doing it since the first time I set up my booth, so it's the only thing she knows during the summer. After shutting the car door, I walk ahead of them and go to the entrance of my studio. Quickly unlocking and opening the door, I allow him to step in first.

Leading him over to the area where we sleep, I show him the bed I share with Josephina, and he places her down on it. He covers her up with the blankets, staring down at her as he stands up, admiring her while she sleeps. After a couple of seconds he turns to slowly take in the surroundings.

I don't have much of a living space. It looks more like a large working studio than a house, but to me it's perfect. It allows me to work on my projects and keep Josephina within a close proximity, so I can always see her. It might be small, but it was better than nothing.

I walk towards my work area, with Joseph closely following behind, as I lead him to a couch that is near the wall. It's usually where Josephina colors or does her activities during the day while I work. He takes a seat next to me and it instantly brings back the memory of the last night I'd seen him. I force myself to push it aside.

"So what is it you do?" he asks, still curiously looking

around my studio.

There are several tables in the middle of the room, with items scattered across them. A large table is off to the side with several burners holding large pots and ladles. Against another wall, shelves are lined from top to bottom; it's where I store items. There are large tubs of containers taking up half of the other walls. It's what I store the finished soaps in, so the scents don't mix. .

"I make soaps. I was taught how to make them when I first moved here to Wisconsin."

"You said earlier you were sent away. Is this where you came?"

"When my parents found out I was pregnant, they had already made the decision to send me away," I tell him, the somberness taking over my response.

He still looks puzzled by my response, so I explain. "I was sent to live here in Wisconsin with my aunt. She lives in an Amish community right outside of Madison. In the beginning it was very difficult for me, because I was an outsider who wasn't raised there and I was pregnant. They didn't approve of me at first. I had to prove I would be a hard worker and that I wouldn't be an inconvenience to them. Eventually they allowed me to stay, knowing it would only be temporarily. I left a little after Josephina turned one, when I'd finally saved up enough money to move here to the capital with her."

"You said you learned how to make your soaps from a lady?"

"Yeah, she lived on the farm and needed help when I first arrived. She showed me how to make them when I was pregnant with Josephina. I found I was able to make them quickly and I enjoyed doing it. I started selling them to the locals to help with the cost of living. Since it was something I discovered I liked doing, I continued with it. It's not making me rich, but it provides enough for me to put a roof over my head and food on the table for both of us," I say to him as I wring my hands on my lap.

Although I know he's absorbed every word, he still looks perplexed. "I still don't understand why your parents sent you away? Why would they, knowing you were carrying my baby? Why didn't they speak with my parents instead of sending you away?" he questions.

Feeling ashamed I never told *anyone*, I look down at my wringed hands as I convey, "I never told anyone who the father was. Not even my parents. I knew my parents didn't really like your parents, so I didn't think it would help the situation. They wanted me out of the house, regardless. Plus, I really doubt your parents would've believed me anyways, Joseph," I finish saying with a whisper.

Joseph's parents never got along with mine. Our parents were never the typical neighbors you see on TV where everyone gets along. No, my parents were too religious, and Joseph's parents were far from it, making them clash.

Sitting there, still silent, allowing him to absorb the information, I patiently wait for him to say something.

"Do you have pictures of her from when she was little?" he asks, his voice sounding raspy. His emotions are tearing at my heart. All this time I didn't think he cared.

Exhaling deeply, I stand up, heading in the direction of the sleeping area. I go to the dresser that holds our clothes and pull open a drawer in the middle. It's in the same spot it's been for the last couple of years. I reach for the envelope containing the photo. I rarely take it out anymore. The fear of further damaging it, keeps me from touching it. Quietly closing the drawer back up, I return to Joseph.

Returning to him, I hand him the envelope, resenting having to surrender it. I know it was meant for him to have, but when it returned to me, I felt he didn't deserve it any longer; always believing he was the one that had sent it back.

He takes it from my hand, giving me a chance to take a seat at his side. I watch him slowly turn it over in his hands, observing the exterior of the envelope, as he closely studies the address and stamp placed on the front. When his finger brushes over the old ink stating, *return to sender,* my eyes tear up remembering my heartache when I had seen those same words.

That day felt as if my entire world had come to an end, believing I would never see him again. Thinking he wanted nothing to do with Josephina or me, was painful. It made it worse when I received an answer, from the second letter I had written, that same day. It was from my parents.

I had written to them as well, informing them Josephina had been born, foolishly hoping they'd ask me to return home. Instead I had received the opposite. They had firmly instructed me to never contact them again. I was no longer a part of their family because of my sins.

Forcing myself to push the resentment from my mind, I focus once more on Joseph. I watch as he slowly opens the envelope, reaching inside to pull out the photo that is wrapped in the letter. He ignores the letter, folding it up to place it back inside its original pocket of the envelope, keeping the picture in his hand. He's deeply concentrating on the picture as I tell him, "It was taken the day Josephina was born." I have to force out a whisper around the lump in my throat.

My heart feels like it has sunk to the pit of my stomach as I wait for a reaction from Joseph. His silence is nerve wracking and it's tearing me apart inside. I'm so fearful of his rejection.

He's intensely staring down at the picture, never taking

his eyes off it. When I look down at it, I see his finger graze over baby Josephina, and suddenly I see a tear falls onto the picture. Quickly looking back up, I see Joseph rapidly blinking his eyes; clearly trying to fight the remaining tears. With his eyebrows drawn, he looks at me. "You said this was taken the day she was born?" I can hear the confusion in his voice as I nod my head. "Then why was this picture taken at home? Why would they let you go home the same day, isn't that unsafe for you and the baby?" he asks, the worry clear in his voice.

"I didn't have Josephina in a hospital. I had her at home, at my aunt's house actually. The Amish community doesn't believe in using hospitals when they deliver their children," I explain to him.

The concern in his expression is pushing my fear away. "That must have been hard on you," he says, with a hint of remorse.

All I can do is shrug my shoulder at him. "I didn't have a choice, Joseph. It did hurt, a lot. There were times when I wanted to give up, but when they handed me Josephina, it made it all worth it. I would do it all over again for her," I say, stating the truth.

He reaches over, grabbing for my hand to squeeze it. My eyes look down to our joined hands and I can see that his hand looks bigger than the last time I remember it. Everything about Joseph seems larger. When he left he was the skinny boy I grew up with. Now he was a large, muscled man who is now a stranger to me.

My eyes are still looking down at our joined hands as I ask, "What do you do now?"

"I'm still in the Marine Corps. I'm stationed in San Diego. I just got back from Afghanistan a month ago," he answers.

He begins to gently stroke his thumb across my hand,

making me realize they're still joined. I take my hand from his, embarrassed by the feeling that I was getting from his touch. My body was beginning to flutter, as it would consistently do when we were younger. Every time he was near me I grew giddy and excited.

"I hear San Diego is beautiful, but I wouldn't know. Besides the bible retreats I would go on with my parents every year and Savannah, this is the only other place I know," I say with a chuckle, trying to defuse the remorse of having to say it.

Joseph is about to say something, but I see Josephina walking towards us, still looking sleepy as she rubs her eyes. Eyeing Joseph, she smiles and quickly walks over to me, taking a seat in my lap and facing him. I hug her close, taking in her childish scent. Looking back at Joseph, I see him admiring her in my arms.

Josephina reaches down, tugging the picture from Joseph's hand, making me scold her for being rude. Ignoring me, she continues looking down at the picture. Her brow scrunches down as she concentrates on it. "Mommy, who is this baby you're holding?"

"That was you, sweetheart, on the day you were born," I tell her, watching for her reaction.

Curiously she tilts her head to the side as she concentrates on the picture. "Oh," she says, "Why would you have it?" she asks Joseph, still focused at the object in her hands.

"He wanted to see a picture of you from when you were born, that's all." Knowing how curious she'll get if I allow her, I pull the portrait from her hands and hand it back to Joseph. "Why don't we start getting things ready for dinner? What do you feel like eating tonight?" I ask, trying to distract her little mind.

"I want spaghetti with meatballs," she says with enthusiasm, making me laugh knowing it's her favorite.

"Okay, spaghetti with meatballs it is then. You're lucky the meat is already in the fridge. Go wash up," I tell her, giving her a little shove, so she will do as requested. Josephina grabs onto Joseph's hand, dragging him behind her to the bathroom to wash up.

Standing up from the couch, I head to the kitchen and begin to remove the necessary items to start dinner. Within minutes, I see both of them exit the bathroom and join me at the table where I have placed the items Josephina likes to help with. Joseph stands at her side, helping her as she instructs him on what they will be doing. His attention unwavering, he follows her orders of what they will be doing.

I wash my own hands in the kitchen sink and start chopping the vegetables needed to go into the meat, listening in on their conversation at the same time. At first their conversation begins with simple questions to get to know each other. Joseph asking if she goes to school and what she likes to do for fun. With time, I grow distracted with preparing the food and don't hear what Joseph tells Josephina, which causes her to squeal with excitement. From the way she's smiling, I have a feeling it isn't good. She's only that excited when she's been promised something, usually something that is huge and beyond her normal expectation.

"Mommy, mommy, guess what? Joseph lives by the ocean and he said we can go visit him so I can see it," she squeals, the excitement still clear in her voice.

My chopping has completely stopped at this point. The hand holding my chopping knife is gripping it so tight that I feel it digging deeply into my palm. Breathing deeply to control the rising anger inside of me, I have to remember he's still a stranger to her before I turn around and face them both.

I smile to conceal the anger rising within me. "Sweetheart, you know we can't afford to travel right now, but it was nice of him to offer," I say, now glaring daggers in Joseph's direction. Her excitement dies; her expression now that of disappointment. I see her open her mouth to say something, most likely a rebuttal that I'm used to. "Why don't you go wash the meat off your hands in the bathroom," I tell her, grabbing for the bowl with the mixed meat to add the vegetables.

She stands up from the table and does as ordered, her face still gloomy, already knowing I won't let her challenge me. The minute I hear the door close I attack him. "Don't go getting her hopes up about things like that. She's only four. She's going to take those things seriously," I quietly snap at him, trying to keep my tone down so Josephina doesn't hear me.

His eyes grow wide. He probably wasn't expecting me to get angry with him. "I'm sorry. I didn't think it was a big deal. She told me she loves fish and wants to visit the ocean one day. When I told her I live by the ocean, it sort of slipped out. I don't see what the big deal is," he claims, making me angrier.

"The *big deal* is that when you tell a little girl something, she expects it to happen, especially Josephina."

"She's four, she'll probably forget about it in a couple of hours anyways," he casually states, as if it's no big deal.

He might not think it's a big deal because he hasn't been the one raising Josephina. He doesn't understand how her little mind works, or what her expectations are. He's obviously never been around little children long enough to understand that not all of them *will probably forget about it*. Josephina is definitely not one of them.

Before I can tell him as much, Josephina comes running back out of the bathroom with a smile on her face, forcing me to stay silent. I don't want her seeing me fight with him, but I already know she's not going to forget about his promise, and I have a bad feeling Josephina won't be the only one left disappointed by Joseph when he leaves once more.

Chapter 4

Joseph

AS MARK DRIVES away, I see a saddened Josephina waving goodbye to me. Waving goodbye to her hurts. It's the second hardest thing I've had to do in a *very* long time. The first was the morning I had walked away from a sleeping Kasey. That morning it took every ounce of strength I had inside of me to leave. I didn't want to walk away from her that night; the night we had conceived our daughter.

Our daughter. It sounds so surreal.

That night I realized how hard I had fallen for Kasey Wilson. Before then, she'd always been the girl next door. The girl who I'd keep an eye on, knowing that because of her parents, I'd never have a chance at touching her. I wasn't good enough for her. At least I'd always thought that, until the night she gave herself to me. It was then I knew I wasn't going to let her go. I was coming back for her.

When *I did* come back for her though, she was already gone.

That day I felt like my heart had left with her.

Had I known I left her pregnant, I would've searched to the ends of the earth for her. But, it's my own fault for not considering it. I should've known she could've been pregnant, but I was young and stupid. It never crossed my mind.

Still thinking about Josephina, I smile. Knowing I helped create that beautiful little girl brings me joy. I always knew I wanted kids, but I didn't think I'd have to play the absent parent when it came to my children.

I push the thought from my head. I might not have been there for Kasey when Josephina was born, or the last four years for that matter. I do know one thing for sure, I wasn't going to miss seeing Josephina grow up from this day forward. I don't know how I'm going to do it, but come hell or high water, I am going to be there for this little girl. I refuse to play the absent parent.

Ashley turns her body in the front seat to better face me. "So is what Mark told me today true?" I hear her ask, tearing my focus from the scenery outside the window, drawing my attention to her.

Kasey had offered to give me a ride back to Mark's house, but Mark had been hounding me all afternoon with text messages wanting to know more details about this afternoon. I wasn't going to have the detailed conversation he was expecting with a couple of text messages, so I asked him to come pick me up instead. Plus, I didn't like the idea of Kasey going out late at night with Josephina.

"Yeah, she's mine. There's no doubt about it," I admit to her, the guilt feeling like a weight on my chest.

Although it's dark outside, with the help of the street-lights illuminating inside of the car, I can see her satisfied expression on her face. "Good, then when can we meet her? Because if you think for one second that you're keeping that little girl from us, I'll strangle you, Joseph Mitchell," She is using her best stern voice, making Mark laugh.

"You know she'll do it too," Mark replies as he grabs Ashley's hand to bring it up for a kiss.

"Why would I keep her from you guys? You're my family," I tell them, knowing it's the truth, since I have no actual family left.

"Good, then you can invite them over for dinner tomorrow night. I really want to meet her. That way I can also get a feel for this girl that has been keeping your daughter from you," Ashley says.

"She didn't keep her from me," I firmly argue, looking back out of the window, her resentment getting to me.

I can't blame Ashley for thinking that way though. They don't know Kasey like I do. Or at least the way I used to know her. Her actions today showed dramatic changes in her. The old Kasey never once stood up to me; this one did it without hesitation, which made me smile. She was confident and much more beautiful because of it.

Arriving at Mark's house, we all head inside. I go straight to their couch to take a seat, leaning my head back as I close my eyes, trying to absorb the events of the day. Today has mentally exhausted me.

Hearing Mark near me, I open my eyes, seeing him already handing me a beer. Grabbing it from him, I open it and take one giant gulp. As he takes a seat on the couch across from me with Ashley, I see both of them anxiously waiting for me to say something. I don't want to have this conversation right now, but I know they will continue hounding me until I tell them the details. Ashley's hand goes to her swollen belly, rubbing it, making my thoughts drift to how alone Kasey must have felt when she was pregnant. I wish I had been there for her pregnancy.

Our earlier conversation comes back to me. It tears my heart apart knowing the entire time she was waiting for me to show up, but I never did. I must have been the biggest asshole in her mind.

"She didn't purposely keep Josephina from me," I say out loud, the thought rapidly coming out. I couldn't help the cracking in my voice as I said it. I feel like shit over the entire situation.

I see Ashley's face light up. "She named her Josephina? How sweet," she says with a smile.

"She was sent up here to live with her aunt when her parents found out she was pregnant. It's why she was no longer living in Savannah when I got back from boot camp. She tried writing to me, but I never got the letters," I explain to them.

Mark nods his head at me, most likely remembering when I had gone back looking for Kasey, but she was gone. He knew about my last night with Kasey and how much I couldn't stop thinking about her. At the time, Mark told me it was for the best. She needed a better future. I had believed him. I didn't have any other choice.

Ashley's face grows curious, but confused. "What happened to the letters?"

Her question makes me wonder the same. My parents never mentioned a letter when I got back from boot camp. I never found any when I packed up the house. It's a mystery I'm never going to solve with them now gone.

"I don't know, but the last one was returned to her. It must have arrived after I sold the house," I say, already reaching into my back pocket where I had placed the envelope. "It's the one telling me Josephina was born. That's also the last time she tried writing to me," I add, removing the picture for them to view.

Mark reaches for it and holds it up for him and Ashley to view together. "It was taken right after Josephina was born," I tell them, waiting for their reaction.

Ashley automatically smiles as she looks at the picture, but Mark narrows his eyes, looking as confused as I did when I first viewed it. "She had Josephina at her aunt's house, in an Amish community." I clarify to both of them.

Ashley's smile quickly disappears, her eyes growing wide. Mark does almost the same. "Are you serious? As in the Amish that float around here, the ones that don't believe in electricity or anything?" she surprisingly asks, just as shocked as I feel.

Ashley isn't helping with the guilt I'm feeling, but I silently nod my head at her and keep thinking about what she's said. I hate knowing Kasey had to endure being in that situation while she was pregnant. The realization only makes me angrier by the moment.

Taking in Ashley's pregnant form, I know women are pretty much miserable while they're pregnant. I heard about it all the time from my fellow Marines that had pregnant wives, but Kasey never once voiced her complaint of the conditions she was forced to endure. Although it must have been hard on her to go from having all the amenities of a normal life to having limited ones, she seemed appreciative instead, when she explained it to me.

Another thing to blame myself for. *I* was the one who got her pregnant. It is also the reason why she got kicked out of her parent's house. Grimacing to myself, I sit there and start to think about the loss when Mark breaks my train of thought.

"See, honey, you should appreciate the things I've been

giving you during your pregnancy. I bet your complaining about wanting that new Kindle Fire is sounding a bit selfish right now, isn't it?" he says to Ashley in a sarcastic tone.

From the look on her face, the comment only pisses her off and she elbows him to show it. He lets out a grunt as her elbow makes contact and all I can do is laugh at him. He is always being a smart ass.

Ashley looks down at the photo one last time before slowly handing it back to me. When I grab it, I bring it up to look at it again, smiling as I do. It may only be a photo, but it's something I will treasure forever.

"So does she still believe in their ways, or is she back to being normal?" Mark asks, the hesitation of the question surprising me. Normally I wouldn't expect it from him.

"She only went through that because she didn't have a choice," I tell him as I put the picture back into the safety of its envelope.

My phone starts ringing, the ringtone tells me it's Elizabeth calling. Probably to remind me I haven't called her at all today. I had texted her when I landed in Madison letting her know I had arrived, but I told her I would call her in a couple of hours, and I never did. I'm surprised this is the first time she's calling. She usually gets upset if I don't return her phone calls in a timely manner.

Obviously I don't need to look at the screen to know who it is, but I still do, dreading answering the call. Holding up the phone, Mark nods at me as I excuse myself to their backyard to answer it. "Hi babe, what's up?" I answer as I'm shutting the door behind me.

"What do you mean, what's up? I should be asking you that, since you haven't called me all day and I'm left drowning in wedding plans," she whines into the phone. She also sounds angry, so I already know this conversation isn't going to end well. It never does when she's in this kind of mood.

"I'm sorry, babe. Something came up and I haven't had a chance to call you."

"What could have possibly distracted you enough to make you completely forget to call your *fiancée*?" she asks, her tone sounding far from being curious.

With that tone, I know I'm not risking mentioning Josephina. I know I have to tell her, but *I'm not* going to do it over the phone, especially to Elizabeth.

"Nothing much, just something with Mark," I lie to her.

Knowing it's best to distract her, I change the subject. "By the way, I asked Mark to be my best man today," I tell her.

"I thought we agreed you were going to ask my brother. *He is family,* so he should be your best man," she demands, taking my mind right back to the small argument we had the last time this conversation came up.

Sighing over her statement, I brace myself. "I told you I would think about it, which I did. Your brother is *your* family and Mark is mine, so I feel he should be my best man," I inform her, trying to stay firm to my decision, but I already know that won't win me the argument.

"My brother is going to be your family soon so I don't see why he can't be your best man," she argues back. "My best friend, who happens to be his girlfriend, is going to be my maid of honor. It only makes sense that they are partnered together," she claims.

I'm already grabbing the bridge of my nose to ward off my headache, as she adds, "He can be one of your groomsmen, but I'm not adding his pregnant wife. She'd be too fat by the wedding and I don't want fat people in my wedding. It would make for ugly pictures."

"Look, Elizabeth, I'm tired and I really don't want to argue with you tonight," I throw back at her, knowing if I don't end the phone call soon, we'd only end up arguing about the subject all night.

She must have felt the same way, because we end the phone call with our usual goodbyes. I'm more irritated now than when I starting speaking with her. I turn around to head back into the house when I notice Mark standing inside the doorway, staring straight at me with a raised eyebrow. I wouldn't be surprised if it's from hearing my conversation.

"Ashley is getting tired so I'm going to head to bed with her."

"Yeah, sure dude. Did you put my stuff in the extra room already?" I ask him, feeling tired myself.

"Yeah, it's in there. I brought it in earlier. If you need anything get it yourself," he says, as I follow him down the hallway to the rooms. He gives me one last wave goodbye with his hand above his head. I watch him disappear into his room, leaving me to make my way to mine. Reaching my room, I grab a pair of clothes and head to the guest bathroom to take a quick shower. Once done, I'm back in the room, heading straight to the dresser where I placed the envelope that Kasey gave me. Taking it with me to bed, I get comfortable to finally read it. I had wanted to be alone when I first read it. That's why I waited until now.

Turning it over in my hands to fully take it in, I run my fingers along the front. It's in a typical white envelope. The lettering now looking aged, making the envelope look distressed, as if Kasey had repeatedly held this letter.

The first thing I noticed, after she had handed it to me the first time, was that it was still sealed. It surprised me knowing she hadn't opened it back up to remove the picture, especially since she said it was the only one she had of Josephina's birth. It's almost as if deep down inside she knew I'd eventually come to retrieve it.

Opening it back up, I take the letter out and gently unfold it, not wanting to damage it. I'm scared of what it's going to say. Bracing myself, I begin to read as Kasey's neat handwriting pops out at me.

Dearest Joseph,

I've tried several times to contact you, but haven't received word from you. I hope you aren't too upset with me. If you are, I truly am sorry for whatever it is I've done. I've missed you so, but I've already told you that before, so you must already know. I hope all is well and you are happy. As for me, things have been difficult, but I thank God everyday for my good health, and the blessings that I do have. I pray the same for you as well.

The reason for this letter is that I was blessed with a miracle from our one night together; a night I will forever hold dear in my heart. I never wanted to tell you this way, but being that you haven't come or answered my letters, I am left with no other choice.

You now have a daughter, a little angel in my eyes, an angel that God has gifted me to always remember you by. She was born a little after midnight, on March 11th, and I've chosen to name her Josephina, to remind me of the person that helped create her. She'll always have a part of you with her, in case she never gets the chance to meet you.

I've included the only picture I have of the night she was born. I feel you deserve it more than I do. I only hope you will treasure it as deeply as I treasure her.

I will pray for you every day, for your health and well being, in hope that God answers my prayers and looks out for you. I will wait every day, praying that you change your mind. Hoping someday you will wish to meet her, but until then, I vow to keep her safe.

Keep safe, my dearest Joseph, and remember that I will always be thinking of you.

Yours truly,

Kasey

Closing my eyes to try to ward off the tears, I fail. They begin to slowly trickle down my cheeks. Clutching the letter to my chest, I hold onto to it tightly, picturing it was Kasey I was holding instead.

As I read every single word, I could feel the pain coming through what she wrote. Even as she claimed she was being strong, deep down inside, I know she was hurting as she wrote the letter. I know I would be.

My heart feels as if it's dropped into the pit of my stomach. No matter how many times I think about it, the regret of never showing up will live with me forever. When she needed me the most I wasn't there. The guilt will stay with me, every day of my life.

I may not have been there to save her the first time, but I wasn't going to leave her behind. I was going to make it up to her, somehow, someway. This time I was coming back for her *and* Josephina.

Chapter 5

Kasey

CHECKING THE ADDRESS on my smart phone one final time, I make sure it's the right house I should be pulling up to. Confirming that it is, I park on the street and put my SUV into park.

"That house is huge, right mommy?" Josephina exclaims from the backseat.

Unbuckling my seat belt, I respond, "Yes it is, sweet-heart."

I don't want to be here, but I'm only doing it for Josephina. Joseph had called yesterday begging me to join him and his friends for dinner, but I had to decline the request due to a delivery I needed to make. It was to a local boutique that helps sell my soaps. Since those profits were the most important, when I wasn't selling at the Farmers Market, I had to pass on the first request. The boutique's sales are made year round. It was the monthly order that helped put food on my table. In my eyes, it was much more important than keeping dinner plans, even if they were with Joseph.

Of course he was disappointed, but he clearly understood when I explained. Although I managed to get out of dinner plans last night, I couldn't escape them a second time, especially since Josephina overheard my conversation with Joseph. She was excited about the dinner. Actually, I think she's more excited about seeing Joseph than anything else. That alone was the *only* reason why I'm here.

Taking a deep breath to calm my nerves, I open my car door to get out and I'm instantly frightened when I see a large man in front of me helping hold my door open. It takes a moment, but I finally recognize that it's Joseph, and I am able to relax, but my heart still feels likes it's racing from the sight of him. I don't know if it's from the fright or the fact that he's smiling down at me.

"I'm sorry. I didn't mean to scare you," he apologetically says to me. "I saw you pulling up, so I thought I'd come help you with Josephina," he says, looking at me with a smile as he shuts my car door. He quickly goes straight to Josephina's to take her out.

Josephina's face lights up at the sight of him as he opens her door to get her out. She's already unbuckling herself, anxious to get out of her booster seat. "Hi Joseph, we're here," she excitedly shouts.

Chuckling at her response, he says, "Yes, I see. I'm so glad you are." Allowing him to help take her down, I go to my passenger side door taking out the gift basket I had brought for Mark's wife. I knew Joseph was a guest in the house and felt bad that they had to cook dinner for us as well. I decided to bring something for the host.

The idea of arriving empty handed, at a house where I

was invited to dinner, didn't sit well with me. Since Joseph had mentioned she was pregnant, I knew exactly what to bring. He mentioned during dinner with us the other night how close he was to Mark and Ashley, and I had felt happy for him that he had such a close relationship with both of them. If it wasn't for them, he wouldn't have been here and I would've probably never had seen him again.

I watch closely as Joseph walks with Josephina, hand in hand, up to the house. He's clearly distracted by the non-stop chatter coming from Josephina. I don't blame him if he's already feeling overwhelmed. Taking in the sight of both of them melts my heart. I never thought I'd see the sight in front of me, them together. *Ever.*

Hesitantly I follow them into the house, immediately spotting Mark, Joseph's friend, whom I met at the Farmers Market. At his side is a pregnant woman.

This must be Ashley.

She comes straight towards me with a smile. "Hi, I'm Ashley, Mark's wife," she says, with a beaming smile. "Mark said he'd already met you the other day," holding out her hand for me to shake. I shake it, still feeling extremely nervous.

Standing with his face expressionless, Mark gives me a short nod. "Hello, Mark," I nervously say, before he turns and disappears into the house following behind Joseph.

"This is for you," I say, handing her the gift basket. "They're some of the soaps I make. Joseph had mentioned you're pregnant, so I've included most of my calming scents to help with any stress you might have. Some of them are in salts in case you like to take baths. I apologize if they're not as well made, but I'm still in the testing phase with those," I tell her apologetically.

She looks down at the basket wide-eyed, then back up at

me. "That's so sweet of you. You didn't have to bring me anything, but thank you for the thought," she expresses with a genuine smile on her face when she replies. Her smile is all I wanted in return. I love knowing something I've made makes someone happy.

"It's my pleasure since you're kind enough to invite Josephina and I to dinner," I tell her, already searching past Ashley's shoulder for my daughter. She has somehow managed to disappear with Joseph into the house, worrying me.

Smiling, Ashley leads us to a living space that is connected to the kitchen where I immediately spot them in front of the TV. Josephina is dancing along to a video game, laughing along with Joseph.

"Joseph insisted on buying it for her when he knew she was coming over. That way she wouldn't grow bored," Ashley tells me as I watch Josephina giggle to some dance move Mark is trying to mimic on the screen. The thought that they bought the game system for the sole purpose that Josephina was coming over, doesn't sit well with me.

Storing the thought of speaking with Joseph about it later, I ask Ashley, "Can I help you with dinner?"

"Oh, I'm pretty much done. I just have to throw the salad together and we should be ready to eat."

Eagerly wanting to help, I try once more. "Please, why don't you take a seat and I can do that," I insist. "You've already done enough tonight by cooking dinner for us," I inform her, already walking into the kitchen area without asking, going straight to the salad items on the island.

Her face lights up as she takes her seat in a chair, thanking me for the offer. While she instructs me where everything is located, I begin making the salad. Before long it's done and we're all seated at the table ready to eat.

As we're about to start eating, Josephina screeches, "Wait, you can't eat until you say grace!" as she stretches her arms out to catch everyone's attention.

My eyes go wide from her rudeness, but everyone else looks shocked with their eyes just as wide as mine. I don't know if it's from what she's said or the fact that they weren't expecting to say grace. Being that she's sitting on the other side of Joseph, I can't pinch her, which is something I would normally have done. However, she's won her way when everyone puts their forks down and bows their heads, preparing to say grace. Josephina quickly takes over and does the honor, leaving me to sit there mortified by her behavior.

When she's done, Joseph leans towards me. "You didn't make me say grace the night you made me dinner," I hear Joseph whisper into my ear, making me blush.

"You were already eating when I was going to begin. So I said it silently in my head. I prayed that you'd live through boot camp," I tell him, earning me a smile from his lips that makes my insides melt.

Focusing once again on dinner, we eat. Dinner goes quickly with the normal light conversation, although most of the questions were focused on me. Before long, I realize what they're trying to do. I didn't mind too much, but it did feel as if someone's parents were scrutinizing me. Their questions were never once rude, or made me feel uncomfortable, so I had to be grateful for that.

It wasn't until we're all eating dessert that Ashley starts asking Josephina questions and the conversation grew agonizing.

"So Josephina, what do you like to do for fun?"

"I like to read books," she answers, before eating a spoonful of ice cream.

It obviously isn't the answer everyone expected as I see their eyebrows go up in amazement from her answer.

"Oh really?" Mark says to her, looking skeptical. "What kind of books do you like to read?"

"I like books with lots of words," she tells him, before adding, "Did you know babies really like it when you read to them? It makes them move a lot when they hear voices," she states looking over to Ashley.

"How would you know that?" Ashley curiously asks her.

"Mrs. Anderson, the lady at the market, has me read to her stomach sometimes. The baby always moves when it hears my voice. I think it likes me," she says, before taking another spoonful of ice cream into her mouth.

"How old are you?" Mark asks her, clearly confused.

"I'm four, but I'll be five in March," she states, puffing her chest up to him, trying to make herself look bigger than she is.

"I've been teaching her to read since she was three, but she has been reading on her own for the last few months," I clarify, feeling proud of Josephina. "She goes through books so fast now, the librarians already know to reserve books for her before her next trip in."

"Mrs. Anderson says it's all the organic vegetables mommy was eating when I was baking in her tummy. They made me smarter," she proudly claims. "Maybe you should eat organic vegetables so your baby will be smart, too," she suggest with a smile, making us all laugh.

Ashley turns, narrowing her eyes at Mark. "See, there's proof of why it's good to eat organic," she says to him, waving her hand at Josephina.

Mark, rolling his eyes at her, turns back to me. "Is there anything else you'd like to tell my wife that she can use against me?" he questions, sounding more like a scorn than a joke.

With the look he's giving me, I know he's upset, "I apologize for my daughter's remark," I apologetically say, feeling remorseful for Josephina's comment.

From the corner of my eye I see Josephina grow confused. "What did I say wrong?" she asks, making me look at her, smiling to reassure she hasn't done anything wrong. She goes back to eating her ice cream, content with my answer.

Ashley looks over at me. "Kasey, don't listen to him. He's just being a grouch because he says I make too many demands now that I'm pregnant," Ashley says, glaring back at Mark demanding he stay silent.

"I think I would've taken full advantage of it as well if I had the chance," I mumble.

Joseph reaches for my hand under the table, squeezing it gently. "I'm sorry, Kasey," he quietly says to me, regret clear in his eyes.

The expression on his face when he said it makes me realize how misguided and rude my comments must have sounded to them.

"I'm sorry, I shouldn't have said anything. It was very rude of me," I guiltily say as I hang my head in shame. I really should think before I speak.

I'm instantly distracted from my thought when I hear Josephina ask, "Mommy, may I go play the video game again for a little bit before we go home, please?" Her sweet little voice breaks the awkward silence drifting through the room.

"Yes, you may," I reply.

She gets up from the table, excited, and heads to the living room area to continue playing the video game. As much as I want to leave already, to avoid any further embarrassment, I don't want to deny her request.

Mark quickly gets up to follow close behind her, with Ashley starting to remove the remaining dishes from the table, leaving Joseph and I alone. I can already feel the awkwardness between us as he continues to hold my hand with his. He's staring directly at me now, with the same smile from earlier. The one that makes me ignite with excitement all over when he looks at me that way. Just as I'm about to say something, I hear singing coming from his back pocket, clearly obvious his cell phone is ringing.

He gently lets go of my hand, reaching for his phone with a scowl forming on his face. "Sorry, I have to take this. Will you excuse me, please?" he says, already standing up from the table as he walks away without waiting for my response.

My eyes follow him as he makes his way to the backyard through a set of double French doors. I get up to head into the living area to join everyone else, wanting some sort of company while he's gone.

Twenty minutes later I notice Josephina starting to rub her eyes as she continues to play. I know it's a sign she is growing tired. I glance back in the direction of the doors that Joseph disappeared through and I can only see his silhouette by the door, pacing back and forth.

I know it's best to start heading home before it gets any later. "Josephina, I think it's time we get going, sweetheart. It's past your bedtime," I inform her, earning me a small whine in return. Her protest at first is expected, but when Ashley tells her that she can come back, anytime she wants, it helps convince her to leave.

Standing up to take Josephina's hand, I thank Mark and Ashley for dinner and start walking to the front door. I can't resist taking one quick glance back in the direction of the backyard for Joseph. Mark notices, immediately saying, "I'll go get him," before quickly walking to the backdoors without hesitation.

Josephina and I wait by the front doors and within minutes, a distressed looking Joseph emerges with Mark from the backyard. He walks over to us with a forced smile on his face.

"I'm sorry about that. I had to take that phone call. I didn't think it would be that long," he apologizes.

Ashley simply groans, but Mark's lips go flat as if he's not happy with Joseph's apology. "I'm sorry we have to leave, but it's past Josephina's bedtime and I'd really like to get her home to bed."

He doesn't hide his disappointment, but doesn't argue as he walks us to the car. Quickly buckling Josephina in, she immediately starts to close her eyes; her exhaustion taking over as her head tilts to the side and falls asleep.

"She must be really tired," I hear Joseph say behind me, startling me.

Turning to face him, I nod my head in agreement, realizing he's standing extremely close to me, merely inches from my body. His head is slightly tilted to the side and I watch his eyes grow hooded, as he looks back at me.

My body instantly freezes up, my breathing becoming unsteady, as I grow nervous from having him so close. I can smell him, and although he's not wearing cologne, he has a unique scent that I can't identify, but it smells good as I breathe him in.

My body starts to hum with excitement. The mere thought of knowing I'm so close to him makes me remember how good it felt to be wrapped in his arms. A feeling I've been craving for years.

I remember his earlier statement and I nod my head as I swallow the lump in my throat. "Yeah, she's usually asleep by now, but I didn't want to be rude by leaving earlier," I tell him.

"So how long are you in town for?" I curiously ask him.

I'm still nervously standing rooted to the spot by his deep voice. "I'm scheduled to leave on Thursday," he replies, now looking nervous as he rubs the back of his neck with his hand. "I'd like to see more of Josephina while I'm here. If that's okay with you?" he nervously asks, sounding hesitant at the request. His face grows worried as he waits for my answer.

"Of course you can see her, Joseph. I would never keep you from spending time with her," I immediately respond.

He lets out a breath as he briefly tips his head up to the sky, as if he was holding it in, relief clear on his face when he looks at me again. "Thank you, Kasey. It really means a lot to me," he quickly replies.

We both stand there silent, as we continue to stare at each other. His eyes narrow down into a slit as he focuses on me, making me light up inside. I see him slowly begin to lower his head and the anticipation of knowing he's about to kiss me excites me. I can feel my heart racing. My body braces itself as I prepare for his kiss. As I slowly start to close my eyes, remembering what it felt like to be kissed by Joseph, it rouses my desire, but I'm left disappointed when I hear the ringtone from earlier in the night.

Joseph quickly draws his body back, taking a full step away from me as he lets out a curse. "I've got to go. I'll give you a call tomorrow to set up a time to see Josephina," he clips out, turning his body to walk back up to the driveway without a backwards glance at me. I watch him disappear back into the house, the rejection piercing me inside.

I'm left there in shock, leaning my body up against the

side of my SUV for support, wondering to myself if he regretted trying to kiss me. From the look on his face and the explicit curse he let out, I'm pretty sure he did. Sighing to myself, I climb into my car, knowing the best thing to do now is drive away.

Chapter 6

Joseph

WHAT THE HELL just happened? I don't know, but I'm confused as fuck. If Elizabeth hadn't decided to call, I'm pretty sure I would have had Kasey in my arms, kissing her. Still kissing her because I'm pretty sure I wouldn't be able to stop once I started. I wouldn't want to either.

I don't know what came over me, but seeing her sweet innocent face like I remembered her, made me loose all coherent thought. My only focus was her, as always when she's around. She didn't have to do anything to make me feel this way. It was the same when we were young and apparently she still had the power to do it.

Remembering I was engaged had left my mind while I was looking down at her. Shit, I couldn't even remember my own name. She had me hypnotized. All I could remember was how good her lips felt against mine. It was something I'll never forget. Ever. I also couldn't stop remembering how I had held her in my arms wishing I didn't have to leave. That alone was repeating itself in my mind. A non-stop loop since the day she came back into my life.

Running my hand over my head and down my face to help clear my mind, I walk into the house, immediately seeing Mark next to the window. He's looking at me with his eyebrows raised, analyzing me. I'm familiar with the view from the window. He probably saw everything, being that Kasey had parked across the street. Our bodies were facing the house, giving Mark a clear view.

He's casually standing there with his hands in his pockets, a smirk on his face as he declares, "So, I take it you have a dilemma on your hands now?"

Scowling when I look at him, I ask, "What dilemma would that be?"

He steps away from the window, as he walks back into the kitchen area without a response, leaving me to follow. I know he's right. I do have a dilemma on my hands. My mind has a habit of wandering back to the memories I have with Kasey. Even knowing I was soon going to be marrying someone else, I can't stop thinking of her and Josephina now. I am determined to be a part of their future, but I needed to figure out a way to get Kasey from my mind before I get myself into trouble.

When I enter the kitchen area, I see Ashley loading the last of the dishes into the dishwasher and closing it up. Mark goes to open up the fridge and retrieves two beers, handing one to me. I take it without hesitation, opening it to take a sip, hoping the cold liquid with help calm my heated blood that I was left with from just moments ago.

Leaning my body against the kitchen counter, I already see Mark ready to state his case. "From what I saw a minute ago, I'm pretty sure you still have feelings for her. It doesn't take a genius to figure it out by the way you were looking at her either," he says, before taking a sip of his beer, his eyes challenging me to differ.

I stay silent, unable to deny his words.

His eyebrows go up in confirmation when I don't say anything. "Just *how* serious was it before you left? I know from the stories you told me there was nothing much going on, but when you came back after boot camp you looked like shit. Did she have you wrapped around her little finger even back then?" he jokily asks, his cocky smile mocking me.

Groaning, I ignore his remark and walk over to the living area, taking a seat on the couch. Mark and I are close, but the last thing I want to do is lay my feelings that I had for Kasey out on the table for him to mock me about. She's my past; Elizabeth is my future now, and it is something I am going to have to learn to live with.

Ashley and Mark follow me, taking a seat on the other couch, and by Ashley's impatient expression, she wants an answer as well. Looking over to Mark I respond, "Not as wrapped as Ashley has you," I tell him with the same cockiness he'd given me. "Actually, now that I think about it, I'm pretty sure she has you by the balls, too," I add, before taking another swig of my beer.

Ashley laughs, but Marks only scowls as he asks, "How serious *was* it?"

"Kasey and I never dated because of her parents. She wasn't allowed to at all," I say, raking my hand over my head desperately trying to clear the irritation from my mind.

"So she was the prize you couldn't touch?" Mark's jokes, making me scowl at him.

"She was more than that," I mumble, wanting to punch him as well.

I hate the way it sounds, but it's true. Of course I've heard the saying, *you want what you can't have,* but Kasey was always more than just a prize I couldn't have. She was different. She always listened without hesitation when I had a problem, never judging me for my faults. She was the one who always helped me with my schoolwork when I couldn't get it through my thick head and my grades started to take a plunge, to the point of failing. She never gave up on me. That's when I started noticing her as more than just the girl next door, but the girl I wanted to date. The girl I wanted to fall in love with. Or maybe I already had.

"It still doesn't explain how you ended up getting her pregnant," Ashley says, breaking my trance of the memory and taking me back to another.

"Kasey cooked me dinner the night before I left for boot camp. Her parents weren't home. One thing led to another and we ended up sleeping together that night. I had to leave the next morning and I kept thinking she'd be there when I got back, but she wasn't," I say, my voice now sounding raspy as I try to control the grief of the words deep within me.

"Her parents told me she left out of state when I asked them where she was at, and I believed them," I explain.

Ashley's looks as if she's ready to cry. I have to turn away from her to look out the back window, needing the distraction of the darkened sky to clear my mind.

But Mark's next question brings my attention back. "So what do you plan on doing now?"

"I don't know," I truthfully tell him. "I haven't really wanted to make plans until I get to talk to Kasey. I don't know how I'm going to handle leaving them when I go back home, though," I say, twisting the beer bottle in my hand, trying to distract myself.

The silence in the room grows heavy, making me feel uncomfortable.

"Well, whatever it is you plan on doing, we're here for you," he sincerely says to me.

Smiling at both of them, I feel better knowing I have their support. Mark can be an ass most of the time, but he's always had my back, and there was no doubt that he'd have it with whatever decision I make in this situation as well. The only problem is, I have to figure out what it is I plan on doing.

"Does Kasey even plan on telling Josephina that you're her father?" Mark asks, making me think about it.

Knowing Kasey hasn't told Josephina worries me, but I've been trying to take things one day at a time with her, not wanting to frighten her. The last thing I want is for Kasey to try keeping me from seeing Josephina, especially since Josephina doesn't know I'm her father. My focus is getting to know her, slowly trying to gain Josephina's trust, as I wait for Kasey to inform her. I want to be part of this little girl's life. I just haven't figured out how the hell I was going to do that.

There's a lot I need to discuss with Kasey; the sooner, the better.

"Does Kasey know that you're engaged?" Mark curiously asks, most likely already knowing the answer.

Shaking my head at them, I feel the guilt returning as it builds up inside of me.

I hear Ashley grumble, but Mark chuckles at my response.

I planned on telling Kasey about Elizabeth tonight, but the right moment never came up. I know well enough not to try to explain the situation to Elizabeth over the phone. Telling *her* was going to have to wait until I got back to the west coast. That was something I was going to have to do in person with her, which I wasn't looking forward to either. I know I'm in deep shit with this whole situation, but there wasn't anything I could change about the past or the outcome of it.

Seeing Ashley starting to yawn, I excuse myself to my room, wishing them a goodnight so they can head off to bed as well. Reaching my room, I lie down in the bed and stare up at the ceiling, trying to figure out how the hell I was going to fix all this.

Looking down at the screen of my phone, I see the time, realizing that Kasey should be home by now. Without hesitation I search for her number in my contacts and I press call, waiting for her to answer. She quickly picks up on the third ring and when I hear her voice a smile forms on my lips, loving the sound of her voice.

"Hi Joseph, is something wrong?" she asks, her worried tone making my smile grow wider.

"No, nothing is wrong. I just wanted to make sure you made it home okay," I tell her. "Did you put Josephina to bed already?"

Her voice drops down, almost into a whisper as she responds. "Yes. I think she fell asleep the moment I put her in the car. She was really worn out from tonight. I think it was that video game system," she says with a chuckle. "Maybe I should buy her one of those things if this is the end result."

I laugh along with her, remembering how much Josephina loved dancing around to the music. "Technically I did buy it for her, so it's hers to keep."

"Joseph, I wanted to talk to you about that. I don't like the idea that you bought it solely because we were coming over," she tells me, sounding distraught.

"Kasey, it doesn't matter. Seeing how happy it made Josephina made it worth buying. That's all that matters," I tell her, trying to defuse her unhappiness. "I'm going to drop it off before I leave, that way she'll have something to wear her out every night while you're working."

"No Joseph, you don't have to do that. Mark looked like he enjoyed himself as well. I'd hate for you to take it from his house. I'll figure out a way to buy her one," she answers, making me chuckle as I remember Mark playing with the game system. Although he *did* enjoy himself, I had bought it for Josephina, not Mark.

"I'm pretty sure Ashley wouldn't like it very much if Mark got hooked on video games, especially with the baby coming soon. She'll probably insist I take the thing to you anyway," I tell her, hoping my insistence will change her mind.

It's then I realize Kasey hasn't changed from the girl I grew up with. She's always been selfless, always thinking of other people first, even back then.

The line grows quiet. I know she's considering my offer. Closing my eyes, I remember what Kasey looked like when she knows you've proven your point to her. When she was no longer able to argue any further, she'd always take her bottom lip with her teeth, nervously chewing on it. Her eyes would dart back and forth to avoid locking eyes with you. Within a couple of seconds she'd sigh in defeat when she knew she'd lost.

"Thank you. Josephina would really like that," she quietly says, making me smile as I open my eyes.

My smile just as quickly turns into a frown when I remember what it was I wanted to discuss with her. "Kasey, there's something I've been meaning to ask you. Do you plan on telling Josephina I'm her father, or did you want to keep it from her?" I ask, bracing myself as I wait for her answer. I'm practically holding my breath at this point, not knowing what her response will be.

"Of course I plan on telling her, but I'm scared of how she'll react to the truth. You live in San Diego, Joseph. In a couple of days you'll be going back. Imagine the disappointment she'll be feeling when you leave," she points out, her reaction telling me she doesn't plan on telling Josephina.

I feel angry. I want to tell Josephina. She has every right to know the truth, but deep down inside I don't have the courage to say it. I might be Josephina's father, but I've been the absent father who only showed up a couple of days ago. Up until now, Kasey has been forced to play both roles of parenting. She has every right to make the decision for both of us of when she will tell Josephina the truth. I'm worried if I'll ever be a part of Josephina's life.

"Joseph, you both deserve to know each other, but please remember that she's a little girl and I'd hate to have her heart broken," she declares. I can hear the pain in her voice. It's most likely the same pain she's been carrying with her since the day I left.

"I'm sorry, Kasey," I quickly whisper to her.

I hear the beep on my phone announcing another call. When I look at the screen I see Elizabeth's name and I silently curse to myself. She always manages to call at the most inconvenient times. It reminds me that I need to tell Kasey about Elizabeth. Something I will have to do soon.

Before I can consider continuing the conversation, I hear Kasey say, "Joseph, it's late and I'm kind of tired from today. I think it's best we discuss this more tomorrow, okay?"

"I'd really like to spend tomorrow with you girls. Can we start with breakfast?" I quickly ask, hoping she'll agree.

"Sure," she answers. "Josephina wakes up around seven, so why don't we meet here at eight?"

"Sounds perfect, I'll see you then."

Ending the call, a couple of seconds later, I call Elizabeth back. Even as she answers, I brace myself. "Why haven't you been answering my calls?" she snaps at me, clearly irritated.

"I'm sorry, babe. I've had a lot going on, that's all," I tell her, still thinking about the conversation I just had with Kasey as I ignore her irritation.

"What can be more important than talking to your fiancée?" she whines, making me realize that Josephina doesn't whine as much as she does. Actually, now that I think about it, I don't think I've ever heard Josephina whine. Kasey always manages to keep her from doing so.

"Well?" she asks, still waiting for me to respond, breaking my thought.

"Nothing," I lie to her.

The only way to distract her is to start asking her questions about the wedding, which I do. Before long, she settles down and we're soon making more plans. An hour later, I have a headache, but I'm finally hanging up the phone.

The entire time I was on the phone, I was wondering how I was going to break the news to Kasey about Elizabeth. One thing was clear; I *was* going to have to tell her before I left.

I already knew Elizabeth wasn't going to take the news about Josephina too well, but somehow she was going to have to accept it. Elizabeth will soon be a permanent part of my life and Josephina is too. She's my daughter and with Josephina came Kasey. There was no doubt about that.

Chapter 7

Kasey

IT'S NOT QUITE eight a.m. yet and I see Josephina's excitement as she's looking out of the window, which means Joseph has arrived. I told her that he would come over when she awoke this morning and of course she was excited about the notion of spending the day with him. She immediately got up and dressed herself faster than I've ever seen her do before, making me laugh.

Now that I know he is here, I'm beginning to grow nervous. I don't know why it keeps happening, but it does. I didn't sleep much, from tossing and turning most of the night. The conversation I had with Joseph kept repeating itself in my mind.

The more I thought about it, the more I was seeing how selfish I was acting by not telling Josephina the truth. The truth is, I'm scared of the repercussions that will come from telling her. She's so young. I would hate to have to break her little heart when she finds out that he needs to leave. I have to keep reminding myself that I am doing it to protect her. Her emotions and well-being come first, no one else's.

Watching as Josephina flings open the door that leads to the driveway, I follow her out and see Joseph already scooping her up; a huge smile on both of their faces. Josephina immediately begins to bombard him with plans for the day. He's probably already feeling overwhelmed from her non-stop chatter, but he doesn't once interrupt her; instead staying quiet as he nods his head in agreement, taking in every word she says.

He briefly looks at me as he walks both of them in my direction with a smile across his face that makes my body light up inside from head to toe. He stops directly in front of me, with the smile still on his lips, "Are you ready for breakfast?"

I can feel my body heating up. A spark is igniting, that I can feel rapidly roaming throughout my body. I'm rendered speechless when he makes me feel this way. I can only nod my head in agreement to his question as we continue staring at one another; our eyes locked with each other's.

Josephina's eagerness to leave reminds me that we have plans, so I quickly head back inside for my purse and lock up; meeting both of them outside. We decide it would be easier to take my car for the day, since it already has Josephina's booster seat. Before long we're headed off to the diner I like to frequent for breakfast. During the two hours we're there, Joseph continued to listen to Josephina's non-stop chatter. The entire time she's been giving him a recap of her life, at least what she could remember, with Joseph sole interest focused completely on absorbing every…single…word.

With breakfast done, we soon leave and I'm asking Joseph what he'd like to do for the day. Upon hearing me ask him, Josephina decides to make a suggestion. "Mommy,

mommy, can we take Joseph to the zoo so I can show him the giraffes?" she enthusiastically asks, her eyes desperately pleading her request as well.

Looking over at Joseph, I wait for his answer. Without hesitation, he nods his head in approval, making Josephina squeal: "Yipee!" She is so excited. Her reaction makes both of us laugh.

Looking down at her as we walk back to my car, he asks with interest, "Do you like the giraffes?"

"Yes, they're my favorite animals," she tells him, "And, the best part is you get to feed them at this zoo. We should hurry since it's still early and it's not that hot today. If we wait too long they'll go into their houses and stay there," she finishes saying as she continues to tug Joseph towards the car.

Half an hour later we're all feeding the giraffes their lettuce, listening to Josephina laugh as they eagerly gobble it up from her hands. The entire time, Joseph is laughing along with her as he looks down at her in adoration. He does it often and it comforts me knowing I can see him like this with her. It's something I thought would never happen at one point.

"Do you girls come here a lot? I noticed Josephina knew her way around without needing a map," Joseph asks as we begin to walk away, moving on to the next exhibit as we both closely watch Josephina skip a couple of feet ahead of us.

"I try to bring her as often as I can, when time permits. I've been bringing her since we moved here. I don't have very much money and am unable to go on vacations. This is the next best thing for her to expand her mind. I also take her to the library often. I have to go a couple of times a week, so I can use their computers and she can get new reading material," I tell him.

In the corner of my eye, I see Joseph grow confused.

"You don't have your own computer at home?" he asks, the shock evident in his voice. "How do you do it with your business? I would think you'd need a computer."

"No, I don't have my own computer. I do things the old fashion way. I still use pen and paper to keep my records. I didn't have the money for a computer when I first began, so that's how I started keeping track of everything. I've kept with it," I explain.

"I've depended on the computers at the library since I moved here. They've been doing fine since then. I don't see why I need to spend the money on a computer."

He's still skeptically looking at me as we reach Josephina, who is at the polar bear exhibit. "Is it because you don't know how to keep records on a computer?"

Mortified, I answer, "If I recall, Joseph Mitchell, I was the one who ended up doing all your work during computer class. If it wasn't for me, I'm pretty sure you would've failed that class," I remind him.

Instead, he tilts his head as his lips go up into a sensual smile that melts my insides. He continues to stare down at me with his hooded eyes locked onto mine. "Of course I remember. It's the only class I looked forward to going to because I got to sit next to you," his husky voice sending shivers down my body.

My earlier feelings return, rooting me in place with his stare. His eyes are weakening me as they always do, making me grab onto the rail in front of me to keep myself upright. I can feel my breath hitch and my body starting to tingle. I can't take my eyes from his. It's as if he's hypnotizing me, demanding they stay focused only on him.

His lip curls up to one side causing my heart to speed up; it feels like it wants to jump from my chest. He's about to say something when we hear, "Look, look! They put a big block of ice in the water for the polar bear to play with!" from an excited Josephina, now at our side, tugging us both to the window to watch.

Taking advantage of her request, I follow her over to the window, eagerly looking at the polar bear as a distraction to break eye contact with Joseph. Knowing that he's once more standing at my side, I chance a quick glance back at Joseph out of the corner of my eye. Instead of looking at the polar bear, like I expect him to be, he's looking directly at me. His eyes are hooded as he focuses on me.

My eyes find his and Joseph gives me a full smile, making me return one to him as well. My smile is out of shyness. His smile though, looks as if it has other intentions, making me wish I knew exactly what those intentions were.

FOUR HOURS LATER, we're leaving the zoo. As we head towards the exit, Josephina started acting tired, whining that she wanted to be carried. I don't carry her anymore, she's getting to heavy for me to do so, but Joseph easily gives in to her request and scoops her up. She immediately falls asleep in his arms, which allows me to admire the priceless moment.

When we arrive at my place, I park my car in the driveway next to my building. Joseph once again helps me carry her from the car and into my building. I watch from a distance as he places her down in the bed for the remainder of her nap, tucking her in, and giving her a kiss. I can't help but smile at the sight. The way he's taken to her so quickly, as if they weren't strangers before this week, but father and daughter the entire time, makes me tear up. I have to turn away so I don't break down. Walking over to the couch, I sit and wait for Joseph. Before long he's joins me; the awkward silence growing heavy between us as we sit together.

He breaks our silence by saying, "Thanks for letting me tag along today. It really means a lot to me," his voice sounding raspy, as if he's nervous.

I nod my head at him. My mind is still stuck on a particular question that Josephina asked him a couple of hours ago. It's been on my mind since she asked it. I'd held my breath waiting for his answer, which never came, due to the loud trumpeting sound coming from the elephants we were looking at; frightening all of us into laughter.

Finding my courage, I remind him of the question. "Joseph, you never did get to finish answering Josephina's question on whether you have a girlfriend or not," I tell him, bracing myself for his answer.

When she'd asked, I'd noticed right away how Joseph's body immediately tensed up, as if he didn't want to reply. The panicked look on his face accompanied with his reaction worried me. I had already sensed his response, but I was still dreading hearing it from him.

The agonizing look on his face tells me he's most likely going to say yes. However, I never expected the answer he gives me instead. "I'm actually engaged, Kasey. It happened recently, when I got back from Afghanistan. Her name is Elizabeth and we're supposed to get married soon," he tells me, looking down at the ground as if he's afraid to face me.

I can't clearly see his face, but I can tell by the way he's raking the top of his head with his hands, his head still lowered, that he clearly isn't happy about his declaration. I can only sit there, shocked from his admission. I wasn't expecting it, but now that I've heard it, my heart is aching.

He turns his head in my direction. His eyes look dark and saddened, almost as if they are lifeless. I can only sit here, frozen and unable to say anything, as I stare back at him. I feel like the blood has drained completely from my body and my heart has plummeted into the depths of my stomach. The pain of hearing he's engaged is still stabbing at my heart. I don't know why the news of hearing that he's engaged would make me feel this way. He was never mine to begin with. Ever. But the news hurts regardless.

"Congratulations." I force a smile as I say the words.

"Thank you."

Taking a deep breath, I make myself ask, "Have you told her about Josephina yet?"

I know he's only discovered the news, but it's only fair his fiancée knew he had a daughter. When he removes his hands from his head, he looks over to me looking torn. "I don't want to tell her over the phone. Elizabeth isn't going to take the news to well, so I need to tell her in person, but I do plan on telling her," he defensively states, as if he's reassuring me out of doubt, as he leans his head back once more.

With my lips formed into a tight line, I take in his response. "Joseph, I think it's best we wait to tell Josephina," I tell him around the lump lodged in my throat.

He whips his head up at me, his furrowed brow conveying his frustration. "Because I haven't told Elizabeth about Josephina yet?"

"When you choose to tell her is between the two of you, but I have to protect Josephina's feelings. She's my responsibly and has been since the day she was born. I'm only trying to tell you that I don't think it's a good idea to tell her, especially knowing that you're going to leave soon," I declare.

He looks angry as he replies. "How can telling Josephina she has a father not be a good idea, Kasey? She has a right to know. You've kept her from me this long, it's not fair you continue doing so," he practically growls at me.

I'm about to argue his point on me keeping her from him, but I hear a surprised gasp come from the bed area making both our heads snap in that direction. We see Josephina standing there, holding her teddy bear she sometimes sleeps with tightly against her chest, her eyes wide in shock. I immediately stand up to go to her side, picking her up in my arms when I reach her.

Holding her in my arms, I try to comfort her. She faces Joseph with a small smile spread across her lips. "You're my daddy?" she questions him with a raspy voice. Unshed tears are evident in her eyes as I hold her. It's as if she's trying to keep herself from crying.

Joseph somberly answers her. "Yes, princess, I'm your daddy," he says as his hand reaches up to tuck her hair behind her ear. "But I didn't know until the day I met you," Joseph calmly mummers to her.

She lays her head on my shoulders, still staring at Joseph as she absorbs the news. I can tell by how quiet she is being that she is most likely trying to comprehend everything. I didn't want Josephina to find out this way and it's making me angry that she has. I walk over to the couch to take a seat with Josephina, Joseph right behind us.

"I didn't want you to find out this way, but it's best you found out before I have to leave," he quietly tells her, his voice sounding apologetic.

She pulls her head up and her eyes grow wider. "You're leaving? But you just got here. Where are you going?" she frantically asks, thinking he plans on leaving this very moment.

Forcing her to look directly at me as I say, "Sweetheart, Joseph lives in San Diego remember? He's only here visiting, which means he has to go back to his home soon."

I see her grow extremely saddened. I know she's taken in what I've said, but she looks over in Joseph's direction choosing to ignore me. "But why can't you move here? With my mommy and me?" she pleads.

He reaches for her, pulling her from my lap to place her into his. "I'm a Marine. It's a special kind of soldier and we are told to live in certain places of the world. We don't have a choice where we want to live. They told me I had to live in San Diego for the next couple of years, so that's where I have to stay. Remember when I said you can come and visit me?" he tells her, waiting as she nods her head. "Whenever I can't visit you I'll make sure you and your mommy can come visit me. Okay?" he declares, giving her a forced smile, as if that is going to take all her worries away.

Her eyes are locked onto his. "When do you leave?" she numbly asks in more of a whisper, as if she has to force herself to ask him. It's the type of question she would have eventually asked, so I'm not surprised. Although I already knew the answer, I brace myself for her to hear his response.

"The day after tomorrow, really early in the morning. So we only have the rest of today and tomorrow to spend together," his answer paining me as I watch her absorb his response.

The unshed tears I'd seen in her eyes earlier are streaming down her face. My heart feels like it's once more plummeted to the pit of my stomach. She wraps her little arms tightly around Joseph's neck, burying her face in the crook of his neck to continue crying. The sight making my own tears come down.

He continues holding her as he rubs his hand up and down her back. I can only sit here, allowing them to comfort each other. I understand the pain she's feeling right now, knowing that he has to leave soon. I never wanted my little baby to have to experience the pain of knowing that he's leaving her as well. I had gone through that pain once when Joseph left the first time. When he was finally gone it tore at my heart for days, even months, waiting to see him again.

I never wanted my Josephina to have to experience the same thing, but no matter how hard I tried to prevent it, it's happening. My poor little girl's heart was going to be broken at such a young age and I have no control of it. As I continue watching them, I know I'm going to have to stay strong for the both of us. I'll have to force myself to glue the shattered pieces together when he leaves. Just like the first time.

Chapter 8

Joseph

I ARRIVE AT Kasey's place, walking up to the front door with the large bag of items I had brought with me to surprise Kasey and Josephina, the Internet guy following closely behind me. I called her an hour ago to tell her I would be arriving soon. I'd left out the part that I had scheduled an appointment for nine a.m. for her Internet to be installed. I didn't want to give her a chance to protest my decision.

Knocking as I reach the door, with the technician standing at my side, I wait for Kasey to open her door after firmly knocking on it again. I glance at the technician and he has his eyebrows raised as he questionably looks at me. I ignore him and continue to wait.

Within seconds Kasey answers and when she sees me, her eyes light up. I love seeing this reaction from her. It reminds me of the Kasey I grew up with. Something I've loved seeing the last couple of days I've spent with her and Josephina. However, when she sees the technician standing next to me she grows concerned.

"Good morning, Kasey. Can I come in, please?" I politely ask her, hoping to distract her from staring at the technician.

Taking another quick glance at the both of us, I see her body relax, opening the door to allow us both in.

The technician follows me in the building, but I stay at Kasey's side when she closes the door. "Kasey, this guy is here to set up your Internet," I say, pointing my chin at the technician looking around the interior of the building.

I watch as her face grows confused, "But, I didn't order Internet," she says, looking at me, obviously irritated. Her hands are on her hips as she narrows her eyes, most likely already figuring out what I'm doing.

I've seen her do it with Josephina to silently scold her. Although it might work with our little girl, it isn't going to work with me. That expression doesn't scare me. It only makes me smile seeing how cute it makes her look. She looks like a fierce little pixy fairy planning my demise.

Holding my chuckle in, I tell her, "I know. I did. I want to be able to chat with Josephina through *FaceTime* when I go back to San Diego and I can't do that if you don't have Wi-Fi," I inform her, still standing my ground. "I called and made an appointment to have it set up."

Still holding her stance, she looks doubtfully at me, then down at Josephina who has made her way over to our side. Right as Kasey is about to say something, Josephina quickly speaks up by asking. "What is *FaceTime*?" her curious little mind taking over as she studies the technician awaiting orders. From the look on her face, I can see the little gears in her head coming up with all kinds of justifications.

Crouching down so I'm eye level with Josephina, I explain, "I'll show you what it is if your mommy lets this man install the Internet," I tell her, earning me a grumble from Kasey. I know exactly what I'm doing and I'm pretty sure it's going to work.

Josephina's eyes light up as she looks up to Kasey. "Please mommy?" her pleading blue eyes begging her as she tugs at her arm. Her lip is now pouting, making me chuckle when I also look at her.

She looks torn as she looks between Josephina and me. "Joseph, I don't have a computer or device that requires it and I can't afford the Internet. It would just be an extra bill for something I won't use," she argues.

Standing up to speak with her, I take a deep breath. "Kasey, you don't have to worry about paying for it. I made sure to put the bill in my name. They have my credit card information on file so I'll get the bill directly. You don't have to worry about anything," I inform her, my eyes now pleading with her. She looks back up at me and I quickly add, "I already thought about the other things you mentioned and I've come prepared," I say holding up the large bag I have in my hand.

Her lips go flat and she looks skeptical. I know I'm close to bringing her walls down, so I continue trying Josephina's approach and simply beg. "Please? It would really mean a lot to me to be able to chat with Josephina every day," I say pouting my lips for good measure, which only earns me another grumble.

I see her sigh as she shakes her head at me while smiling. "Fine, you win." She accepts her defeat as she looks back down at Josephina giving her a nod, making Josephina jump up as she pumps her fist in the air. Kasey and I both laugh at her reaction.

Looking over to the technician, she asks him, "What do you need from me?"

Turning my attention over to the technician, I see him smiling with satisfaction.

"I need to know where your cable outlets are, ma'am," he tells her.

She looks at me doubtfully, before rolling her eyes, as she begins to walk towards the living area.

The technician takes one look at me before saying, "Good way to break her down man," he says pointing his chin at an eager looking Josephina standing next to him, waiting for him to make his next move. He walks away as she follows him, curious to see what he's going to do. He looks down at her following him and chuckles.

Yeah, I know I played dirty to make her cave, but I would do anything possible to keep in touch with them. Going straight to the couch I start pulling out the new iPad mini I bought for Josephina and a MacBook Pro for Kasey. I lay them out on the coffee table, since the X-box I had purchased the other day is still in the bag. I'll set it up for them in a couple of minutes. Josephina has soon returned to my side, curious at all the new gadgets I've brought. I quickly begin explaining how to use the iPad mini to her and within minutes, she's maneuvering her way within the apps with an excited smile on her face.

Half an hour later the technician is leaving and I've already set up everything for them to start playing with their new toys, including the X-box, to the small flat screen that Kasey has.

Kasey makes her way back to the couch with me; her eyes go wide in amazement because of the things I've brought with me. "What is all this?" she confusedly asks, taking in all the objects.

"Just some presents I bought for you," I casually say.

She takes her lip in between her teeth as she continues to take everything in. "Joseph, I've already told you, I don't feel comfortable accepting these expensive gifts from you." She conveys her discomfort by looking down at the laptop like it's going to bite her any minute. Josephina is already playing a game from one of the apps on her new mini, and from the excited squeal she makes, I know she's passed the level.

Kasey is still hesitantly standing to my side, glancing down at everything, then at me. "Kasey, please. I don't care how much money I spent on them. All that matters is how much we're all going to benefit from them. I know you said you didn't need a laptop, but I didn't like the idea of you not having one of your own for your business. I've already set up the software you need to help you manage your expenses and it comes with a video tutorial in case you need it. I have an iPad, as well as an iPhone like you. So I'll be able to *FaceTime* with you girls every day. That way I won't feel left out with Josephina," I explain. She's still looking at me with uncertainly, so I continue. "Kasey, please? I might not be able to be here physically, but if I can at least see her on a screen, I wouldn't feel so guilty about being two thousand miles away," I declare, the resentfulness of knowing it will only be through a screen is clear in my voice.

Seeing her quickly sigh makes me smile because I know I've won. I like winning in these kinds of situations with Kasey. They might not be huge victories, but they're big enough to make me feel better about leaving; even if just a little.

"Okay, but at least let me pay you back for the laptop. I can't pay you for the full amount today, but I can send it to you in installments," she sternly demands, but I only chuckle as I shake my head at her.

She's about to argue, but I cut her off with a stern, "No,"

as I hold my hand up to stop her from speaking.

I watch her grow irritated, but I only ignore her as I reach for her hand to force her to sit on the couch. She doesn't protest, but does grumble as she pulls the laptop towards her. With a smile I turn my focus on Josephina, acting as if I'm concentrating only on her, but in the corner of my eye I'm still watching Kasey.

Her once tense body now relaxes, and she proceeds to explore the features on the laptop. I can see her eyebrows drawn down in concentration, making me smile knowing it's another victory to add to the list.

An hour later after I've showed both of them how to use the *FaceTime* feature and seeing the smile of Josephina's excited face when we test it, proves every penny I spent was worth it.

We play with their new toys for another hour and Kasey decides to cook lunch when Josephina voices her hunger. After we've eaten, Kasey and I play the X-box with Josephina for another hour. I take in their smiles and laughter, trying to absorb them deep into my memory; knowing it will be a while until I physically see both of them in person. The thought hurts more than I expected it to.

We spend the rest of the day together. We take a walk around town as Josephina shows me all her favorite places to explore, followed by eating dinner and ice cream for dessert. The day couldn't have gone better, but on the way back to Kasey's I see Josephina starting to get tired, her eyes growing droopy as she rubs at them. I can tell she's desperately trying to fight off falling asleep and I know why. It's the same reason why I don't want the day to end. It's the last night I get to spend with them.

Upon arriving, I ask Kasey to allow me to put Josephina

to bed. I selfishly want to be the last person she sees before she goes to bed tonight, but it's more so I can keep the memory for myself as well.

I sit with Josephina holding her tightly in my arms. The dreaded conversation I was trying hard to delay comes up as her eyes grow glassy looking back at me. "Do you really have to leave tomorrow, daddy?" she asks, a tear escaping her eye. I wipe it away with my thumb, feeling just as torn as she looks.

I can't answer around the lump that's formed in my throat. The only thing I can do is nod my head. Hearing her call me daddy melts my heart. It's still new to my ears, but it's the sweetest name she can call me. She only started calling me *daddy* this afternoon on our walk. When she said it for the first time, it shocked us both, but it was soon followed by a giggle; making us all smile. Deep down inside I felt like crying the moment I heard her say it. It only made each passing hour unbearable, knowing I was going to leave.

I continue hugging her against my chest, wanting to hold her close to me. My heart refusing to acknowledge that I'm soon going to leave.

"When will I see you again, daddy?"

I pull her away to look at her. "I'll try to come back in a couple of months, princess. If I can't come then, I'll be here for Christmas for sure. I'm not going to miss my first Christmas with you," I tell her almost at a whisper. The thought of knowing how many holidays I've missed with her makes me more determined to be here.

Her lips start to tremble. Her eyes quickly tear up and my heart shatters seeing her this way. I cradle her head in my palms, trying to calm her from crying. She wraps her arms around my neck as she tugs me tighter and I return her embrace, holding her against my chest, refusing to loosen my hold. I've only just found this little girl. A little girl who is a part of me and I have to leave her. I hate it.

Fighting the pain I feel in my chest, I brush her hair away from her face so I can better look at her. "We'll be able to talk every day, no matter what. I might not be able to hold you like I'm doing right now, but we'll be able to see each other. You'll be able to tell me about your day and I'll tell you about mine. We'll talk every night. I'll make sure of it," I whisper to her.

She nods her little head in understanding. "I love you, daddy, and I'll miss you so much," she whispers back to me, the pain of hearing the words piercing my heart.

Pulling her back to continue comforting her, I say, "I love you, too, princess. Don't you *ever* forget that," as I fight back my tears.

She eventually falls asleep in my arms, and although I don't want to let her go, I do. I tuck her in under the covers, kissing her one last time on her temple, savoring the feeling of her soft head against my lips. The pain is tearing at my heart. I fight to keep myself from crying as I stand up, taking one last glance down at her as I walk away.

I make my way over to Kasey's workstation where I see her pouring a new batch of scented liquid into molds. The aroma is taking over, as I get closer to her. She hears me approaching and looks up at me, her face looking sympathetic, but goes back to her pouring. I stand at the workbench. My arms stretch down onto the wooden table as I watch her concentrating on how much to pour into each container, her eyes narrowing down to make sure it reaches the precise amount. She finishes pouring the last of the batch, placing the pot into a giant sink near the wall, and washes her hands before coming over to my side. Slightly turning my body to look at her, I see her wringing her hands in her apron, looking nervous and skittish.

"Did she take it okay?" she quietly asks me. I was barely able to hear her question. It had come out more of a shaky whisper than a question.

I nod my head. "I think so. I don't know who it's going to hurt more that I'm leaving. I hate knowing I have to leave you again, but I have to do it," I explain, feeling the need to plead my case. "I felt guilty doing it the first time and it feels worse having to do it again," I guiltily say, dropping my head down to look at the floor.

I feel her place her hand on my shoulder, drawing my eyes to look at her. "Joseph, you leaving the first time wasn't your fault. We both knew you were leaving the next morning and I made the decision to give myself to you that night. We were young and yes, we should have been more responsible and used protection. You couldn't have known that I was pregnant when you left. I don't blame you for leaving. I never did, but I don't regret the outcome. I got the most precious gift that I could have ever asked for from it. I was blessed with Josephina."

I listen to her words. Absorbing them, I still feeling guilty for leaving her the first time. No matter what she says, it won't ever change how I feel about that night. As I'm about to re-spond to her words, I feel my phone vibrate in my back pocket. I don't need to look at the screen to know who it is, but I'm not going to pull the phone out in front of Kasey. Ignoring the vi-bration, I hug Kasey one last time and tell her I'll text her to-morrow, so they both know I made it back safely.

We say our goodbyes and then I'm in Mark's car driving away from Kasey's building. I still feel like shit as I drive fur-ther away. Kasey may not blame me for leaving her the first time, or this time around, but it doesn't matter. I still feel so much guilt. Leaving both of them for the second time is tearing me apart. I know I shouldn't be doing this, but I have to. All I can do now is find a way to make it up to them.

Chapter 9

Kasey

THE MORNING BEFORE Joseph left all those years ago, I had silently cried to myself most of the night. I remember my body being entangled with his as I lay next to his warm body. I had lied awake, draped across his chest, dreadfully waiting for morning to come, as I quietly listened to his heart beating in my ear, tears slowly flowing down my cheeks.

I didn't sleep at all that night. He assumed I was asleep when he quietly snuck out of my room, but I couldn't bear to watch him leave. It hurt knowing he was leaving back then and it was hurting to know he was going again.

It hurt worse than the first time.

He had a fiancée now, someone else who owned his heart. I knew I shouldn't be allowing myself to feel this way. I had no right to be pinning for him like I did the first time.

It was another reason why I forced myself to let go, to watch him walk away this time. It hurt to see him walk out the door tonight, but I had to let him go. He was never mine to begin with, nor would he ever be in the future.

It still didn't take the pain away, though. No, the pain felt ten times worse this time. I had a little girl to share the pain with me. The thought of knowing she would be feeling the same pain as I am is tearing my heart apart. I had hopes last time that I would see him soon. Although it never happened, I was left with hope, but now I'd only see him because of Josephina; he belongs to someone else.

I wasn't going to allow myself to cry this time. I'm stronger this time around. I knew if I was able to watch him walk away once, I could do it again. I had to stay strong for both Josephina's sake and my own.

I WOKE UP this morning, already dreading what the day would be like. I knew I would have to keep Josephina occupied, so she wouldn't think too much about Joseph leaving, especially when she first woke up. But I didn't have the chance. The first question from her lips when she awoke was, "Has he left yet?" her eyes desperately begging me to tell her no, but when I answered her with a "yes," the loss was evident on her face.

Although I was trying my best to be stronger this time around, it was proving difficult to do, but I kept my head held high. I forced a smile on my face as I kept us entertained throughout the day. I saw it in her eyes, though. Every time she looked at me, I knew how badly she was hurting inside, because I was hurting too.

Knowing I needed to get my batches made for the upcoming week, I had her help me in an effort to keep her little mind distracted. Before we knew it, the sun had set and she was growing more anxious, hoping Joseph would call.

As I was cooking dinner she constantly kept checking her iPad for any missed calls, which would have been impossible because she kept the thing at her side, refusing to let it go. It wasn't until we were done with dinner that the much-awaited call finally came through. The smile on her face as she slid her little finger across the screen to answer the call was all it took to make my pain from the day disappear.

"Hi daddy!" she excitedly answers into the screen as I walk over to take a seat next to her.

Looking down at the screen, I see Joseph. He looks exhausted, but just as quickly a smile forms on his lips with a hint of glee in his eyes, as he stares back at Josephina. He's lying back against what looks like a headboard, his arm behind his head emphasizing his large bicep as he relaxes against it. "Hey there, princess. What did you do today?"

Knowing how much Josephina can carry on a conversation, I leave so I can continue cleaning up the kitchen from dinner, giving them their privacy. Thirty minutes later they're ending their little chat, with the insistence from Joseph that Josephina get into the shower and ready for bed. Although she's disappointed, I catch her yawning and already know why he insisted. With the promise of speaking tomorrow, she ends the call and I take her to the bathroom to wash her up.

After her shower, I tuck her into bed and wish her a goodnight.

I'm about to fall asleep myself, my eyes already drifting closed, when I hear ringing coming from the iPad. Confused, I go to pick it up, noticing it's Joseph calling again. I reluctantly answer the call, thinking he wishes to speak to Josephina once more, contemplating ignoring it, but instead I give in and answer.

As soon as his face appears on the screen, I immediately say without hesitation, "She's asleep, Joseph." It comes out closely to a whisper, since I don't wish to wake Josephina up.

Although he's in the same position as earlier, the first thing I notice is he's now shirtless and his hair looks wet, as if he also just took a shower. He still looks tired, making me wonder why he's *really* calling.

"I would hope she's asleep, it's past her bed time," he says with a mischievous smile.

"Then why are you calling?" I watch as he shrugs his shoulder. His expression worries me. He looks disappointed with my response. "Is something wrong, Joseph?"

He shakes head. "No, nothing's wrong, I just wanted to talk. That's if you're not tired," he hesitantly adds.

The thought that he was calling to speak to me both confuses and excites me at the same time, but from how exhausted he looks, I feel guilty wanting to talk.

"No, I'm not that tired, but you look it. Are you sure you want to talk? Or is there something you needed to discuss that can't wait until tomorrow?" I carefully ask, worrying at the same time.

He quickly responds, "I'm not too tired. I just wanted to talk to you. Tell me about your day," he states with a smile, the worry fading from my mind.

At his insistence I tell him. "I wrapped up my projects needed for the rest of the week earlier today with Josephina's help. I think she made more of a mess than help, but she always enjoys working with me. If she wasn't my daughter, I would've fired her a long time ago," I jokingly tell him.

He chuckles, making me smile with him. I take in how carefree his smile now looks. "Yeah, she told me how you had her working like a slave today," he says with a teasing smile.

I gawk back at him, but just as quickly realize he's going along with the joke by the teasing look in his expression. "Well, slave or not, it was the only way I could think of to distract her from focusing on you being gone," I tell him, realizing how hurtful the words must have sounded the moment after I say them.

His once gleeful smile has now turned somber and I'm soon duplicating his expression, now regretting I said the words. "I'm sorry, Kasey. I know how hard it must be on her. It was hard getting on the plane this morning knowing I had to leave," he says, his voice dropping low and raspy.

The pain is clear in his voice, and being able to see the pain on his face doesn't make it easier for me. Seeing just how hard it was for him as well made me feel selfish thinking Josephina and I were the only ones hurting. I'd never once considered how much it was going to hurt Joseph to leave. It was obvious he was hurting too. This wasn't easy on any of us.

Knowing it was best to change the subject, I start to tell him about the upcoming project I had planned involving expanding the scents I had for the bath salts. Ironically, the more we spoke, the more I noticed how easy it was to have a conversation with him, like in the past. The whole time he was attentive to my conversation, seeming interested and being responsive. It felt like when we were young all over again. When he would occasionally walk me home and the entire time we'd carelessly laugh and tease each other, making me miss those days. My days have felt lonely since then.

An hour later, we both stifle our yawns and end the call. As I'm about to fall asleep, I hear the ping of a text message on my phone. Picking it up, I immediately notice the message is from Joseph.

Joseph: *I forgot to ask you to give my little princess a kiss from me. Can you do it?*
Kasey: *Of course*
Joseph: *I already miss you girls so much.*

His message takes me by surprise. I never expected him to say he missed the both of us. Josephina yes, but to include me as well... I was left in shock. Thinking maybe he didn't really mean to say the both of us, but not wanting to sound greedy with wanting clarification if he really meant it, I simply ignore it and give Josephina her promised kiss from Joseph. Getting myself comfortable, my once tired state is now gone as I lay there wondering if he really meant those words the way they were written. I pick up the phone and open up the text message he sent, staring at it.

I miss him dearly already myself, but I know I can't tell him that. I would only be sending him mixed signals, or sound like an idiot if he didn't really intend to say those specific words. Knowing he's engaged makes me push my feelings aside, especially since someone else will soon own his heart forever.

I HEAR MY phone ringing. I already have a pretty good idea who it is. When I look at the screen and see that it's Joseph, I push the ignore button as I grumble to myself. I don't want to speak to him right now. I'm still harboring the resentment that's been building up over the weekend, especially since he's now deciding to call.

It's Sunday evening. The weekend having come and gone without a phone call or *FaceTime* call from him until now. The last time Josephina spoke to him was Thursday evening. As usual, he'd promised to call the next night, just like he had been doing every night since he'd left. Only he never did call.

At first I had thought he'd merely forgotten, hoping he would make it up to her by calling in the morning, but he didn't. She had gone all day Friday trying to call him instead, but he never did answer. The poor thing was watching the iPad all day with longing eyes, waiting for his call. It hurt to see her full of disappointment as I laid her down to sleep that night and still did not receive an answer. I grew worried about him not following through with his promises at first, but I was convinced that Joseph wouldn't give Josephina false hope through empty promises.

Josephina had kept insisting that I call him to make sure he was okay. I *was* just as worried as she was. So I finally gave in and called him on his phone Saturday afternoon after the Farmers Market, but as before, we didn't receive an answer. The call went straight to his voicemail. I was worried after that, until I received a text message a couple of hours later stating he would call when he could. I immediately grew angry as the realization hit me that he was ignoring our phone calls. I should've known he wouldn't keep his promise, but I was the idiot for believing him.

I didn't tell Josephina the truth, of course. Instead I told her he was probably not answering because he had to work. My answer made her sad, but she accepted it without any further questions, which made me angrier with him. How can he think it was okay to promise her something and not keep his word?

When she started moping around the building, I couldn't take it anymore. This morning when we woke up, I decided to get her out of the house to help distract her from waiting for him to call.

Apparently, now that it's the end of the weekend, he decides he wants to talk to her. Well, he was going to be the one waiting, because I was not going to give him the satisfaction of waking her up to speak to him. My mission for the day had worked. She was both distracted and exhausted by the time we finally ended the day, which made me happy. She had only asked twice if he had called, but I was able to quickly distract her after answering her with a quick "No."

Pulling into my driveway and taking a sleeping Josephina out of my car, I head inside and tuck her into bed. While I'm giving her a kiss I hear the phone ringing, growing irritated as I did earlier. I grab for the phone and quickly remove myself from the bedroom area to the farthest end of the building. I don't want to risk waking Josephina up when I speak to Joseph.

"She's already asleep," I snap at him in frustration as I answer the phone, not bothering with a simple "Hello" when I answered.

"I'm sorry, I forgot about the time difference. I'll remember for next time," he casually says as my anger builds up inside of me.

I can hear the tiredness and exhaustion in his voice when he tells me, but it doesn't stop me from snapping back at him. "Fine, I'll tell her you called," I clip out, ready to end the call. I'm unable to when I can hear him quickly pleading, "Please, Kasey, don't hang up on me. I really am sorry." The desperation in his voice making me pause and feel guilty for snapping at him.

My mind is torn between staying mad at him and wanting to hear his explanation. Needing to know why he's barely calling, sighing I tell him, "Joseph, you haven't called all weekend and she's been waiting to speak to you the entire time. You can't do that to her. I won't allow you to hurt her like that."

I hear him heavily sigh on the other end of the phone. "I'm really sorry about not calling Josephina. She's all I kept thinking about all weekend, I swear," he states, sounding frustrated. "I went to Vegas to see Elizabeth, so I could finally tell her about Josephina. She didn't take it too well at first, but I think I got her to come around," he declares.

Although he's stated it, I can tell by the tone in his voice he's not telling the truth, but I'm not going to argue with him now. I don't have the energy to do so. I already knew she wasn't going to take the news well at first, so it didn't surprise me he was masking her reaction.

He tries to further explain, "She took advantage of me being there to help her make some last minute decisions for the wedding. I was busy pretty much from the moment I got there until the moment I left. I just got back a little while ago. I tried calling you, but you didn't answer and I started to get worried."

Remembering how worried Josephina and I were about him not answering *our* phone call, only makes me feel remorseful for not answering his the first time. "I'm sorry for not answering. I was driving. I really hope your fiancée will come around," I say to him, not knowing what else to say.

As if sensing how uncomfortable I feel about the conversation, he quickly changes the subject by asking what we did over the weekend. Giving him a quick recap, we easily fall into a conversation as I begin to tell him about an upcoming delivery I need to make. Shortly after, we are ending the phone call as we say our goodbyes.

I lay down in bed that night with Josephina, repeating Joseph's words in my mind. His fiancée's response keeps me awake for several hours as they repeat themselves in my thoughts. Although Joseph states he's going to be a part of Josephina's life, it still worries me whether he'll keep his promise. How can I *really* know he'll stay true to his word once he's married? He will start a family with her, making it easy for him to forget about Josephina. He's only just met her; both still strangers to one another. He can claim that he'll continue to be part of her life, but with Elizabeth at his side, with a new family they make together, his promises can easily be forgotten.

As much as it had warmed my heart to see both of them together, I know it can easily go back to being how it used to be, Josephina without a father around again in her life. The only thing I can do if it happens will be to reassure Josephina that no matter the outcome, we were going to be fine, just like before Joseph came back into our lives.

"MOMMY, WHERE IS Mrs. Thompson?" Josephina impatiently asks as she stares out the window she's been looking out of for the last twenty minutes.

Placing the lid on the last box needed to go into my SUV, I take another glance at the clock looking at the time. If Mrs. Thompson doesn't get here in the next ten minutes, I'm going to be late. She was supposed to be here fifteen minutes ago. I try calling her again but the phone call goes straight to voicemail. Same as it did earlier.

I'm starting to grow worried. I really don't have any room for Josephina to come with me. With all the boxes that are in the SUV, she doesn't fit. I had to take her booster seat out of my car so I can load this last box. There is *no way* she is going to fit.

This is the one shipment I make every month without hesitation because of the recipient. It was for Mrs. Berry, the lady who originally showed me how to make soaps to begin with. Due to her arthritis, she stopped making the soaps two years ago, leaving the task up to me. In return for her selling my soaps, I give her fifty percent of the income, which helps provide for her family as well. It's why I couldn't afford to take fewer products with me. If I did, it would affect us both.

I'm surprised Mrs. Thompson isn't here yet. I've always made this delivery around the same time every month; she knows being that she always watches Josephina for me. She'd even confirmed with me over the weekend about today.

Sighing, I begin to look through my contact list in hopes I can find someone else to stay with Josephina, but I quickly come up short from the list of people I usually use. They can only watch her at night or on the weekends if they have advance notice.

I'm about to give up when I come across Ashley's name. I consider the possibility of calling her. Joseph had made me put both hers and Mark's cell numbers, along with their house number, in my phone before he left. Just in case of an emergency.

Although this wasn't an emergency, it was close to it for me. Looking back at Josephina, still staring out of the window,

I think really hard before I make the decision to call her. Taking another deep breath, I press on her number and pray that she'll answer.

As I listen to the ringing coming into my ear, I'm nervously biting my lip. "Hello," a confused Ashley answers.

Realizing she probably doesn't recognize the number, I say, "Hello Ashley, it's Kasey."

"Oh, Kasey. How are you?"

"I'm good, thank you. I'm really sorry to be calling you so suddenly, but I was hoping I can ask you for a really huge favor," I hesitantly ask, waiting for her response.

"Of course. What can I do for you?"

Feeling like the worst person in the world for even asking, I say, "I was hoping you'd be able to watch Josephina for me today, only for the next four or five hours. I have a really huge shipment I have to deliver to the next town over and I don't have any room to take Josephina with me."

I go on, further explaining. "The lady who usually watches her hasn't arrived and I'm already running late. I wouldn't normally ask, but I can't afford not to make this shipment. I'm sorry to have to call you last minute like this, Ashley, but I really don't have anyone else who would watch her right now," I desperately add.

"I'm about to head home from the grocery store. It's around the corner from your place. I can swing by to pick Josephina up on the way if you'd like?"

I let out the breath that I was cautiously holding while waiting for her answer. "Thank you, Ashley. Thank you so much."

She chuckles, telling me not to worry and within ten minutes she's at my front door. Quickly loading Josephina's booster seat into her car, I give Josephina one last kiss before I watch them drive away. I just as quickly jump into my car and drive away myself.

It usually takes me an hour drive to get there and an hour back, but I always give myself two extra hours because I like to spend time visiting with Mrs. Berry.

The dreadful thing about the drive is I have to take a narrow two-lane highway the entire way, in both directions. Most of the time it's a boring drive, the Amish community prefers to be in their own secluded area of the state, keeping to themselves.

Arriving and quickly unloading everything from my SUV, I have my usual coffee with Mrs. Berry as we catch up. She always likes to know how Josephina is doing and of course this visit is more emotional when I tell her about Joseph.

The entire time I lived in the community, I was always questioned about where the father of my child was, but not knowing the exact answer, I always refused to answer. It only made the community isolate me even more. Mrs. Berry was the only person who stood by my side, never once judging me for it, even when my own aunt did so. Because of that reason alone, I was determined to help Mrs. Berry with an income. Without her, I wouldn't have the gift to give back.

Knowing that I needed to get back to Josephina, I say by usual goodbyes, promising to see her next month. I finally get back into my car and pull out of town to head home.

I'm almost back into Madison when a song I despise at the moment comes on the radio. Scrunching my nose at the melody, wanting to change it, I take one last glance at the road ahead of me and I see it's still empty and safe to change the station. I look down at the radio to change the station and I quickly glance back up to see a huge truck pull out from a side road without stopping at the intersection. I jerk my car to the side to avoid hitting him, but I lose control of my car, swerving into the opposite lane. My heart stops. The fear of not knowing what to do takes over and I scream in fright. I feel my car hit something head on, the air bag deploying into my face, instantly sending a jolt of pain throughout my body. I can only sit there and let it take over, and immediately I'm dragged into darkness.

Chapter 10

Joseph

I'M FINALLY GETTING off of work. *TGIF!* The end of the day felt like it would never come. I'm exhausted from having to deal with the bullshit of the week. On top of that, I told Elizabeth I would go back to Vegas this weekend to do some fucking tasting for the wedding. I don't know why she needed me there for that. My only requirement for the wedding was I get a steak that night, everything else I didn't care two cents about. The wedding was technically all for her anyway. If it were up to me, we would've been married the night I asked her. We were already in Vegas when I proposed. I didn't see anything wrong with going to the local chapel and getting it done, but she refused, saying that she wanted the fairytale wedding every girl dreams about.

Right now, I just want to get home and get something to eat. Plus, I wanted to speak with Josephina and Kasey really quick before I left. I've been looking forward to it all day. There's nothing I wanted more than to see their faces, even if it's on a screen.

I'm climbing into my truck when I hear my phone ring and I'm already dreading seeing who it might be. In my head I'm thinking it's Elizabeth, asking if I've already left. All week she insisted I leave work early so I could get to Vegas sooner, but I couldn't manage it. There was too much going at work, which made it impossible, but it also made for an angry Elizabeth. Another reason why I was dreading going this weekend. I knew I would have to hear her non-stop complaining about it. I look down at my phone and see that it's not Elizabeth, but Mark's house number instead.

"Hello," I answer, wondering why they'd be calling me. Usually Mark would text me for anything.

"Joseph, have you heard from Kasey at all today?" Ashley worriedly asks in a rush as I start to drive away from the parking lot.

Confused, I wonder why she'd be calling me about Kasey. She also sounds desperate for an answer. "No, I haven't, but I was about to call them when I got home. Why?"

The groan she gives me doesn't calm my nerves. Instead I start to panic, especially when I hear Josephina on the other end of the line desperately asking Ashley if I've heard from Kasey. "Ashley, what is my daughter doing at your house and why is she asking if I've seen Kasey?" I demand.

"I'm babysitting her for Kasey. She called this morning needing me to watch her while she made an important delivery out of town. Kasey told me she couldn't fit everything in her car with Josephina too, so she asked if I could watch her and of course I offered, but she also said she would be back in four hours. That was supposed to be one this afternoon. I tried calling her cell phone, but it keeps going to voicemail. Josephina is really worried because she hasn't shown up, and to tell you the truth Joseph, so am I. I was hoping she would have called you," she finishes, her voice sounding frantic as she rambled on.

I look down at the clock on my dashboard to see it's almost five, Pacific Time and since they're two hours ahead, it's well after six. I know Kasey would have called already had she not been able to make it on time. It's unlike her not too. That alone worries me. The feeling in the pit of my stomach tells me something is wrong.

"Has she called *at all*?" I ask, hoping for something, anything at all.

"She called me this morning when she arrived to speak to Josephina. She said she would be running a little behind, but she hasn't called us back since. That's why I'm calling you," she indicates.

"Ashley, let me speak to Josephina."

Within seconds I hear the rustling of the phone, soon followed by a worried little whine. "Hi daddy. Has mommy called you today?" she desperately asks. "She hasn't come back to get me and I'm really scared now," she utters, her raspy voice making me picture her crying on the other end. I hear her sniffle, confirming the picture in my mind.

The worry and guilt is beginning to build inside of me, knowing that I can't be there to comfort my little girl makes it worse. I hate not being able to be there to take her worry away.

"I'm sure she's fine, princess. I'm going to try calling her and as soon as I get a hold of her I'll tell her to call you, okay?" I tell her, listening as she sniffles while giving me a muffled "Okay."

"Why don't you go and color a pretty picture for her, that way you'll have something to give her when she shows up," I cheerfully tell her, trying to mask my worry.

"Okay, daddy. Will I still to be able to *FaceTime* with you tonight?" she asks, before adding, "Ashley says she has an iPad like mine and I can talk to you on it," she says, while still trying to get her sobbing under control.

"Of course, princess. We'll talk as soon as I get home. I'm driving there right now. Now let me talk to Aunty Ashley, that way you can get started on those pictures for your mommy."

I hear the rustle of the phone before Ashley asks what she should do. The calm collected self that I disguised myself to be for my daughter is gone and my worried, panicked self is back. "Ashley, I need you to keep Josephina calm. I'm already pulling up to my place and I'm going to try calling Kasey myself, if I can't get a hold of her I'll start calling the hospitals, just in case."

She loudly gasps on the other end of the line. "Oh, Joseph, you don't think something has happened to her, do you?" she asks, almost at a whisper.

"I don't know, but I'm pretty sure Kasey wouldn't go this long without checking up on Josephina. It isn't like her. I'll call you as soon as I get any news."

It's now Ashley who is whimpering through the phone, forcing me to say, "Ashley, please calm down. The stress isn't good for you or the baby. The last thing I need is Mark getting on my ass because you go into early labor over all this," I tell her, remembering how Kasey had mentioned stress wasn't good for her or the baby.

As she tries to mask a sniffle, she says, "Okay, but please keep me updated or I'm going to continue being worried."

"I will."

As soon as I reach my apartment complex I practically jump out of my truck running straight up into my apartment. I boot up my laptop and immediately start searching for numbers of the local hospitals in Madison. There are several of them, but I try the first number hoping that they'll have some news for me. I have to lie to the front desk in the emergency department, telling them I'm Kasey's husband, to be able to even ask if she's been admitted. When they confirm the nightmare I was dreading, my heart stops. Kasey had been brought in earlier from a car accident and she was currently still in surgery.

I sit there, shocked, without words, feeling as if I can't breathe. The only thing I can think of is getting to her and it can't be fast enough. Ending the phone call, I sit there trying to catch my breath. My heart has resumed its beating, but this time it feels like it's rapidly racing, as if I can't get it under control. I'm panicking knowing she's in surgery, fighting for her life, and I'm not there.

Without thinking, I immediately start making phone calls to my commanding officer, demanding he give me leave. He's reluctant at first, but I remind him I still have mandatory leave available he kept insisting I take. He didn't like the idea of the short notice, but after a little explaining, he gives it to me. Even if he hadn't agreed, I would have left regardless.

Quickly booking an overnight flight back to Madison, I start packing my bags, waiting as the minutes tick by. I call Ashley as promised to give her an update, informing her that I'm on my way. Although I promised Josephina I would *FaceTime* with her this evening, she soon forgets when I explain to the news of Kasey's accident to her. She doesn't take the news of the accident very well, but I didn't expect her to. She's still a little girl. This is harder on her than anyone else, because it's her mother. Ashley promises to take care of her until I get there before we end the call. I continue packing my bags, frantically wanting to leave already.

Packed and ready, my phone starts to ring and I panic thinking it's the hospital with an update: one I might not want to hear. Demanding they keep me updated with any news, I left them my number, but in my mind I'd only wanted them to deliver good news, nothing more.

Bracing myself, I look down at the screen to see it's only Mark calling and I already feel relieved. "What's up Mark?" I clip out, looking around my room one last time to make sure I'm not forgetting anything important.

"I wanted to tell you I'm at the hospital. I was already on my way to the grocery store when you called Ashley. She called me to tell me what hospital Kasey was at and I headed straight over here. When I got here they thought I was her husband that called earlier. Do you happen to know who that would be?" he sarcastically asks, trying to mock me, but the somber tone in his voice overtakes his attempt. "Knowing that they wouldn't give me any information unless I was family, I told them that she was my sister-in-law," he says with a sigh. "She's still in surgery Joseph, but they came out a couple of minutes ago to tell me that she had complications. They'd originally thought it was only her spleen, but when they got in there they found some internal bleeding and they're trying to get it under control."

My body drops down onto the bed behind me, my legs collapsing from under me, as I close my eyes and force myself to breathe. Running my hand over my head, I pray that she'll make it. I'm having trouble fighting to keep the tears from coming. I can't see. My vision becomes blurred from the tears I'm holding at bay.

I feel like I'm about to throw up. The feeling of losing her any moment is killing me and I hate being clear across the county from her, instead of at her side.

"Joseph, you still there man?"

Deeply sighing, I answer, "Yeah, I'm still here," I force myself to say around the lump still lodged in my throat.

"Joseph, you need to calm down. It's not like what happened to your parents. Her accident wasn't as bad. She came out of it alive and she's currently in surgery, which is a good sign. Your parents never made it that far," he assures me, reminding me how my parents died. He's right. They died in their accident. Kasey didn't.

Attempting to calm my racing heart, I let out the breath I was holding. "You're right, but it still fucking sucks being so far away from her," I declare. "I've booked a flight already and I'm leaving tonight. I'm going to have someone drop me off at the airport, but I won't be there until morning."

"Alright, text me the details and I'll be there when you land."

Ending the call, I make a quick phone call to a buddy to take me to the airport.

After checking in and passing through security, I'm soon sitting and waiting at my terminal's waiting area. Thinking I finally have a chance to breathe, I hear my phone ringing again and the breath is just as easily lost thinking it's the hospital. However, when I look down at the screen, instead of seeing a Wisconsin number, I see Elizabeth's house number.

Cursing under my breath I answer the phone, already dreading the conversation. "Hello."

"Joseph, are you almost here?"

Silently I curse to myself. I had completely forgotten I was supposed to be on my way to Vegas right now. "I'm sorry, Elizabeth. I've had a change of plans. I'm actually going to be heading back to Madison," I inform her, bracing myself for the scolding I know she'll be giving me for not showing up this weekend.

"As in Madison, Wisconsin?" she screeches into the phone, making me pull it away from my ear. "Why are you going back to Wisconsin? Didn't you just come back from there?" she continues to yell into the phone.

"Yes, Elizabeth," I growl, as her voice makes the pounding headache from earlier return.

"Then?"

"Then what?" I ask.

"Why are you going back?" the seething anger evident in her question.

Closing my eyes, I grab onto the bridge of my nose hoping the darkness behind my eyelids will help calm my headache, but it isn't working. "Something happened and I have to go back. I'll call you when I can," I calmly state, not feeling I need to further explain myself, but Elizabeth still insist for more information.

"Are you going back because of the little girl?" she demands to know.

"She's my daughter, Elizabeth. And yes, I'm going back because of her," I state, not lying at that particular detail.

She mutters something on the other end, but I can't quite make out what it was, and at this point I really don't care anyway. "Well, I guess while you're there you'll be able to get the test we talked about done."

Now I'm mumbling a curse. Remembering our conversation when I told her about Josephina only makes my anger return. Elizabeth demanded I have a paternity test done. She'd easily claimed maybe Kasey was lying about me being Josephina's father. Elizabeth didn't like the idea that Kasey never tried contacting me to tell me I had a daughter. I tried explaining the situation between Kasey and I, but she kept insisting on the test, regardless of how much I refused to agree to it.

"Elizabeth, I'm not discussing this again," I growl into the phone.

"Well, whether you want to discuss it or not, you have to face reality that this little girl might not be your daughter. The only way to find out for sure is to have the test done. I just don't understand why you refuse to have it done. My parents have offered to pay for it," she adds, as if it's going to get me to agree.

Groaning, I hear the announcement to board my plane, and it couldn't have come at a better time. "Look Elizabeth, I have to go, they're announcing my boarding call. I'll talk to you tomorrow," I say before I give her a quick goodbye, then pressing the end button on the screen and turning off the phone as I board the plane. My head is now pounding harder than it was when I arrived at the airport and I'm already looking forward to getting some sleep.

Eight and a half hours later, with one layover in Salt Lake City, I'm finally arriving in Madison. As promised, Mark is waiting for me when I exit the airport and without hesitation he drives us straight to the hospital. When we arrive I don't wait for him to park the car, insisting he drop me off at the front doors. With him having already told me where Kasey was at, I start running straight there, taking the stairs because I'm too impatient to wait for the elevator.

As I get closer to the ICU department I see the waiting area and immediately spot Ashley with Josephina sitting in a set of chairs. The minute my little girl sees me she comes running towards me, catapulting herself into my arms. I scoop her up, holding her tightly in my arms, feeling like I'm whole again. It's only been a few weeks since I've held her, but it's feels like forever since then.

"Hey, princess. I've missed you so much," I whisper into her hair, my nose inhaling her sweet childlike scent at the same time.

I feel her squeeze her little arms tighter around my neck, as if she doesn't want to let me go. I can hear her sniffling and I can already feel the wetness of her tears running down my neck.

"They won't let me see her, daddy. I just want to see my mommy," she whimpers.

It's tearing me apart hearing her heartbroken voice; knowing how badly she must hate not being able to see Kasey. "I'm sorry, princess. As soon as your mommy is feeling better, I promise you'll be able to see her," I tell her, as I rub her back trying to comfort her.

I feel a hand on my shoulder drawing my attention. I turn to see a teary eyed Ashley staring back at me. "They've got Kasey in a room now. Did you want to see her?"

I calmly nod my head, but I already know I have to let Josephina go in order to do so. Pulling her back so I can see her face to speak to her, needing to make sure she understands as I say, "Princess, I'm going to go see your mommy now. Is that okay? I'll make sure to tell her that you're here."

I wait until she nods her head. I give her a kiss on her temple before I hand her to Mark, who is now standing next to Ashley. They inform me which room number Kasey's in and I hesitantly make my way there, dreading what I'm going to see. When I enter the room, my breath hitches and my heart skips a beat as I take in the sight of her.

Kasey's hooked up to machines that are quietly displaying her vital signs. She has a tube coming out of her mouth, which must be helping her breath. She's lying there, motionless, with her eyes closed and her body stiff. If you were to get past the sight of all the wires and machines that are surrounding her, you would think she's peacefully sleeping.

I force my feet to move, slowly taking one step after another, to reach her. Pulling the chair next to the bed, I take a seat as I take Kasey's hand into mine, needing to hold some part of her. Bringing her hand up to my mouth to place a kiss on the back of it, I pray that she'll wake up soon. She looks so fragile lying there and the sight of her like this is scaring me. What if she never wakes up? I can't bear the thought of losing her.

The silence of the room is broken when I hear someone walk in, making me turn towards the doorway to see a doctor walking in. "Are you her husband?"

I simply nod, unable to speak.

He goes straight into explaining what happened during the surgery, informing me of the details. Although they were able to find the tear and repair it, it is too soon to know whether there would be any more complications from the surgery. Only time would tell, he informed me. I absorb the words as I continue holding Kasey's hand, needing to know that regardless of what he said, I know she's still here.

He soon excuses himself, leaving me alone with Kasey in a silent room with my thoughts. I sit at her side hoping she'll wake up; needing her to wake up soon, for all of us.

An hour later Mark enters the room looking like he hasn't gotten much sleep either. He looks tired and exhausted, with darkened rims around his eyes. "Since they won't let Josephina back here to see Kasey, Ashley and I are going to take her home. She's restless from having to be in the waiting room. Do you need anything before we leave?"

"I'm fine," I tell him, but just as he's about to turn away

to leave, I quickly add, "Mark, thanks for being here last night. It really means a lot to me that you stayed with her."

His somber expression stares back at me. "Don't worry about it, man. I know you would've done the same for Ashley had the tables been turned."

I could only nod my head in confirmation, agreeing with his words as he walks out.

Looking back at Kasey, I watch her chest slowly rise and fall as she takes her shallow breaths with the help of the ventilator. For the last eight hours, all I've had is time to think about Kasey and Josephina. I don't know what the hell was going to happen from this day forward, but I'd already made one decision. I wasn't returning back to San Diego without the both of them. I couldn't.

Chapter 11

Kasey

"YOU BOTH REALLY need to stop fussing over me, it's not like I'm dying," I mumble, as Joseph tries to fluff my pillows. When done, he stands tall, looking down at me, waiting for me to request something of him.

On the other side of me, Josephina stands as well, the same look on her face. The difference is she's been verbally asking me if I needed anything. As much as I love how they're both putting forth the effort to nurse me back to health, it's making me feel guilty and useless. It's been like this for the last hour since we got home from the hospital and I'm beginning to realize it might just get worse.

It's been a week since I woke up from my accident. According to Joseph, I hadn't awoken immediately after surgery, but two days later. I'd felt every single ache that was a result of the accident the day I woke up. I still did a little, but it was tolerable, and I wasn't going to complain. I was alive and in good health compared to most.

At first when I had awoken, I'd forgotten what had happened. I was confused and it had taken me a couple of seconds to remember where I was as I took in my surroundings, realizing I was in a hospital.

What surprised me the most was seeing Joseph at my side. The sight of him confused me. I thought I was in a dream when I'd first seen him next to me. It was the main reason why I felt so disoriented. I kept wondering how long I was asleep and how long I had been there. I would have never expected him to be there at my side.

He was sleeping with his body hunched over mine, completely lost in his slumber. The position he was in looked very uncomfortable, but I didn't want to wake him, wanting to watch him for as long as I could. Quietly admiring him next to me, he had my hand tightly wrapped in his as his head rested at my side. He looked so peaceful lying there.

It was when the nurse entered to take my vitals that he had awoken. He had rapidly awoken at the slightest sound, as if he was trained for it.

When he looked up at me with sleep-laced eyes, the smile that spread across his face was all I needed to make me feel better. The pain instantly disappearing as his excitement of seeing me awake lightened up the room. From the state of his wrinkled clothes and five o'clock shadow on his face, I could tell he had been there for a while. His body looked worn and exhaustion clear on his face. Even after waking up, his stubble was something I hadn't seen on Joseph before, which made me feel guilty wondering how long I'd been asleep. I was completely shocked when I had later learned from the nurses that he had refused to leave my side, resulting in the state he had been in.

"Are you sure you don't need anything? Anything to make you feel more comfortable?" Josephina's enthusiastic voice brings me back to the present.

Seeing her desperate little face patiently waiting for me to request something, I smile at her eagerness to please. "If you don't mind, I'd like a glass of water."

Although I'm not truly thirsty, I already know how persistent Josephina can be until she feels she has accomplished her task. She briskly returns handing me the glass of water, already asking if I need anything else. "No, sweetheart. You're doing a really great job of taking care of me already. I haven't needed anything else since a minute ago when you asked," I tell her, earning me a triumphant smile.

Joseph laughs at my side, and when I look up at him, he's shaking his head with a smile. "Princess, why don't we give your mommy some time to rest?" he proposes, scooping her up into his arms.

Taking in the sight of them both, I can't help but notice how small Josephina looks in his arms, but the way he holds her, it takes my breath away. He does it as if she's the most precious artifact in the world, as he holds her with care. He also looks at her with such adoration. It is clear in his eyes and actions just how deeply he's grown to care for her in the short amount of time he's known her.

"Why don't you go with me to the pharmacy so we can pick up mommy's medicine?" he suggest looking back down at me to give me a wink. The thought that he's trying to keep Josephina entertained for my sanity is sweet. I watch as her eyes light up as he walks away with her to leave the building.

Taking advantage of them being gone, I take a quick shower, loving how good it feels to finally be home instead of still being at the hospital. With some difficulty, I manage to dress myself and brush out my hair, soon making my way back to the bed to lie back down. I'd told Joseph I wouldn't get up, but I had desperately wanted to take a shower. The sterilized scent of the hospital was still strong on my clothing and body, even after we left, and I wanted it off of me. Climbing back into bed, I am now trying to look like I had never moved, hoping they don't take notice in my change of clothing, since I'm wearing the same color tank top. With only a couple of minutes to spare, I hear them walking into the building and I immediately notice they've brought back more than just my medicine.

Josephina quickly runs in my direction, handing me a beautiful bouquet of flowers. "You didn't have to buy me anymore flowers," I utter to both of them as I take in the floral scent of the roses in my hands. Joseph merely shrugs his shoulders as he casually stands at the end of my bed, his hands in the pockets of his jeans, looking shy as a schoolboy, as he looks back at me.

Although he is no longer the schoolboy I grew up with, but now a very muscular man, he still looks at me with the same eyes I grew up crushing on. His body was the opposite of the scrawny boy I grew up with, now more defined. No matter how much I take him in, I'm still left amazed at how much he's changed. I liked this Joseph so much more.

"Josephina wanted to buy you some more. Who am I to deny her request?" he shyly conveys.

"Her father," I sternly remind him. "Which means you need to learn to tell her no every now and then, or else she's going to learn that she can easily control you. You'll come to regret it if she ever realizes it."

"We'll worry about that later. Right now I just want to take care of my girls," he states, his eyes narrowly locked onto mine as his lips go up to one side into a smile.

His words shock me, leaving me confused as to the meaning behind them, as I slowly repeat them in my mind. My mind wants clarification, but my heart doesn't have the nerve to question him. It's obvious from the look he's giving me he knew exactly what he'd said, but I doubt he meant them. He couldn't have.

Left sitting there confused, I bring the flowers up to my nose to take in another smell, allowing it to calm my disoriented thoughts. I can't complain about the flowers. I do like them.

Wanting to put them in some water, I swing my legs off the bed and attempt to stand up, but I'm startled when I hear Joseph shout to me. "What do you think you're doing? Lie back down," he scolds, as he rushes to my bedside to gently shove me to lie back down.

He's been treating me like a child since the day I awoke. It was beginning to get annoying. "I'm not an invalid, Joseph. I'm getting up. I want to put the flowers in some water," I snap at him, still trying to push myself up, easily failing.

"I could do that for you," he says, taking the flowers from me.

"I hate that you're treating me like I'm not capable of doing anything at all. I can walk perfectly fine. They wouldn't have let me come home if I wasn't allowed to," I clip out, still resenting his irrational behavior.

He doesn't argue, but his face looks guilt ridden as he stares down at me. Even with protest, he won't truthfully tell me why he insists on acting this way with me when I asked. His lack of response only made me want to recover faster. The sooner I was back to taking care of myself, the sooner Joseph can get back to his own life, because truthfully, the longer Joseph stayed at my side, the more I was growing attached to the idea of him always being there. I had to keep reminding myself if wouldn't be forever.

With determination, I returned to walking not too long after waking up. Joseph wasn't happy with the idea at first, but regardless was at my side the entire time I wobbled around. It may be slower than normal, but I was still walking. Plus, I really couldn't afford to take it easy anymore. Not for the sake of my business. I was already too far behind.

In the corner of my eye, I suddenly see Josephina take the flowers from Joseph. "I'll put them in some water," she says, already heading in the direction of the kitchen.

My eyes find Joseph's. He's staring at me with a frown on his face, his eyes looking woeful, making me feel guilty. It's the same face Josephina gives me after I've scolded her. It was merely days ago when Joseph gave me the same look, that I discovered where she got it from, and the thought only made me smile, pushing the resentment I felt at the time away. Between the two of them, I already know I won't be able to continue to stand my ground if they keep giving me those looks.

"I appreciate everything you're doing for me, Joseph, I really do, but I've never had anybody fussing over me," I say, still attempting to push my body up and out of the bed. I finally manage to stand up.

Placing his hand on my elbow to help steady me, he leans down to bring his mouth next to my ear. "Well, maybe it's time somebody started doing it," he calmly says in his husky tone, sending shivers down my body and leaving me frozen in place as each word caresses my skin. His warm breath is still running down my neck as it continues to send the bolt of electricity straight down my spine, all the way to my toes.

His words have taken my breath away leaving me immobile, unable to speak, taking all coherent thoughts from my mind. Instead of breath, it's replaced with thoughts of what my body is craving. Something only Joseph awakens inside of me. Closing my eyes, I imagine all the possibilities.

"Kasey," I hear Joseph saying my name, making me open my eyes to look at him. His eyes have a hint of laughter while his mouth curves up to one side.

"What are you thinking about, Kasey?" His husky voice mocks me as our eyes lock onto each other.

"Nothing," I flatly respond, because the last thing I'm going to admit is how I was daydreaming about the both of us together, especially to him. Composing myself, I glare at him. "Look, whether you like it or not, I'm going to walk around a little. I've been lying in a bed for the last week and I swear my legs are feeling stiff already."

His lips go flat as he considers my request, but he soon nods his head as he steps away, allowing me to walk past him. It's slow at first, but I start walking towards my workstation with eager determination, but I'm soon brought to a halt when Joseph blocks me from taking any further steps, once I'm near the tables.

"If you think for one minute, Kasey, that you're going back to work, then you're wrong. You're supposed to be resting and taking it easy. I'm not letting you work," he sternly states in a distressed tone as he now glares back at me.

My mouth gapes open in shock. "Who are you to tell me what I can and cannot do, Joseph? Don't you dare say you're going to pay my bills because if you do, I will scream," I snap at him, my finger pointed at him daring him to try to say another word to me.

The entire time I was in the hospital, the stress of knowing I was falling behind on work was building inside of me. It was evident on my face, making Joseph grow curious to ask what was wrong. When I told him, he automatically responded for me not to worry, he'd take care of it. I didn't like the idea. I've been responsible for myself since the day I was forced to leave my house and I wasn't going to change just because I was injured.

I knew deep down inside it wasn't a good idea to allow Joseph to take responsibility of me. He was engaged. He should be focusing his attention on his fiancée. From the small conversations I managed to get from him, in regards to her, I was starting to get the idea that he hadn't told his fiancée the real reason why he was in Madison, which only annoyed me. It's as if he was keeping me as his dirty little secret and it wasn't sitting well with me. Another reason why I was so determined to recover was so Joseph could leave again.

Every time the ringtone announcing her call came through, he would excuse himself and always returned looking worried. I'd asked several times if she knew why he was truly here, but he refused to answer. He'd instead change the subject, annoying me with his lack of answer, so I stopped asking.

Returning my thoughts to the subject at hand, I remind him, "I need to work in order to pay my *own* bills and provide for myself and my daughter."

Stepping closer to me as he takes my face into his hands, he forces me to look directly at him. I'm still so infuriated from the thought of him refusing to allow me to work, that I'm practically shaking with agitation, but the moment his hands touch me it all disappears. It's as if I had never been upset.

"You can scream all you want, Kasey, but I *am* going to take care of you, regardless. The sooner you realize it's more important for you to rest, the sooner I will be happy and leave you alone," his calm collective voice conveys, telling me he's not going to budge on his decision.

As much as I want to stay angry with him, I can't. I don't have the energy left in me anymore to do so. Sighing to my-self, I stand there nodding my head in defeat, earning me a smile. His smile should make me feel bitter, but instead I shyly smile back to him, causing me to think. I don't know what I'm going to do with him, but I better figure it out soon, because there is no way I'm going to be able to keep pushing him away; especially when he acts this way.

Chapter 12

Kasey

I'M STILL FROZEN in place as he continues to stare back at me, still holding my face within his hands, making me feel like I'm the most important thing he sees, like I'm something worth caring about. I want to believe I am, but I remind myself this is Joseph, and my heart and mind are telling me to keep fighting him; it's for my own good.

He's left before, twice in fact, and he will leave again. Knowing I was now out of the hospital, it would be soon, which is why I was already mentally preparing myself for it. But what I couldn't handle was these mind games he was beginning to play with me. He was giving me false hope. Forcing myself to focus, I'm about to argue with him, to let him know I make my own decisions and that he has no right to make them for me when, of course, his phone rings. It doesn't surprise me. It's been happening more often the last two days.

He rapidly releases me, as if my face has burned his

palms, scorching his skin. He takes a step back, his eyes still locked onto mine as if he's waiting for me to react. Instead I keep my eyes locked onto his. I'm waiting to see what he'll do next. His reaction to the ringtone doesn't surprise me. It's been the same, as it always is, every time it rings. The musical sound from the phone shocked me back to reality, like a bucket of cold water being dumped on both of us, awaking our senses back to the reality of our life, reminding me of the reason why I can't have hope. Instead I avert my eyes away from his, already feeling ashamed of what was happening just moments ago. The troubled look on his face is the only answer I need to confirm what we were doing was wrong. Elizabeth calling is a reminder that Joseph needs to get his priorities straight, and his main priority should be her, not me.

The melody has now stopped, but just as quickly, it repeats itself, notifying him she's not giving up this time, like she usually does. I watch his body tense, his eyes closing as he lifts his head back to let out a deep breath, accompanied by a scowl on his face. He opens them up to look at the phone. "I've got to take this," he says, walking away to the door that leads outside, without a backwards glance.

Standing there, I watch him walk out of the door, my thoughts wondering if he's going to tell her this time. Pushing the thought aside, I make my way over to the couch to join Josephina while she watches TV. It allows me to continue thinking. Something I need to do.

I tried talking to him about the phone calls, giving me an excuse for something to discuss as we grew bored in the hospital, but he would keep his answers short and to the point, making it obvious he didn't want to discuss her; never showing any real emotion, either.

It worried me.

The curiosity got the better of me. Even if it hurt a little deep down inside to know that she would soon be his wife, I wanted to learn more about the person he was about to marry. I kept telling myself I only wanted to know for the sake of Josephina. She would soon be a permanent part of my daughter's life. Whether I liked it or not, she was Joseph's future. That's if Joseph had plans to continue being in Josephina's life after he married Elizabeth. It was another subject still lingering in my mind. I know Joseph hasn't told his fiancée the true reason he was here. I could see the frustration in his eyes when he was done speaking with her.

I kept wondering if he spent most of the conversation dodging her questions about him being here. I didn't like the idea of him hiding things from her. If I were in her place, I wouldn't want it done to me. For that reason alone, I was upset he was still here. I told him countless times to go home, but he'd refused, stating he didn't have a reason to go back. It only made me question what kind of man Joseph really was.

"Is daddy talking to his friend again?" Josephina's question draws me to the present, making me turn my attention to her.

"Yes, sweetheart, he is," I say brushing her hair back off her face.

Joseph hasn't told Josephina about Elizabeth, but from the look on her face, I have a feeling she knew his friend was more than a friend. Josephina was a smart girl, she'd noticed the phone calls as well, but when she had originally asked, my only answer had been he was speaking to his friend.

I know deep down inside I should have told her the truth, but I couldn't bring it upon myself to tell her. It hurt too much, considering what she would think when we'd have to explain that Joseph was getting married to someone else; someone who he'd soon have a family with, if that is what they decided. My thoughts are broken when I see Joseph come back in looking frustrated, as he usually does, when he's done talking to Elizabeth.

He walks straight back to us, taking a seat next to me on the couch, forcing me to be in the middle between him and Josephina. Being that my couch is small, my body is closely squeezed up to his, leaving him to throw his arm over the back of the couch behind me. He leans his head back as he rubs his closed eyes with the thumb and forefinger of his other hand; another common thing he does after the phone calls.

"She's still not coming around?" I curiously ask him.

He stays quiet, and the silence is my answer.

He lifts his head back up to look at me. "Ashley called while I was on the phone with her and invited us to dinner," he states, changing the subject, as if trying to distract me.

I cringe at the thought of going to their house for dinner. It isn't that I *don't* want to see them, it's the fact that I already feel guilty for everything they've done for me while I was in the hospital. It's another reason for me to feel guilt ridden.

"I don't know," I tell him. "I don't want to impose on Ashley anymore than I already have. She's done a great deal for me, with watching Josephina while I was in the hospital. She must have felt overwhelmed watching her so much," I state, still looking over at Joseph who looks exhausted.

The day I awoke, I had insisted he start going home at night to properly rest. Although he did leave upon my insistence, he would leave really late and return really early, usually before I'd awaken. I felt bad for him, but he wouldn't leave my side for more than a couple of hours, which was usually to pick Josephina up or drop her off at Mark and Ashley's.

That was another benefit of waking up. They were able to

move me to a regular room, allowing Josephina to visit with me. However, she would grow bored in my hospital room after four or five hours, which left me to depend on Ashley to watch over Josephina.

Joseph stands up from the couch, extending his arm down towards me so I can take his hand to help me up. Taking it, my hand wraps into his, reacting with an excitement that travels throughout my body. Ironically, it's been happening more often whenever he touches me.

I don't know what the hell is happening with me, but I know deep down inside that I couldn't allow myself to feel this way with Joseph. I just couldn't seem to get my body to understand it.

Still sitting, I look up to him. "Are you sure you wouldn't rather just rest. You're welcome to use the bed if you'd like," I offer, as I have been doing, hoping he'll say yes, but of course I already know the answer he'll most likely give me.

He wearily looks at me, this time actually smiling when he says, "If you think it will get you out of going over to Ashley's for dinner, then the answer is no."

Rolling my eyes at him, as I give up the notion of trying to be considerate, I allow him to pull me up. When he does, it's with a little too much force, causing me to stumble. He catches me, though, by wrapping his arm around my waist and pulling me up against his body to steady me. My arms are locked in between us, making me place my hands on his chest as I feel the warmth of his body radiating on me. I easily lose my breath, being so close to him. My heart feels like its racing as it pounds within my chest as I inhale him in, my mind starting to swirl. I can only stare up at him, hoping I don't make a fool of myself by giving away how badly he affects me.

It's uncontrollable.

"Mommy, are we going to Auntie Ashley's house?"

Joseph breaks eye contact with me as he looks down at Josephina. "Yes princess, we're going over there for dinner," he says down to her, his gaze eventually meeting mine again.

"Yay." Is the only thing I hear in the background as Joseph wearily smiles down at me, making me realize it's happening again. He's making me feel things I shouldn't be feeling, but I can't seem to control myself.

Pushing myself away from him, I quickly step my way around him, needing to put as much distance between us as I can. I need to stop letting myself have these feelings.

Even with protest, a couple of minutes later we're all piling into the rental car my insurance company provided me with, and on our way to Ashley and Mark's. Being that Joseph is driving, I'm able to stare out my window, refusing to look at him. My body is still humming from him holding me earlier, so I'm desperately trying to get it under control.

I couldn't be more relieved when we arrive at Mark and Ashley's, soon making our way up to the front door. I need other people to help provide a protective barrier between us. The minute we walk in, Josephina runs straight into the living room that is connected to the kitchen, looking for Mark. I shouldn't expect anything different, she did spend more than a week here. It probably feels like her second home now.

I shyly make my way towards the kitchen with Joseph at my side as he guides me with his hand on the small of my back; another thing he's been doing a lot of. He claims it's in case I need him to help steady me.

When I reach the kitchen, Ashley spots me and rushes over to give me a tight hug. "How are you feeling?" she asks, her voice sounding concerned, even though I've reassured her plenty of times I'm feeling better.

"I'm fine, thank you. It's good to see you," I say, still embracing her.

"I'm happy to see you, too."

I pull away to say, "Ashley, I want to thank you and Mark for everything you've done while I was in the hospital, I really appreciate it."

Her face beams as she gives me a smile. "Kasey, I would do it again in a heartbeat. Josephina was very helpful. You did a really great job of raising her. Plus, it felt good to have someone around to have a conversation with."

I can only chuckle at her response. Josephina *is* really good at holding conversations, I should know, she does with me all day long. It is helpful when I'm working sometimes.

With a nod, Ashley returns to what she was doing in the kitchen when we entered and it allows me to search for the subject of our conversation. I quickly find her sitting in between Joseph and Mark watching TV, her body leaning against Joseph as he embraces her. Those sights are what I'm going to miss most on Josephina's behalf. Seeing her with her father is bittersweet. It's hard to believe that he was simply a stranger to her weeks ago, but he will soon be gone again.

Turning my attention back to Ashley, I ask if I can help with anything. She dismisses my offer, making me take a seat in the chair at the kitchen island. Ten minutes later, we're all enjoying dinner. Almost two hours later, dinner is done and everything is cleaned up, allowing Ashley and I to speak alone. It's when the conversation of my business arises, that I don't hesitate to tell her the dilemma I had with Joseph earlier in the afternoon

With a roll of her eyes, she simply responds, "That doesn't surprise me about Joseph. If he's anything like Mark, and I'm pretty sure he is, then he's going to be overbearing.

You just have to let him think he's winning."

Grumbling to myself I take in her words. I've already fig-ured that part out. Even if I didn't like the idea, she was right. "I don't know how much longer I can go without working, though. My income depends on it. I have *some* money saved up, but it's going to run out if I don't get back to work. I'm going to end up losing the only customers I currently have and I can't afford to do that. My future depends on them," I mum-ble.

"Have you ever considered selling your products over the Internet?"

I take in her question and remember the one time I did. "I did, but it's so expensive to hire a web designer and trying to build a website on my own sounds too difficult. I wouldn't have a clue how to make my own webpage if I tried it myself. I might know how to use a computer, but designing a webpage is out of my league," I admit, already sighing from the dis-couragement of knowing it's not possible.

"I only ask because I gave my mom and sister each a soap from the basket you gave me. I hope you don't mind," she states before she continues on. "But, after I used one, I knew they would love it too. You're really good at what you do, Ka-sey. I think you'd be a great success if you were to expand by selling over the Internet."

Sighing to myself, I tell her, "I know, but I just don't have the money to do it. Thanks for the idea, though."

Her lips go into a triumphant smile. "Well, good thing I'm a web designer and I can do it myself," she informs me, her eyes beaming with pride.

I'm left shocked. "But, I thought you were a housewife?" I say, feeling embarrassed by my own words.

I'm mortified by my assumption, and it must be showing

on my face, because she chuckles at me. "I work from home. It's convenient and I can run my own business how I choose. You know how convenient it can be to work at your own pace and when you want to. It will especially help when the baby comes," she states, rubbing at her swollen belly.

"Ashley, there is no way I would be able to afford your services," I sadly admit. "Thank you for the offer, but like I said, I really can't afford to pay you what you probably charge. I barely have enough to keep afloat some months. That's why I have to be really froogle with what I do earn," the disappointment clear in my voice.

"I'll make a deal with you. How about in exchange for me designing your webpage, I get a supply of soaps every month. With my help it will be fantastic. I'll update it with new products and merchandise, when needed, so you don't have to worry about it," she offers, hesitantly waiting for a response.

She looks as if she's holding her breath as she waits for my answer, and I feel the same way as I consider her offer. "Oh come on, Kasey. What would you have to lose? Try it for the next couple of months," she enforces, to try and convince me. "You can still do the Farmer's Market thing for the rest of the summer. If you're not happy with the profits from the website sales we can always take it down. It's worth taking the chance on, isn't it?" she states, looking like she isn't going to take no for an answer.

Considering her offer, knowing I should take the chance, I smile with a nod. "Okay, we have a deal."

She squeals with excitement, embracing me to give me a hug, reminding me that I'm still sore, making me flinch. "Oh, I'm so sorry. I forgot," she says as she releases me.

Still excited, she's claps her hands and starts rapidly making plans for the website. I'm still in a daze at how lucky I am that's she's willing to do it.

Joseph and Mark come over to inquire what the excitement is all about and Ashley quickly tells them of our plan. Joseph looks skeptical at first. "I don't know. It sounds like it would make her busier and the plan was for her to relax more, not put more pressure on herself," he says, his eyes scolding me.

"Oh come on, Joseph," I hear Ashley say to him. "Lighten up a bit. If she does well from the Internet sales, which I'm sure she will because I'll be designing her website, then she'd probably be able to stop having to sell at the Market," she informs him with a mocking grin.

I'm about to correct her, stating that I would never stop selling at the Market but Joseph speaks up, stopping me from responding. "Okay, that's sounds like a plan," he says before looking sternly at me. "As long as you don't overdo yourself," he finishes stating, wrapping his arm around my body as he gives me a kiss on my temple.

All coherent thoughts have disappeared with his simple gesture, leaving me speechless and wondering why he did it in the first place.

I need to speak to him about his actions, like the one he just did, but I wasn't going to discuss it in front of everybody. No, it was something we were going to have to discuss just between us.

Until then, I'm left more confused than before. I hate this feeling.

Chapter 13

Joseph

I DON'T KNOW what the hell happened at Mark and Ashley's, but Kasey has been quiet ever since the conversation about her business... too quiet. She has barely spoken a word now that we're driving back to her place. It's beginning to worry me.

Forcing myself to push the worry to the back of my mind, I focus on the real problem in front of me, needing to go back to San Diego. I didn't like the idea of leaving Kasey so soon, but Elizabeth was growing more demanding since I wasn't giving her much information as to the real reason why I was here. The only response she kept getting was, "For Josephina." Nothing more, which only upset her.

She was demanding I get back to help with the wedding plans, especially since she knew I was currently on vacation. She wanted to take advantage of my time off. I was starting to dread answering her calls because she'd bombard me with wedding details.

It didn't help with every phone call she'd remind me about the damn paternity test, another thought sitting in the back of my mind.

This last week has been an eye-opener for me when it came to Josephina. With every added day I spent with her, I realized how much more I love her, but I was growing scared. With Elizabeth reminding me of the paternity test, I was left wondering what would happen if she wasn't really my daughter. Was I going to be able to walk away from her without looking back?

At first, I had never doubted Kasey's word about Josephina being my daughter. It wasn't a concern until Elizabeth had inserted the thought into my mind. Since then, I couldn't stop thinking about it. I knew there was only one way to get it out of my head. I needed to have a talk with Kasey, if only to extinguish my doubt. I hadn't wanted to do it while she was in the hospital, but now that she was home, it was getting harder for me to approach the subject. I didn't want to hurt Kasey's feeling by asking, but I knew deep down inside I would never be able to live with myself if I didn't at least ask.

I needed to make sure, at least for my own sanity.

Still driving back to Kasey's place, I'm a nervous wreck, more so than I was when I first showed up. As I pull into her driveway I'm practically sweating bullets. I've got more nerves this week than when I had to enter a dangerous bomb laden building. I didn't know how Kasey was going to react when I asked her for a paternity test. For all I know, she will explode with emotions. She can even go as far as refusing to allow me to keep seeing Josephina. Or worse, admit Josephina wasn't really mine, which was my biggest fear of all.

Making our way into the building with a sleeping Josephina, I tuck her into bed before giving her a kiss goodnight.

When done, I look over to see Kasey watching me with a smile on her face. I dread asking her the next question. "Can I talk to you?"

Her brow furrows, clear with worry. She nods her head and turns to make her way over to the couch. I follow her, taking a seat next to her. Her eyes are intensely staring back at me, her expression blank, but still worrying me with every second that ticks by.

"Joseph, is something wrong? You've been acting strange since we left Mark and Ashley's house and it's starting to worry me," she calmly conveys. "If it's about my business, then there isn't anything else to discuss. It's my business and I'm the one who is going to make the decisions I feel are best when it comes to it," she sternly states.

I smile as I watch her facial expression change from being worried to now looking infuriated, making me smile at how strong she is. This is a side of Kasey I'm still learning to adjust to. This is nothing like the Kasey I grew up with. That Kasey was sweet and innocent. A girl that wouldn't fight back, but she clearly isn't that girl anymore.

It made me proud of her.

Shaking my head to answer her earlier question, I start to explain as best as I can. "Kasey, there's something that's been on my mind for a while," I say to her, trying to calm my nerves that are returning. "I was wondering if you'd consider allowing me to do a paternity test on Josephina, to confirm she's really mine?"

With her eyes growing wide, I see her breath hitch, her mouth gaping open in shock. Her body automatically stiffens up. It doesn't surprise me she's reacting like this. I would too if she would have thrown a doubt like this at me.

"Joseph, what would make you believe that Josephina

isn't your daughter?" she questions, in a sharp low tone. I know she's desperately trying to stay calm, but by the way she looks, it isn't working. Her body is lightly trembling as she opens and closes her fist, taking slow deeps breaths as she looks off into the distance.

She must think I'm the worst human being in the world right now. I deserve for her to think like that. "I need to know, Kasey, if only to erase the doubt I have in my mind. You have to see it from my point of view. I haven't seen you since the night before I left for boot camp. Then when I see you again, you throw at me that I suddenly have a daughter. I have a right to have my doubts, Kasey," I tell her. "I don't know what happened after that night. For all I know you could've been with someone else and gotten pregnant and now that I'm back in your life, you're trying to pin a child on me," I state, immediately regretting the words after they've left my mouth.

She turns to face me, her eyes glaring daggers at me. She's not hiding one ounce of her anger as she abruptly stands up from the couch heading straight over to the workstation as quickly as she can walk. I follow closely behind, keeping some distance between us as she stops in front of her workbench, her body hunched over it as she leans her arms on the edge of the table. At first I think she's in pain, so I reach over to try to help her up, but she just as quickly shoves me away. There is no doubt in my mind if looks can kill, I'd be a dead man right now.

"I would never have thought about lying to you, Joseph, or even considered betraying you in that way. Josephina and I were doing perfectly fine before you even came back into our lives. If you think for one minute that I would want to pin her on you, so I could easily claim a father for her, then you've got some damn nerve," she seethes through clenched teeth.

I'm left speechless. Her eyes turning dark with anger and her breathing becoming labored, but she continues on. "I don't need a damn paternity test to know she's yours because I haven't been with another man since I've been with you. I didn't have the time, or the need, because I was too busy trying to raise *my* daughter," she says, pointing her finger at her chest. "*I made sure to put her first*. I found a way for both of us to survive. I did it all without your help and I will continue to do it from this day forward," she growls.

I stand there, shocked by her words as I absorb them. I wasn't expecting her to say what she just said. I'm left standing frozen to the spot, still trying to comprehend the entire situation. "Kasey, if what you say is true, then what's so hard about taking a paternity test? I'll even pay for it. I just need to know for sure, for my peace of mind that's she's mine."

Her eyes are filling with tears. "You still doubt me, don't you?" she whispers, the agony clear in her voice.

Still silent, I continue standing there, not wanting to say anything more I'd regret. I've already said enough. She begins walking in the direction of the door leading outside, swinging it open as she says, "Fine, I'll have Josephina take the damn test, but until you get the results, I think it's best we don't see you. Call me to let me know when and where I need to take her. Until then you should focus on the real reason why you're requesting it," she growls at me.

Her words feel like they've stabbed me in the chest, but what could I have expected? It's as if she knows it's Elizabeth behind the request. I should've known this was going happen when I asked her. Knowing there is nothing more I could say, or do, I decide to leave. As I slowly walk my way over to the door, my heart is heavy and feeling as if it's been ripped apart, and there is no one to blame but myself.

The drive back to Mark and Ashley's goes by in a blur, as if it never occurred. The whole time I kept repeating Kasey's words in my head, but the one line that sticks with me the most, is the one where she stated she hasn't been with anyone else since me. To think she never once tried looking for someone else only makes me regret asking for the test in the first place. I should have expected nothing less from Kasey.

Slowly dragging myself inside the house, I see Mark in the living room watching TV. He takes one look at me, his eyebrow curiously rising up as he turns the TV off. "I haven't seen that look since the day you came back from boot camp," he says. "Please don't tell me someone died," his sarcasm not affecting me at all.

I drag myself over to take a seat in one of the armchairs facing him, throwing myself into it. My body sinks into the cushion as I rub my hands down my face, trying to wipe away the pain. Now that he's said it, it's exactly how I felt the day I found out Kasey was gone the first time. I'd thought back then that I had lost her forever and tonight I feel like it's happening all over again. Only this time, I've pushed her away. Knowing I had to tell Mark the truth, I come out and say it. "I asked Kasey for a paternity test," the statement feeling like a heavy weight crushing me on the outside.

He looks shocked "Why the fuck would you do that? What would make you have any doubts now?" he asks, sounding shocked from the request I gave Kasey. "Let me guess, Elizabeth?" he states, as if he already knows the answer.

My silence is his confirmation, as he shakes his head in disappointment. "I don't know, man. It's your life, but I am going to say one thing," he says as he leans forward to rest his elbows on his knees. "I really doubt Kasey would lie to you. She doesn't seem like the type. You know for me to say that, says a lot. You know I don't trust very easily and when I first met Kasey, I had my doubts about the whole situation. I've since changed my mind. Another thing, I've come to love that little girl. So you better pray to God you don't fuck this up, dude, because it'd be a damn shame if you did. Ashley and I aren't going to lose having Josephina in our lives. She's special and so is her mom," he tells me as he stands up. "I'm off to bed. I was just waiting for you to get home."

He starts to walk away, but briefly stops as he takes one last glance at me. "I hate to sound like an asshole when I say this, but if Elizabeth can't accept Josephina now, I really doubt she ever will. So you better think long and hard about what you really want. Is she worth marrying if you have to give up Josephina?" he states, before turning away, going straight down the hallway without waiting for an answer.

I watch him walk to his room as I take in his words. He's right. Since the day I told Elizabeth about Josephina, she hasn't tried to accept her. How the hell was it going to be after we got married? I sit here, left alone to ponder over the events of the night. Left with no choice but to think hard about what I need to do.

With the night growing late, I finally stand up and head to my own room. I had planned to stay at Kasey's, so I could help her out while she was recovering, but I've managed to screw up those plans as well. Entering my room, I go straight to my duffle bag with my things, reaching inside to search for the one item I know will help push my doubts aside. Within seconds I find it, digging it out and walking over to the bed, to toss myself onto it, to open up the envelope. Slowly pulling out Kasey's letter, I couldn't bring myself to travel without it. For some odd reason, my gut kept telling me to bring it back with me that night, and now I know why.

Staring at the picture of Kasey and Josephina, on the day she was born, my thought instantly goes back to the one regret I've grown to have. Not being there with Kasey when our daughter was born. I take in the picture, staring at it long and hard as I finally pick up the letter to reread it. The tears freely fall as I read it this time, knowing that Kasey poured her heart and soul into it when she wrote the letter, telling me I had a daughter. I should have known from the words alone that Josephina was mine. I shouldn't have doubted it.

I don't know how the fuck I am going to fix this, but I damn well was going to... even if it killed me.

Chapter 14

Kasey

WATCHING JOSEPH WALK out the door was making me wonder if my words were going to keep him from coming back. I hadn't asked him to come back into our lives. I had tried that once and fate had made that decision for me. I had accepted her decision. I had no other choice. I'll admit I felt blessed when he'd found us again. Thinking it was fate's way of giving Josephina and I a second chance, so she could have a father, but now I was beginning to doubt my own theory.

Had I known Joseph had his doubts about being Josephina's father, I wouldn't have told him. I wouldn't have allowed him to weasel his way into her heart, making her believe he *really* cared for her, like a father would do. He could have easily walked away, never looking back, and I would have understood.

Because of that, I was angry with him.

Still leaning my body against the door, I stare at my

workstation with the large block table sitting in the middle of the room, and only one thing comes to mind: working. It has always helped release my stress. It's the only thing that has always helped keep me calm, as I get lost in my own world of creations. The only place my mind can escape without anyone judging me.

I know I should be resting, but if I *did* try to lie down in bed, I would only end up tossing and turning, unable to sleep. I'm too mad at this point. The anger is coursing through my veins and heating my blood, like a fire that refuses to be extinguished. Joseph has a way of doing that to me, but usually it's from another reason completely. I had much preferred that reason, even if I know it's wrong.

Slowly making my way over to my stove, to prepare to heat my batch, my mind immediately begins to escape to my world of blissful ecstasy. With the ingredients boiling, I start pulling and gathering the materials needed to get my molds done. It's a much slower process this time, since I have to move carefully as to not over do my body and injure myself, but I'm determined to get it done.

I've perfected how to work quietly while Josephina sleeps, managing to make as minimal noise as I possibly can; most of the time I continue working late into the night, well after she's fallen asleep. It's the best time for me to work. The quiet hours relaxing me as it allows me to work better.

When I had first started working on my own, I found myself staying up into the late hours of the night, experimenting until I had the perfect creation. Now I have most of those creations memorized; no longer needing to measure anything anymore. But tonight I wanted to try something new, needing the distraction of not knowing the outcome, to pull me further from my thoughts.

It's been a while since I've stayed up this late, but I'm pretty sure with the frustration I have inside of me, I'm going to be up most of the night. There's only one reason for it, to get Joseph out of my mind, and this was the only way I could think to do it.

Six hours later, what I thought was going to happen, didn't. The stress of getting caught up on my orders did fade, simply because I managed to fill them all. In fact, I was now caught up for the next two weeks, including the next order going to the local shop. However, what didn't manage to leave my mind were Joseph's words. No matter how badly I tried to push them aside, I failed miserably. They were branded into my mind and I doubt they will ever leave. I'm still so angry with him. He was completely clouding my mind to the point that I was able to make that new scented soap because of him. It consisted of a sandalwood accent that I fantasized smelling on Joseph. The entire time I was making it, I was thinking of Joseph smelling of it.

I remember buying the scented oil the day I had went to buy my usual scents I use for my orders. At the time it'd been an impulsive buy, thinking I might not ever use it, but I bought it anyways in hopes of one day making the new scent. Again fate. I wouldn't have considered using it if it wasn't for Joseph.

I start to cut up, divide, and wrap up my soaps. I then place them in the designated bins, which are labeled with their specific scent, so none get mixed up accidentally. I'm so tired at this point that I leave the buckets on the worktable, telling myself that I'll move them another day. Knowing that I shouldn't be lifting anything heavy helps make the decision to leave them easier.

Taking in the time, I realize it's already close to dawn as I finally crawl into bed. The exhaustion of working through the night finally takes over my body, reminding me why I was supposed to take things easy. The moment my head hits the pillow I close my eyes and fall asleep, my mind going into a dreamless slumber.

I AWAKE THE next morning still feeling exhausted, but the couple of hours of sleep I've managed to get helped clear my mind. That is until I hear a deep voice coming from the kitchen area. My mind already recognizing it the minute I hear it. It's soon followed by Josephina's soft giggle. Knowing Joseph is here, after I told him last night not to return, makes me irritated. My entire night of relieving stress is completely gone.

Josephina most likely let him in this morning.

Forcing my body to sit up, it immediately notifies me it's upset with me for not resting last night. My body feels stiff and sore, just as badly as it did the first couple of days I was in the hospital. I can already tell from the extreme discomfort, I will be punished for not listening when I was told to rest. Managing to finally get my body to sit up, I swing my legs over the side of the bed, but that's proving more difficult than I'd thought with the tenderness.

Taking in a deep breath as I try to stand up, a sharp pain travels through my body, with an ache in my chest where the stitches used to be. It's the primary source of the pain. I let out an excruciating groan as I wince. My body just as quickly collapses back down on the bed, causing me to sit on the mattress in defeat. I'm forced to take deep breaths to push the throbbing away. I'm so lost in the pain I don't notice Joseph has rushed to my side and is now kneeling in front of me, his face looking worried and torn. He frantically rakes his hands over my body, as if searching for something.

"What's wrong? Where are you in pain?" he asks, his voice matching his worried eyes. His hands reach for the hem of my shirt to lift it up and I quickly push them away, refusing to allow him to lift it.

"I'm fine," I snap at him, more from a reaction of the pain than anything else.

Our eyes lock as I take in his concerned expression. "I only want to check your wound and make sure it hasn't opened up," he calmly states, already reaching for the hem of my shirt again.

"My wound is fine. I'm just sore."

His lips go flat as his eyes narrow at me, as if he's debating whether to argue with me or not. He sighs as his hands rest on the sides of my hips, lightly gripping me, as if to keep me from moving. I learned my lesson from my earlier attempt, my pain still reminding me of the mistake.

With his eyes gazing at me, the pain has now disappeared. It's now replaced with the heat traveling through my body from his touch. It's making my body come alive with excitement. The butterflied feeling is floating in my stomach as I close my eyes to allow the sensation to flow throughout my body.

Joseph's sobered voice makes me open my eyes back up. "Kasey, please tell me what's wrong? I can see it in your face that something is wrong," he mumbles, also sounding worried, making me feel guilt ridden for making him feel this way.

It's heartbreaking to see him this way. I hate how he can easily make me feel torn between staying angry with him and wanting to reassure him that he has nothing to worry about. If only I could tell him it's not the physical pain that's making me look this way, but the pain from wanting him so badly; knowing I have no chance at all.

Remembering he's not supposed to be here in the first place, overcomes my thoughts. "What are you doing here, Joseph? I told you last night not to come around until you had the results for the test and I meant it. I refuse for you to be playing mind games with Josephina," I angrily relay to him.

His face turns regretful as he deeply sighs. "You're right, Kasey. There doesn't need to be a test to prove that Josephina is my daughter. I don't want one now, or ever. It was a mistake to ask for one. I should have never doubted that Josephina is my daughter," he soberly states as he lifts his hand to tuck my hair behind my ear, our eyes deeply locked onto each other. "You would have never lied to me about something like that and I should have listened to my gut when it told me so," he says, his voice laced with the pain matching his pleading expression, begging me to forgive him.

Regardless of how much he regrets asking for the test, I simply can't forgive him for asking in the first place. Not yet. "You think it's that easy? You change your mind and everything will go back to the way things were before? I don't think I'll ever forgive you for asking in the first place, Joseph," I say, my blood already boiling. I allow it to take over, needing the reminder of why I'm angry with him in the first place.

His shoulders slump forward. He turns his head to look at Josephina sitting at the table eating her breakfast, my eyes averting to the same direction. When she notices us both looking at her, she waves to us with a mouth full of food and a smile already forming on her little face.

My eyes find Joseph's again and I see them filled with

threatening tears. "Please, Kasey. I already regret asking. I know it was a mistake, but please don't make me pay when it comes to Josephina. I'll do anything you ask, but don't keep her from me."

His plea brings tears to my own eyes. My vision is now blurred as the tears begin to fall down my face. Speaking around the lump formed in my throat, I tell him, "You have every right to be in her life, Joseph, but it has to be *your* decision, not one that I forced on you."

"I won't ever feel forced to be her father, Kasey. That I promise you."

The truth of his statement is clear in his eyes as he holds his gaze on me, making me smile. When he returns the smile, the fluttering resumes, making me hate how easily my body surrenders to the simplest things he does. I'm jealous of his fiancée, knowing she'll be able to feel this way everyday.

"I'm fine now. Please let me up," I firmly tell him, dislodging his hands from my waist. My mind knows I need to put as much space between us, before I give into my temptation of doing something I'll regret.

Allowing me access, he pushes his body away, helping me to stand with him. I purposely keep my eyes averted from his, already knowing if I don't, I will succumb to my weakness.

Both standing now, his face grows serious. "Kasey, I see what you did last night," he says, breaking the silence between us as he points his chin at my workstation. "You're supposed to be getting your rest and obviously you're not listening," he scolds me as if I'm a child, his voice growing deeper with disappointment as he reprimands me. He's shown me exactly how Josephina feels now.

"I couldn't sleep. To tell you the truth, there is no one to blame for that but you," I throw at him, feeling the need to defend myself. "So I figured I'd get caught up on work."

I hear a low growl come from deep within his chest. "You're right. It is my fault," he mumbles.

Hearing him admit I'm right should make me feel overjoyed, but I don't, it only saddens me to remember why I'm upset in the first place. Yet, he finishes by saying, "You're not resuming your work until you're completely healed up, or until I say you can."

My mind is racing with ways to argue with him. I'm about to protest when he places his finger on my lips, preventing me from speaking. "Anyway, you can't work if you're not here," he says with a mischievous smile.

Now I'm confused. Where the hell would I be if we're not here? "You're both coming back to San Diego with me. I thought about it and you're right, I need to keep my word to Josephina and show her the beach," his confidence in my accepting his decision clear as he shrugs his shoulders. "Whether you want to come or not is up to you, but I'm keeping my promise to my daughter," he declares without a challenge.

My eyes again go wide in shock. "You can't do that," I practically shout at him.

"I already purchased both your tickets last night. You have until tomorrow to decide if *you* want to come with us," he declares with a smile before turning to leave me gaping at him.

I open my mouth to dispute his decision, but I see Josephina already running towards him. He catches her as she launches herself up at him, her eyes beaming from excitement.

"Is it true? Are we really going back to California with you, daddy?" the question filled with an animated squeal.

Joseph chuckles at her, his eyes looking just as excited. "Yup," he says to her before looking back to me. "That's if your mommy says it's okay."

They're both looking at me with pleading eyes, waiting for an answer. Why is he doing this? He knows if I say no, her disappointment would be aimed at me. I don't want to see her disappointment return if he leaves without us. I'd barely been able to endure her sorrow the last time he left. My heart wouldn't be able to handle it again.

"Yes, we're going to California," I say to her, the words practically burning my mouth as I say them.

Joseph's eyes beam back at me as his lips go into the widest smile I've seen him give me. Josephina wraps her tiny arms around his neck, happily squeezing him. With his eyes still locked onto mine, he silently mouths, *"Thank you."* Making me weak all over again, this time for another reason completely.

Chapter 15

Joseph

I SWEAR, THIS morning I feel as if Kasey is testing my patience. It's the day we're scheduled to fly to San Diego, but the trials these two girls put me through are going to break me. They're lucky they aren't one of my Marines, or else I would've had them crying mercy from the punishment I'd be putting them through.

At least her clients wouldn't be missing anything. Kasey had me running around like a damn errand boy yesterday, making sure everyone got their deliveries. Kasey insisted everyone have their orders before she left.

I'd lost count of how many times I had to lecture them this morning, reminding them we needed to be at the airport early. But Kasey would simply ignore my demands, pushing my limits.

Another thing Kasey kept doing was double checking to make sure she had everything she and Josephina would need for the trip. I lost all patience with her, finally scolding her. I told her whatever she was missing I would buy it for them in San Diego. I just wanted to leave already, earning me the silent treatment from her. Regardless if she was quiet or not, she was still cute when she was mad.

I caught her sticking her tongue out at me when she thought I wasn't looking. It happened more when I continued to lecture her to bring only what she absolutely needed as she was packing yesterday. What she didn't know were all the times she made me smile when she was doing it. I couldn't resist keeping my eyes on her, though. My eyes were always drawn to her like a magnet, wanting to watch her. She still had the same pull on me she had when we were growing up.

Now at the airport, with the rental car now dropped off, I'm finally able to relax a little. Although we made it to the airport on time, it's only because I'd practically rushed Kasey and Josephina out the door this morning, fearing we would miss our flight. These darn girls would never make it in the military with the way they drag their heels. They had no concern for being on time. I wanted a quick direct flight back to San Diego, needing to get them there as soon as possible. So I'd made sure to book our flights out of Milwaukee, not wanting them to deal with any layovers along the way. It was the reason why we needed to be out of her door on time.

Looking to my side, I see Kasey staring off into the distance. She's no longer ignoring me, but quiet for another reason completely. I had another dilemma on my hands; Kasey was terrified of flying. Something I didn't know until today.

"Daddy, do you think I'm going to be able to sit by the window? I really want to see the sky," Josephina enthusiastically asks from the other side of me, as I take a peek in her direction, making me smile at her eagerness of wanting to get on that plane. "I made sure of it, princess," I answer her.

My eyes look over to Kasey. She's biting her nails. Her breathing looks labored as her eyes continue staring off into the distance. This isn't the first time I've seen her like this to-day. She had that look on her face the whole two-hour car ride here. That's when I'd discovered her fear of flying. She was a nervous wreck and her nervousness was escalating as the clock drew closer to our departure time. It was clear on her paled face she had no desire to get on the plane.

Seeing her with that expression made me want to take her nervousness away, so I'd reached over and grabbed her hand, holding it tightly within mine. With Kasey's hand in my own, I'd forgotten the true reason why I was holding it: to help calm her nerves. I was so lost in the thought of how good it felt to actually hold her hand. It was the first time I had ever been able to do it. I was instantly addicted to how it felt, not want-ing to let go.

Remembering how I wanted to do it again, I reach up to take her hand from her mouth, entwining our fingers together hoping it will help calm her nerves. She looks over to me, a forced smile plastered on her face, making me grin. She doesn't give me the same reaction though, but narrows her eyes at me with a fierce scowl. I bring her hand to my lips placing a soft kiss on the back of it, ignoring her expression. I know why she's mad, but there's nothing she can do about it. She's getting on that plane.

With a forced smile still on her face, I know she's still trying to hide her fear.

"Kasey, are you going to be okay with the plane ride?" I hesitantly ask her, already knowing from how wide her eyes grow and the terrified look on her face, she isn't. I have to force myself to bite back the laughter that is building up inside of me right now.

With the mention of the word *plane,* her eyes go as wide as saucers and her face grows pale. I know it's not from excitement, which is the reason why I want to laugh.

I didn't know this was her first plane ride. I thought she had taken one when they shipped her up here to Wisconsin, but she informed me her parents had sent her by bus. It led to the conversation about her non-stop sickness from the smells on the bus. It added to my list of reasons to feel guilty for not being there for her during her pregnancy. I swear it feels as if the list of things to feel guilty about is never going to end with every new fact I learn.

Kasey forcefully nods her head as I squeeze her hand, trying to calm her nervous state. I want her to know I'm here for her. She gives me a genuine smile, making me return the same to her. A couple of seconds later they announce the boarding call for our flight and her body stiffens, her saucer eyes returning.

Shaking my head, with a smile on my face, I pull her up with me as I stand, keeping her hand tightly in mine. Josephina jumps up with excitement when she sees us stand, already understanding we're finally ready to board. Kasey groans as I try to pull her towards the gate door refusing to move with me, attempting to keep her body rooted to the spot.

Laughing as I reach down to pick up Josephina's booster chair off the ground, I hear Kasey say, "I don't know what you find so funny, Joseph," she scolds. "What if something is wrong with the plane and it malfunctions? What if it happens to be my luck that this plane has a bomber on it? I don't want to die in the air." She practically shouts.

Dropping Josephina's chair, I grab Kasey's face within my palms, forcing her to look at me. She grabs for my wrist with her hands, trying to pull them away, but I firmly hold onto her face as I look down into her deep blue eyes. "Kasey, first of all you can't be saying words like bomb or bombers at the airport," I whisper down at her hoping that airport security isn't rushing towards us at this very moment, ready to take us away for her earlier comment. "And I'm pretty sure they wouldn't be allowing us to board if there was anything wrong with the plane. I've traveled many times by plane and I know it's probably the safest way to travel. Safer than a car," I tell her with a raised eyebrow, remembering her recent car accident.

She considers my words. I feel her body finally relaxing while her fierce grip loosens from around my wrist. She briefly closes her eyes, just as quickly opening them as she deeply takes a breath.

I ask one last time. "You going to be okay now?" It takes her a couple of seconds, but she responds with a simple nod, and I'm happy with that.

Looking down I see Josephina standing next to us, looking confused. I let go of Kasey's face to reach down for Josephina's hand, taking Kasey's hand with my other. It forces her to reach down and take Josephina's booster seat before I pull her away, practically dragging her towards the entrance of our plane.

We're in the plane and I already feel relieved I have her inside it. Finding our seats, I go straight to making sure Josephina is safely buckled into her booster seat next to the window, as requested. Of course Kasey takes the aisle seat, wanting to be as far away from the window as she can be, leaving me in the middle. Normally I would hate this seat, preferring the aisle so I can stretch my legs, but I wasn't going to complain this time. As long as it made Kasey happy, and less nervous, she can have it.

The roar of the jet engines grow louder as we begin to taxi down the runway and I feel Kasey's hand start to grip mine with a fierceness that conveys her fear. I allow her to squeeze it as tightly as she wants as I focus on Josephina, who is now starting to look a little frightened as well. The plane starts to gain speed and Josephina grows more excited. The second it starts to climb, I hear an excited gasp from both of them. I can't help but smile because, for the first time, I'm actually experiencing a first with both of them and it feels so good. It's the best feeling in the world to experience it. I can't wait to experience more firsts with them.

With the plane now in the air, I manage to calm Kasey to the point where she is no longer scared. Josephina is looking out of the window, taking in the view of the clouds in the sky, as we start to make small talk about the different shapes and sizes; making it a game between the two of us. The hours quickly go by and when I think everything is going fine for the remainder of the flight, the plane picks up a bit of turbulence, causing it to shutter and slightly drop elevation.

The pilot's voice comes over the intercom announcing for everyone to take their seats and buckle up due to the turbulence. We do so, but the only thing I can think of at this moment is, *why does this have to happen to us?* Especially since I already know Kasey is scared out of her mind, probably thinking the plane will crash down at any minute.

Taking a quick glance at Josephina to makes sure she is fine, I turn my attention to Kasey. She's gripping her armrest with a force that is making her knuckles turn white. Her eyes are tightly shut, the strain clear on her face. From the rise and fall of her chest, I know she's panicking. I try to pry her fingers from their tight grip on the armrest, but it proves difficult with the force she's using. I start to see tears escape her closed eyelids and my heart begins to ache seeing her like this. It's entirely my fault she's going through this.

I reach up to pull her head closer to me as I begin to whisper in her ear. "Kasey, you need to calm down. You're going to scare Josephina if she see's you this way." Hoping she's listening to me as I say the words.

Frantically, she shakes her head, her eyes still tightly shut when I hear her whimper. "Please, Kasey." I desperately plead, praying she'll listen. The plane jolts, the shutter making Kasey's sobs return. On the other side of me I hear a giggling Josephina, the opposite of what I have facing me. Knowing Josephina is still okay, I continue focusing my attention on Kasey.

I need to do something, anything, to calm her down before she has a heart attack on me. I do the only thing that comes to mind. Grabbing her face, forcing her to face me, I don't wait for her to open her eyes before my mouth is descending down onto hers to give her a kiss on her closed lips.

Her eyes go wide, letting out a gasp against my lips. Taking advantage, I deepen the kiss, pushing my tongue into her mouth. My tongue grazes hers and I can feel the warmth of it, making it impossible to hold back. My eyes close as I tilt her head to better kiss her, wanting to taste more of her. My tongue glides against hers, exploring every inch of her mouth with each second that goes by. I feel her moan into my mouth and I swear it's the greatest sound I've ever heard.

The excitement of knowing I'm kissing Kasey again makes me want more. She tastes so sweet. Better than the memories I hold from the last time I kissed her. The memories and dreams I've had for the last five years don't compare to the way it feels as I'm kissing her right now.

I want to keep kissing her forever, but the thought is easily broken. "Are you guys going to be stuck like that forever?" Josephina asks from the other side of me, followed by her cute little giggle.

Kasey shoves at my chest. Our mouths quickly break apart, making me open my eyes to stare at her. Her breathing looks as rapid and heavy as mine. Her lips look swollen and her face is flushed with a pink blush from the kiss. I'm still holding her face in my palms, but when her hands come up and grab for my wrists, she pulls my hands from her face, leaving me disappointed. I'm still in shock from kissing her that I easily allow her to pull away.

The plane's turbulence is gone and the pilot is announcing we can safely move about the cabin now. Kasey leans her body across mine to reach for Josephina to check on her. The feeling of her body rubbing up against my chest isn't helping with the carnal thoughts flooding my mind. They started the moment I began kissing her. Remembering what resulted from the last time I kissed her.

Kasey's calm collective voice breaks my memory. "No, sweetheart, we won't get stuck like that forever. It shouldn't have happened," she sternly states, more like a reprimand.

Hearing her say those words is a stab to my heart.

She leans back into her chair to quickly unbuckle her seatbelt, before she stands up, making her way down the aisle to the restroom. As I watch her walk away, I wonder if she's angry with me. From the way she was returning my kiss, I would have thought she wanted it too, but her horrified expression is telling me otherwise.

I don't know what is going through her mind at this moment, but I know what's going through mine, *that was the best kiss I've had since leaving for boot camp. I don't regret kissing her at all.*

Chapter 16

Kasey

I'M STANDING IN the bathroom of the airplane gripping the counter for dear life. My body is uncontrollably trembling. I don't know if it's from the fear of knowing I'm still on a plane, or the fact that Joseph just finished kissing me. I want to believe it's from my fear, but in my mind I know it's from the kiss. I won't deny the fact he has that effect on me.

My body is burning with a longing to go back to Joseph, to kiss him again. It took every ounce of energy to stand up and walk away from him. I'd forgotten he's engaged to someone else while he was kissing me; my mind was lost in the moment. I was a desperate child with a candy bar. The taste of his kiss was too sweet and addicting to resist. I wanted more with every second our mouths were fused together.

Pulling my face up to look into the mirror, I take in my flushed expression. Bringing my fingers up to my swollen lips, I can still feel them tingling from the kiss. It's like a burning fire I never want extinguished. Closing my eyes, I savor the memory a little longer, embedding it into my thoughts. My lips start to tremble when I remember the first time Joseph kissed me. He's the only person who has ever kissed me. Our kiss that night was no comparison to the one he just finished giving me.

Breathing deeply, to calm my erratic nerves, I force myself to bring my body under control. I need to get back to my seat. Exiting the bathroom, I head back to my seat and see Joseph leaning towards Josephina, their heads closely leaning next to each other as they talk about the clouds.

Taking my seat, Joseph turns, looking concerned when he does. "Are you alright?" he asks curiously, his face expressionless, as if what happened minutes ago hasn't affected him at all.

The lump in my throat is preventing me from speaking. I'm afraid to say or ask something I might regret, so I stay silently sitting in my seat. The thought that he simply kissed me out of pity is turning my stomach upside down. Joseph turns his attention back to Josephina, dismissing me; confirming he no longer has any concern for me. Making me feel pitiful.

A couple of minutes go by, the pilot announces we'll soon be landing in San Diego, and it couldn't have come at a better time. I want to get off this plane. This time for reasons other than my fear.

An hour later, we're waiting at the conveyer belt distributing the luggage from our plane when Joseph resumes speaking to me. "My friend should be here any minute to pick us up. As soon as he does, we'll be on our way home."

I'm confused as I glare at him, standing there deciphering his last words, as if there is any real meaning to the definition of what they were meant to represent.

"You mean *your* place?" I mumble to him, waiting to hear his response. I don't get one though because a young man steps up, distracting us both.

Reaching out to shake Joseph's hand, he has an easy smile on his face. "Hey, Staff Sergeant, how was your vacation?" he cheerfully asks Joseph, already reaching for the bags in my hand. "I can get that for you ma'am," he kindly states.

My eyes are still on Joseph as he skeptically looks at me. "This is one of the Marines under my command. His name is Lance Corporal Jones, but you can call him Michael."

Michael reaches out to shake my hand as I grab a hold of Josephina, pulling her to me. "Corporal Jones, this is my daughter Josephina," Joseph says pointing to her, then over to me. "And, her mother Kasey," he says to him.

The young man is taken by surprise, but he quickly smiles. "So you got married early, Staff Sergeant?" he asks, surprising me with his words.

"I'm not his wife, or the fiancée he intends to marry," I quickly correct. By how surprised he looks, it's clear he wasn't expecting me to say those words as he embarrassedly looks at me.

"I'm sorry, ma'am."

With the awkwardness still in the air, we begin our exit towards the parking lot as Michael leads the way to a large, four door, blue, Chevy Silverado. Digging the keys from his pocket he tosses them at Joseph. He catches them with one hand and disengages the alarm. He opens one of the truck's back doors to place Josephina's booster seat behind the driver's seat, lifting her up into the truck to follow.

Walking my way over to the other side to sit next to her, I'm quickly met with Michael who is already climbing into the back seat, leaving me confused. Where am I supposed to sit?

Looking at the front seat, it dawns on me it's the only seat left. With the confusion still on my face as I look at Michael, I am hoping he'll allow me to take his seat instead. "Oh, I'm sorry, ma'am. I'd assumed you'd be riding in the front with Staff Sergeant since it is *his* vehicle," he says, looking more confused than I felt a moment ago.

Sighing to myself, I give up because he's already buckled himself in and I'd hate to be rude by making him move. I climb into the front seat of the truck, trying not to look disappointed. I can't blame the guy for being a gentleman. Joseph quickly climbs into the driver's side, already starting up the truck as he looks over at me, smiling.

Joseph's smile softens his face, making him look less intimidating. He looks happy and excited about something as he drives away. I could only sit there wondering what it can be, now that he's focused on the road ahead of us.

To distract myself, I do the same. Taking in the sights, while absorbing the scenery that we swiftly drive by, I notice how you have to take a freeway to get anywhere around here. I've lost track of how many different ones we've had to take after leaving the airport. With all the twist and turns, it was easy to do. It was required to get on and off them repeatedly. I would definitely get lost here if I had to drive myself around.

Thirty minutes later, we're pulling onto base to drop Michael off. Joseph then drives us around to give us a quick tour, showing us were he works, telling us about what he does and what it entails. His job doesn't sound very interesting, but I nod my head making sure to indicate I'm interested. I don't understand the military and its ways, but then again I never had to. With our tour quickly over, he starts to drive off base and I suddenly grow confused as we exit the gates.

"You don't live on base?" I ask him, still looking at the

gates behind us as we wait at the light.

Keeping his eyes on the road ahead of him he shakes his head. "No. When I got back from oversees I got an apartment. With my rank I have the freedom to live off base," he simply answers.

"What *exactly* is it you do?" I ask, realizing I never specifically asked. He looks at me with a smile. "I work in communications. It's one of the most important things needed in the military, but with my rank, I pretty much just boss people around every now and then," he clarifies with a chuckle.

Rolling my eyes at his remark I don't question him any further, because really, what more could I ask? I don't understand all the technical aspects of being in the military. The light turns green and he drives off, but doesn't get back on the freeway this time; instead, he takes several different streets that lead us to an apartment complex. Parking his truck, we all climb out. Joseph tells me to leave the luggage and that he'll return for it later. I don't dispute, since I feel tired from the trip, and follow him to his apartment; eager to see where he lives. He leads us to a set of stairs, climbs them, and opens the door at the top.

We enter and the first thing I notice is how simple the apartment looks. It has the basics: a couch, a flat screen on the wall, and a small table off to the side of the kitchen, presumably the dinning area. Even the kitchen looks pretty bare.

Shutting the door behind him, I continue taking in the room. "You and Josephina can have the bedroom since it's the only room. I'll take the couch while you guys are here," he offers before pointing his chin to the only item in the living room.

With a tilt of his chin, I follow him to the room, and I notice it looks just as bare as the rest of the place. There is only a bed and a small dresser against the wall. A door is off to the side, which leads into a bathroom. The sink and vanity are outside the bathroom.

Looking around the room as well, Joseph shrugs his shoulder. "It's simple, but I guess I really don't need much since I'm a guy," he says to me. I agree by nodding my head, being that I don't have much either.

Since we're all exhausted from the plane ride, Joseph decides it's easier to order pizza so we can eat in. With dinner done, we all take turns taking a shower. Josephina, of course, takes her bath last since she likes to linger in the tub.

When it gets dark, we all head to bed. Joseph takes the couch, as he said he would, while Josephina and I take his king size bed. There was so much room on it that there was a huge gap in between the two of us. Normally I would be close to her. It felt strange to have so much room between us. It makes me restless, but since I'm exhausted, I figured I would be able to simply fall asleep. A couple of hours later though, I discover that I can't. No matter how exhausted I feel from traveling, sleep still eludes me. I know if I keep tossing and turning I'm eventually going to wake Josephina, so I need to distract myself. I look over to the clock on the dresser that Joseph has and see it's a little after midnight. Technically, since my body hasn't adjusted to Pacific Time, I know it's more like after two a.m.

Being that I'm a bit thirsty, I decide to get up and get something to drink. I slowly walk out of the bedroom, tiptoeing myself over to the kitchen. I take a quick glance at Joseph sleeping on the couch, taking in his body as he lies there. His arm is thrown over his eyes and I can see his chest slowly rising and falling. Not wanting to wake him up, I keep walking slowly in the direction of the kitchen towards the fridge. The light coming in through the window helps me to navigate throughout the kitchen. Opening the cabinet containing the glasses, I take one out, and then open the fridge to get the water. Pouring some into the glass and slowly closing the fridge back up, I start to walk back to the bedroom trying desperately not to make any noise.

"You couldn't sleep, either?" I hear Joseph's deep mumble from the couch, startling me, causing me to spill half my water over my chest. The coldness of the water makes me gasp loudly, the shock freezing me to the spot. Joseph quickly jumps up from the couch and heads in the direction of the kitchen, returning with a dishtowel. He starts dabbing at my chest chuckling at the same time.

For some odd reason I grow irritated at hearing his laugh, especially since he's the reason why I spilled the water on myself in the first place. Not thinking twice about my next thought, I pour the remaining water down the front of his chest, making him gasp like I did.

"It doesn't feel so good, does it?" I tease, holding up the glass, now chuckling at him. His white shirt looks more saturated than mine.

His eyes are wide in surprise as his shirt sticks to his chest.

"Oh yeah," I hear him say, before he pulls me closely against his body. A gasp escapes my lips when our bodies meet. I wasn't expecting his shirt to feel so cold.

I forcefully try to push at his chest, attempting to shove myself away, but he keeps his arms tightly wrapped around me. I can feel the rumble of his laughter from his chest. It's contagious. I can't help but laugh with him.

Our laughter soon dies though when I stare up at him, I can see his eyes; they're dark with hunger. A hunger I've seen before. It literally takes my breath away.

He leans down and I close my eyes as his lips gently touch mine. I feel him pull back, making me open my eyes. I'm weak from the simple touch of his kiss. My body feels like it's been turned into a pile of mush as I watch his lips go up into a sensual smile. The smile reminds me of our kiss on the plane and the remorse I'd felt earlier.

"No, Joseph, we shouldn't be doing this." My arms try to push him away, but just like before, he keeps his arms tightly wrapped around my body. My eyes are still locked onto his when he asks, "What's wrong?"

"What's wrong? How can you ask, *what's wrong?* You're engaged to someone else, Joseph. Did you forget that?" The anger within me has now replaced the longing I once had for him. He stands in front of me, looking as if what I've said is surreal.

He sighs, his face turning disappointed, as he let me go, my body already missing the loss of his arms. "It's not how you think, Kasey."

I'm unable to stay silent to his response. "I shouldn't have even come. It was a mistake," I whisper, my heart aching as I say the words. I'm torn as I ponder whether I've made the biggest mistake by coming, or would I have been left wondering if I would have regretted it the rest of my life. From the look of disappointment on Joseph's face, I know the words have affected him as well.

"Please don't say that." The pain of my words is clear in his voice.

Waiting for an answer, I question, "Why did you want me to come, Joseph? I have no reason to even be here. How do you think your fiancée is going to feel when she finds out you brought not only Josephina, but me as well? Did you ever stop and ask yourself that?"

"I don't care what she thinks, Kasey. I brought you *both* here because I can't stand the thought of knowing that you're so far away," he utters, raking his hand over his head, looking frustrated.

"What do you expect, Joseph? Madison is where I live. You live here. There will always be distance between us, whether you like it or not. It's the way it's always going to be," I confess, the realization of knowing how far apart we'd always be feels like a punishment to both of us. His first words return to me, leaving me shocked by his declaration. "How can you say you don't care what she thinks? Don't you love her enough to care about her feelings?"

He remains silent, his lips going flat as if he refuses to answer.

"Well?" I demand.

"I don't love her anymore," he whispers, I'm barely able to hear, but I do.

I'm shocked, frozen, and unable to breathe, or properly think as my heart feels as if it's dropped into the pit of my stomach. My body feels as if it's spinning again, leaving me unable to react to his response.

"What do you mean you don't love her anymore?" I force myself to ask. The words rasping in my throat, as I practically whisper them, because I feel like the blood has been completely drained from my body as I stand, waiting for an answer.

I don't know whether to feel excited or disappointed by his revelation.

He slowly stalks towards me, stopping in front of me, as he looks straight down at me, as if waiting for my reaction. I could only stare back at him. My thoughts lost in his eyes as they keep me hypnotized in place. He takes my face into his hands as he leans forward, this time when our mouths meet I can feel his tongue pushing against my lips, demanding I open up for him. I part my lips, obeying his command.

The glass in my hand drops to the floor. The floor lightly vibrates with the thump of the glass echoing throughout the silent room. Wrapping my arms around his neck, he deepens the kiss, pulling his body closer to mine. His tongue explores my mouth as my body ignites from excitement. I can already feel a heat pooling in between my thighs.

I feel my body being lifted off the ground. Joseph's strong hands grip my sides. My legs dangle off the ground as he walks our bodies backwards. We're soon at the couch and I feel my body being lowered down onto it. He pushes his body down to follow mine; our mouths still fused together.

His body is still slightly extended above mine, as if he's fearful he'd crush me, but I want him closer. I want to feel his body against mine. I pull at his shirt, demanding he come down on me. He complies and his body meets mine. His hand starts exploring my body, finding it's way into my shirt, his palms electrifying every inch of my skin with his touch. The warmth of his hand is slowly gliding up my stomach, to reach for my breast as he starts kneading it, making me moan into his mouth. His touches feel so much more intense this time. I had forgotten how much I love his touch.

Wanting to feel his skin next to mine, I start tugging at his shirt, wanting it off. He breaks our kiss just long enough to allow me to remove his shirt. Mine comes off next and his mouth immediately comes back down to mine.

His lips slowly kiss their way down my neck. The heat of his mouth awakens my desire for him, as it grazes its way down to my breast, before he takes my nipple into his mouth, vigorously sucking it. My back arches towards him, wanting to give him more. He moves onto my other breast, giving it the same attention; my moans sound more like a whimper from the pleasurable torture. My hands are holding him in place, refusing to allow him to stop. The feel of his touch is so intense I'm praying he doesn't stop.

His hand reaches for the waistband of my pajama pants. Lifting my hips to allow him to pull them down, along with my underwear, I help him push them off. I don't know what has come over me, but I don't want him to stop.

With his eyes locked onto mine as he stares down at me, he suddenly stops, lifting himself from my body. I whimper from the loss of his body above mine, thinking he's regretted what we're doing. "I'll be right back," he whispers as he places a quick kiss on my lips to walk away.

I'm lying on the couch, confused, as I watch him disappear into the bedroom, but he quickly returns, stopping to stand to the side of me. With the glow of the light from the patio window I see him remove his sweatpants and climb back down above me. His mouth finds mine, as it demands another kiss.

I can feel his hard erection pushing up against my thigh, tantalizing me, before he stops kissing me completely to pull himself away. Every time he pulls away it leaves me frustrated, making me want to scream for him to quit torturing me. But I soon understand when I see him put something up to his mouth, hearing the tearing of a packet. It dawns on me that he disappeared to get a condom. I watch with mesmerized eyes as he rolls it down his hardened shaft, leaving me desperate to touch it myself.

His hands slowly glide up my legs, igniting the fire within me as I let them fall open, allowing him to bring his body down between my thighs. His fingers find the heat of me, rubbing on my clit, intensifying the bliss building within me. His finger finds it's way inside of me, making me moan as I push my hips up to grind against his hand. I'm lost in the sensation, but it's quickly lost when he removes his finger to bring himself down to me, his hips finding mine. His hand reaches under my ass to lift me up, as I feel him slowly entering me. I gasp as inch by inch he stretches me.

Closing my eyes as he continues to push his way in me, my earlier moan is replaced with a soft cry of pain. It's when he fully inside of me that he stops, frozen in place above me. "Kasey, baby, are you alright?" he whispers into my ear.

I can't answer him. The feeling of being completely stretched is distracting me from his words. He places a kiss below my ear, continuing his way down my neck before I hear him ask, "Do you want me to stop?"

His deep husky voice, along with the touch of his hand as it glides up and down my hip to caress me, makes the pain disappear. I try moving my hips, testing how I feel, but I hear Joseph groan, feeling him grow larger inside of me, reminding me that we're still connected.

Slowly, he starts to pump his hips, making me grab onto his shoulders to hold him closer as he increases his thrust, his hand gripping my ass while he glides back and forth inside of me. Wrapping my legs around his waist, I meet him thrust for thrust. His mouth finding its way back to my breast, the sensation of his mouth along with him moving in me makes me moan louder. His lips leave my nipple, coming down onto my mouth, muffling my frantic moans.

My body tenses up. The electrifying wave of pleasure builds through me with each thrust. Suddenly I feel my body strung tight, but just as quickly I explode, crying out in pleasure as Joseph continues to thrust inside of me. I feel as if a hundred firecrackers have been ignited inside of my body. If it wasn't for Joseph's mouth covering my screams, I know I would've woken Josephina.

His body quickens its pumping as I feel him let out a loud groan into our mouths, his body stiffening seconds later. As his pumping comes to a slow stop, I feel his body relax above mine. Our breathing is labored as he pulls his mouth from mine, my heart rapidly racing inside my chest. Bringing his hand up to wipe my hair away from my eyes, I can see his dark eyes staring down at me, a worried expression staring back at me. Reaching up, I kiss him softly on the mouth, feeling him smile on my lips.

His lips slowly trail down my chin, over to my ear as I hear him whisper, "You okay?" The warmth of his breath sends another shiver down my body.

I can't even speak, still out of breath, so I simply nod as I rub my hands up and down his sweaty back. I love how he feels against my body, but the feeling is instantly taken away when he pulls out of me to climb up and off of me. Disappointed, I watch him disappear into the bedroom, hearing the bathroom door shut soon after. Laying there, still trying to catch my breath, my mind dwells over what just happened. Before I have time to regret our actions, I hear Joseph exit the bathroom, making my body freeze up. I don't know whether I should go back into the bedroom with Josephina or stay on the couch with him.

He walks back into the living room, his large body a shadow in the darkened room, as he makes his way back over to me on the couch, lying down next to me.

Thinking he'd probably prefer for me to leave, I try to stand up, but he pulls my body down on top of him, wrapping his large arms around my waist as he entwines our legs. I don't argue, but instead make myself more comfortable, laying my head on his chest, listening to the strong thumps of his heart beating into my ear. My body is completely sated from making love, relaxing without protest as I feel his hand begin to rub my back sending me drifting off into sleep.

Chapter 17

Joseph

KASEY SHIFTS IN my arms, the small stirring of her body awakening me. It's happened several times already, as if her body is restless, or she's uncomfortable. I know my couch isn't the largest. She's draped across the top of my body making it a tight fit, but a pleasurable one. Tightening the hold I have on her, I place a kiss on her head to comfort her; fearful she'll awaken and want to go back to the bed. It's the last thing I want her to do. I don't want to ever let her go. I *need* to hold her within my arms. She feels so good in them.

My mind wanders back to the first night I spent with her, trying to remember if she moved this much. I don't remember her doing so, but then again, we were both too sated to stay awake. I'm surprised I even woke up the next morning to leave.

Reaching down to the floor, I pick up my cellphone, checking for the time. It's only two a.m. It's been a little over an hour since she fell asleep, yet she's awaken me three times.

Closing my eyes I try to fall asleep again. My body is still exhausted from the last couple of weeks. Sleep has eluded me as I stressed about Josephina and Kasey, but now having Kasey next to me, I can finally relax.

Suddenly I hear rattling at the door, soon after, the sound of something being inserted into the doorknob. My only reaction is to get up, dragging Kasey's body up with me as I hear her gasp in surprise. Without thinking, I toss her back onto the couch, rushing to the intruder coming through the door. I'm not expecting anyone, so I'm instantly on high alert, ready to attack whoever is walking through that door.

The door opens; the light from outside the door illuminating a shadowed body, of whom I still can't make out, as it walks in the door. Not caring who it is, I grab for the person bringing them into a chokehold, the instinct of protecting my family taking over as I shove them against the door. Their body slamming the door shut.

A frightened gasp escapes the intruder's mouth as they struggle to speak. "Joseph, what the hell is wrong with you?" I hear Elizabeth choke out, frantically trying to pull my hand from her neck.

"Elizabeth?" My body freezes on the spot from the shock of hearing her unexpected voice, surprising me. What the hell is she doing here?

The kitchen light turns on. The brightness practically blinding me as my eyes try to adjust to the light. Turning to see who's turned it on, I see Kasey standing in the kitchen wrapped in the small blanket I used to cover us. Her eyes are wide open, looking stunned as she stares back at Elizabeth and me, her mouth gaping.

Hearing Elizabeth quietly groan as she digs her nails into my wrist, my eyes avert back to her, and instead of shock, they are fuming with anger. Letting her go, she catches her breath, her eyes glaring daggers at me. "Who the hell is she?" she growls, her eyes finding Kasey, who is turning a bright shade of red all over her pale body, as she tightly clutches the blanket. "And, what the fuck are you both doing naked?" Elizabeth blurts out.

Looking down at my body I realize she's right, *I am* still naked. I'd forgotten, but that was the least of my concerns when she'd walked in the door. Scrambling for my boxers, I quickly put them on, trying to figure out how I'm going to explain this whole situation.

"Did you just fuck her?" Elizabeth shouts, stalking her way over towards Kasey looking like she's ready to attack her. I stop her, grabbing onto her arm to bring her to a halt as I watch Kasey in the corner of my eye. "Who is she?" Elizabeth furiously shouts, fighting to break her hold from my hand, but I yank her body back behind me. I don't want her anywhere near Kasey, not in her state of mind.

"Mommy," Josephina fearfully says from the doorway, rubbing her eyes, looking frightened and confused. I'd forgotten she was asleep in the room.

Without hesitation, Kasey rushes to Josephina's side, picking her up into her arms, making the blanket fall to the ground, exposing her naked body from behind as she retreats to the bedroom with Josephina. Although Kasey is rubbing her back trying to calm her, I can see Josephina's frightened eyes looking back at me as they walk away.

"Daddy, what's happening?" are the last words I hear before they disappear into the room, Kasey shutting the door behind them. My heart sinks into the pit of my stomach. I didn't want my daughter frightened from what's going on.

Elizabeth turns her body to face me. I'm too lost in my

thought that she's able to yank her arm from my grip. "You brought that girl and the slut of her mother back with you?" she snarls at me, the anger radiating from her lips.

"Keep your voice down," I throw back at her. "What are you doing here anyway, Elizabeth?" I growl through clenched teeth, forcing myself to push the anger I'm feeling from her earlier comment to the side.

Her shocked expression surprises me. "I came to see you. I left as soon as I got your text telling me you were back, thinking you'd want to see me," she clips out.

"I told you I was going up there to see you tomorrow. You didn't have to drive all the way down here," I calmly tell her, sneaking a peek at the bedroom door, curious as to what's going on in there.

Bringing my attention back to Elizabeth as she says, "I thought you wanted to see me, but it's obvious you didn't, since you're already fucking someone else."

"I told you to keep your voice down, I don't want you frightening Josephina," I snap at her, the anger of her words already boiling my blood.

This isn't the way I had planned to break things off with Elizabeth. In my mind I was going to sit down with her, calmly talk with her, explain why I didn't want to be with her anymore. I *was* going to try my best to be honest with her. Explaining things were no longer the same. Because they weren't, not since the day Kasey came back into my life. We had a daughter together and in my mind, they were my main focus now.

"Apparently it's a good thing I did. How long have you been sleeping with her?" she snarls, her chest puffing up from her anger.

Sighing, not wanting to deal with this conversation right

now, especially while Josephina and Kasey are in the apartment I answer, only since I have to. "It only happened tonight," I tell her, the guilt of knowing what I've done is morally wrong, even if I don't regret it.

Angry. "I don't believe you," she declares. "She's the reason you went back, isn't it?" her voice dropping low as she asks, the realization in her tone making me sigh. Elizabeth was never stupid, I wouldn't doubt if she suspected it from the beginning. Maybe it's the reason she kept blasting my phone with her calls.

"Yes, but it isn't what you're thinking. Kasey was in an accident and I had to be there for Josephina," I try explaining, but the skeptical look on her face clearly tells me she doesn't believe me.

"That little girl might not even be your daughter!" she screams, still trying to prove her point. "Have you even done the paternity test?"

I stalk towards her, making sure I'm looking directly in her eyes. "Don't even try to make me believe that shit anymore, Elizabeth. The little girl in that room is my daughter," I say, now pointing my finger at my bedroom door, "And I don't need a fucking paternity test to prove it," I growl at her.

The anger in her eyes is replaced with fear. I'm grateful. I'm tired of her placing doubts about Josephina being my daughter in my head. "I'm sorry, Elizabeth, but I can't marry you. Not anymore," I somberly tell her.

Her face turns worried, her head slowly shaking back and forth as she stares down at the floor. "You can't do this to me," the words coming out in a strain.

I don't know what else to tell her. What else can I tell her? Looking back at the closed door to my bedroom, I remember I *do* have a reason why I can't marry her.

"Elizabeth, I don't love you anymore. To tell you the truth, my heart belonged to someone else," I declare. My eyes quickly glancing towards the bedroom door, before I look back to Elizabeth to finish telling her, "I jumped into our relationship and I'm sorry to tell you like this, but I never *did* love you. It took the person I *have always* loved coming back into my life to realize it."

Saying the words, I feel as if the weight of a building has been lifted from my shoulders. Feeling obligated to give Elizabeth everything she wanted was that weight. I always tried my best to please her, to keep her happy, and proposing was one of those things, even if it didn't feel right. I hate knowing I'm hurting her, but I don't love her. I never did.

Elizabeth's eyes are filled with tears, the heartbreak clear in her face, making me feel guilty over everything I've done. "I'm sorry," is all I can say.

Still in shock, I watch the tears running down her face. Slowly she begins to back away, making her way to the door. When she reaches it she takes one last glance at me, her disappointment clear on her face as she turns around and walks out the door.

Standing there, staring at my front door, my body is unable to move. I don't know how I long I stand there, but when I finally came back from my paralyzed state, I make my way to my bedroom, slowly opening the door to find a dark and quiet room. With the light of the kitchen beaming into the room I'm able to take in Kasey's form on the bed next to Josephina. Her arms tightly embraced around her.

Leaving the door cracked to allow the light to glow into the room, I walk over to the bed to climb in behind Kasey. She lightly stirs as I spoon her body against mine. Feeling the warmth of her body soothes me, taking all the tension of the night completely away. Nuzzling her neck as I take in her scent, I close my eyes and pray when I wake up this will not be a dream, because the last thing I want is to know I've lost everything. Including Kasey.

Chapter 18

Kasey

THE SMELL OF bacon wafting through the air pulls me from my sleep, along with Josephina's laughter. My eyes snap open as I remember what happened last night. Slowly sitting up, the blanket falls to my waist, reminding me I'm still naked. Pulling the blanket back up, I sit on the bed trying to fully comprehend last night's events. The scene from last night repeatedly plays in my head, the guilt returning from what I did with Joseph. It shouldn't have happened. I really need to speak to Joseph about it, but I refuse to do so in front of Josephina, fearing we might cause a scene like the one last night.

Although Josephina didn't ask many questions when I brought her back to the room, it was only because I was able to comfort her back to sleep, falling asleep just as quickly with her. I'd forced myself to shut out the conversation continuing outside the door. I didn't care what they were talking about, I already knew I was at fault; I was going to live with the guilt for the rest of my life.

Standing up from the bed, I wrap myself in the blanket to get up and out of bed, immediately noticing how sore I feel in between my legs... another reminder of what occurred last night. Ignoring my soreness as I walk, I make my way over to my luggage for clothes. After finding something to wear I head to the bathroom and quickly dress, hoping to speak to Joseph this morning.

Making my way towards the continued laughter, I stop at the doorframe to take in the scene before me. The sight of Joseph in only a pair of sweats and nothing more paralyzes me in place. My breath hitches as I take in his bare chest. The sight of him heats my body. A tingle soon travels down my body to the area where I'm most sore, leaving me craving to touch him all over again.

The sunlight from the kitchen window is reflecting off his body, making his toned skin glisten from the ray of light. He's breathtaking. I still can't breathe as I continue taking him in.

I'm left weak from staring at him, needing to lean on the doorframe for support as I take in the show. He's tossing pancakes into the air, catching them in a pan as they descend. His dramatic gasp for effect makes Josephina laugh. I can't help but smile seeing the little things he does to keep her smiling. It's clear how much he loves her.

His eyes find mine, giving me a heartwarming smile, his eyes lighting up. If I thought I was weak before, I'm completely and utterly lost at this point. Finding the strength inside of me, I somehow make my way over to the table, trying to disguise the powerlessness I'm feeling as he keeps his eyes on me. Reaching Josephina, I lean down to give her a kiss on the top of her head as she places a forkful of pancakes into her mouth with a smile. Pancakes are her favorite, but I was never able to give her a show like Joseph's when I was making them. Even I'm impressed.

Continuing on to the kitchen area, aiming straight for Joseph, I return his smile, mine making me shy. "We really need to talk about last night," I quietly tell him, looking back at Josephina to make sure she didn't hear me. The cheerful smile tells me she didn't, allowing me to turn back to Joseph, and I'm caught by surprise when he wraps his arm around my waist, pulling me towards him. He leans down to give me a kiss on the mouth, his lips lingering on mine, making me weak as I slump against his body.

He pulls back, compassion overflowing as he looks down at me. "Later," he states with his eyes gazing down at me. "First we eat. Then I have a surprise for both of you," he says, pulling his face from mine, leaving me breathless on the spot.

I'm left standing there with my mouth gaping open, trying to catch my breath, still flush to his body. I don't know what to say, or how to react, as I'm still shocked from his kiss.

"Do you want orange juice or coffee?" Joseph asks, unwrapping his arm from my waist to grab for the plate full of pancakes on the counter, taking them straight to the table

"Orange juice will be fine, thank you," I say, watching him return to grab an orange juice carton off the counter. "Will you grab another set of forks, please?" he says, nodding his chin at the drawer next to me.

His request forces me to move as I open up the drawer, grabbing two forks from the utensil tray before joining them at the table. Even as I attempt to eat, my mind keeps going back to the kiss. It may have been simple to him, but being I'm still confused by last night, his kiss this morning isn't helping solve any questions; it only left me with more. We *are* going to have that talk, today, whether he likes it or not. I need answers, especially after a kiss like that one.

JOSEPH DIDN'T TELL us what his surprise for us was until we arrived at our destination. I was just as anxious as Josephina to know where we were headed, but Joseph wouldn't tell us. The only clue escaping his lips was telling us to put on our bathing suits and grab some towels. At first I'd thought we were simply going to the pool in his apartment complex, but instead he lead us to his truck.

As he drove away from his apartment, my eagerness to know where we were heading was matching Josephina's. It wasn't until we can clearly see the ocean within our view that I realized where we were headed, bringing a smile to my face. I was just as excited to see the beach as Josephina, if not more.

With the day being as sunny as it was, there was no better day than today to be at the beach. Climbing out of his truck, Joseph goes straight to removing Josephina from her booster seat, and the moment her feet hit the ground, she's anxiously tugging at his hand to lead him to the beach. Finding a spot, we lay out the towels, and within seconds, Joseph is picking Josephina up, rushing her towards the water.

With Josephina's laughter fading as they get closer, my heart stops. "Joseph, please be careful with her. Don't let her out of your sight!" I shout to him, the worry already taking over as he turns his body to smile back at me. The chuckle he returns reminds me how paranoid I can be when it comes to Josephina.

Preferring to stay behind to sunbathe instead of following

them to the water, I settle in and get comfortable. Even from where I'm sitting I can hear Josephina's squeals of laughter as I watch them from a distance. I don't think I'll ever get tired of seeing them together. Knowing I have to return to Wisconsin soon tugs at my heart. I already dread having to separate them again; another subject I needed to speak to Joseph about. I already know he was going to protest me leaving, but I *was* going to return to Wisconsin, whether he liked it or not. Every passing day I remained in San Diego was another day I fell behind on my inventory. I have never taken a vacation from my work in my life, and although I wanted Josephina to have these memories, I also had an obligation to provide for the both of us.

The future was still unclear how Joseph and I were going to raise Josephina together, but I wasn't going to hold my breath expecting anything more than a friendship from him, simply for Josephina's sake.

Hoping to take advantage of the sun, I lie on my back and attempt to get a tan, something I haven't been able to do since before Josephina was born. Closing my eyes, my body begins to relax as I slowly begin to drift off into a relaxed state. It isn't long before I feel the sun above me disappear, a darkened shadow standing to my side. When I open my eyes to a slit I see Joseph's shadowed silhouette staring down at me with a smile on his face. With his hands resting on his hips, his body still wet with droplets of water running down his body, he looks as if he could pull off an ad for a swimsuit company with his swim trunks resting low on his hips.

He narrows his eyes down at me. "Why aren't you getting in the water?"

I've heard his question, but my mind is completely lost in another place. I have to force myself to focus on his question, instead of his body and the carnal images swirling in my mind.

"Hmm?" he adds, still waiting for my answer.

Picking my body up onto my elbow, my head goes straight for the water, the realization that Josephina is no longer with him hitting me as I frantically search for her. Spotting her playing on the sand only a few feet in front of us, my mind eases. My eyes skeptically look over at the water, with absolutely no desire to get in, making me look back up at Joseph to answer his question. "I don't want to get in. I'm fine where I'm at," I declare with no further explanation as I lie back down.

He chuckles before saying, "We'll see about that," as he bends down, scooping me up in his arms.

"Joseph, put me down!" I shout at him, struggling against his body as he jogs both of us to the water.

Of course he doesn't listen, as he laughs along the way. Seeing us near the water, my body tenses up, dreading going into the water. Bracing myself I feel my body descending along with Joseph's, as he holds me tight, our bodies both going down into the waves. The water feels cold, shocking me completely as I come up for air. I immediately feel Joseph wrap his arms around my body, pulling me tight to his chest. Pushing my hair from my face, I see Josephina laughing as she rushes towards the edge of the water, making me stiffen with panic thinking she is going to enter. Instead, she stops at the edge of the waves, clapping her hands as she jumps in excitement.

"Don't worry, I told her she isn't allowed into the water without me. She understands. I told her I was bringing you into the ocean," he says into my ear. "I wasn't going to let you avoid the ocean. It's something everyone should experience." His husky voice laces onto my skin as his lips graze my neck. I can feel the warmth of his breath, giving me goose bumps, and making my whole body shudder.

Having to hold onto his arms for support, already knowing my legs will collapse any moment, my heart speeds as he continues to hold me in his arms. My breath hitches, making me light headed when he starts nipping at my neck.

"Since you've managed to dunk me, I think I'm good now. Will you let me go so I can get out now?" I ask, trying to push his body away, but he keeps his arms tightly wrapped around me, refusing to let me go as he pulls me tighter to him. I'm seconds away from losing all restraint of keeping him at a distance.

He pulls his head back forcing me to look at him. His hooded eyes showing me a hunger I've seen in him before as he lowers his face towards mine. Turning my face to avoid his kiss, I shove at his chest. "No, Joseph, no more," I tell him, attempting to force myself from his grip to no avail.

"Kasey, what's wrong?" he questions, completely confused with my reaction.

Glaring up at him, I ask, "Have you forgotten about Elizabeth?" Understanding the meaning of my declaration, he explains. "You don't have to worry about Elizabeth anymore, Kasey. I ended things with her last night," he clarifies with a sigh.

Knowing I'm the cause for him breaking up with her intensifies the guilt I already feel. His behavior over the situation only makes it worse. I couldn't allow him to continue acting as if she never existed by moving on so quickly. "I refuse to be your back up plan. How can you be kissing me after you've just broken things off with her only last night?" I ask him, a dirty feeling settling in the pit of my stomach.

His furrowed brows tell me he's offended by my words.

"Is that what you think you are, Kasey? A back up plan?"

"It's not like I was the original one," I throw at him.

He grows serious before answering. "You were never the backup plan, Kasey," he says, sighing. "I never loved her."

"I don't believe you," I say, still feeling unsatisfied with his answer.

As he's about to say something, Josephina's shouts stops him. "Look, I found a pretty seashell. Can I keep it?" she asks, holding up her prize for both of us to see.

His expression softening for her, he looks back at her with a smile now on his lips. "Of course, princess," Joseph shouts back to her. Letting me go, he begins to walk in her direction. "Do you want to swim some more while your mommy goes and lies back down?" he asks, scooping down to pick her up.

Making my way back towards the spot with our towels, I lie back down. I'm left wondering what he would have said to my response. We weren't finished discussing the subject, but we needed to finish soon.

Chapter 19

Kasey

ALTHOUGH I WOULD have preferred to be alone when I finished my conversation with Joseph, it was impossible to do so with Josephina always around. Taking advantage of Josephina sleeping in the back seat, I continue, wanting desperately to get it off my chest.

"Joseph, we really need to talk," I hesitantly announce. As much as I dread having the conversation, I know I need to get it out. As I look at him, I can already see him grimacing, wanting to avoid the subject. "Don't give me any excuses. We *are* going to have this conversation," I demand.

"Then talk," he clips out, keeping his eyes focused on the road ahead of him. His face still strained from our earlier conversation.

Searching for the specific words I want to ask, I used the first ones on my mind. "Why did you stay with her even though you claimed you never loved her?" I dreadfully ask, hoping the answer he is going to give me isn't one I will regret hearing.

His dragged silence worries me. "I don't know," he simply states.

Letting out the breath I was holding in, I sigh to myself, still unhappy with his answer. "It's my fault isn't it, for allowing it to happen?" I quickly let out. "Maybe if you wouldn't have cheated on her in the first place, you guys would still be together," I guiltily tell him.

He is still staring at the road ahead as he answers. "I'd already planned to break up with her. When you and Josephina came back into my life, I had a reason to end things with her," he says, his words sounding sincere, but not satisfying me.

Bracing myself, I ask, "What reason is that?"

His eyes find mine as he answers, "You were the reason, Kasey," his lips going up into a smile as he stares back at me. The look in his eyes mixed with his words makes my breath hitch, my heart skipping a beat. Just as quickly he tears his gaze away from me, focusing back onto the road ahead of us, leaving me confused to ponder the words.

My cheeks begin to flush as I take in the meaning of his words. "It still shouldn't have happened. You never should have cheated on her," I repeat to him, the words coming out almost at a whisper since I've had to say them around the lump in my throat. I'm hoping my words will make him understand how wrong his actions were.

"There was also another reason why I was going to end things," he conveys. "She refused to allow me to continue being a part of Josephina's life. She wanted me to walk away from her, regardless of the outcome of the paternity test. It wasn't going to happen."

The shock of his words keeps me sitting there puzzled as

I watch him, wondering what the future would have been like for Josephina and I had he done as Elizabeth demanded. I was fine before Joseph came back, but would I have been able to pick up the pieces of both Josephina's broken heart and mine, when he never came back? He looks in my direction, the anger radiating from his face. "*Nobody* is going to keep me from being a part of my daughter's life," he replies.

The indication of the statement worries me; as if he believes I would do the same. "Joseph, you honestly think I would keep Josephina from you? Is that why you made us come back with you?" I say, remembering how determined he was for us to return with him, going as far as buying our plane tickets without discussing it with me first.

His shoulders slump forward, his facial expression relaxing. "No, Kasey. I know you wouldn't keep Josephina from me, but I knew *she* would."

I can't argue with him, nor do I wish to continue having the conversation since we're not coming to a resolution. We're only upsetting each other, so I stay silent, finally giving up.

Soon we reach his apartment, leaving me relieved we've finally arrived, and I immediately begin preparing to cook dinner. Joseph kept insisting he would order in so I wouldn't have to cook, but I simply ignored him, needing the distraction to help clear my mind. With dinner done, we eat and I'm soon starting my normal routine of getting Josephina into the bath and ready for bed.

While I'm bathing Josephina, Joseph informs us he's headed to the gym for a quick workout. His absence finally allows me to breathe and focus on my thoughts of our earlier conversation, going over every word in my mind. Still unable to come to an answer when I'm done bathing Josephina, I push the thoughts aside, and curl up onto the couch with her to watch a movie, waiting for her to fall asleep. I'm already trying to get up with Josephina when Joseph walks in the door. Joseph immediately comes over to take her, lifting her up as if she weighs nothing. She looks like a limp noodle against his hard sweaty body.

I can't help but take in his scent when he'd bent down to pick her up, even sweaty he smells so good. He smelled like the soap I gave him before we left Madison. I would've never imagined how good they both smelled together, or how much I'd enjoy the combination. Unable to resist, I take him in as he holds Josephina, making his arms bulge. They appear larger than I normally see them. I know I've taken in his form before, but for some odd reason, I'm looking him over now with great detail and the sight of him making me weak.

"I'll put her in bed. Why don't you go grab your shower," he whispers, turning to head into the bedroom, leaving me to watch him walk away.

Standing up from the couch, I head straight to the bathroom, needing a cold shower to calm the burn in my body. Quickly undressing and getting into the shower, my thoughts return to the image of Joseph just a few moments ago. Knowing exactly how good he could make me feel wasn't helping with the craving inside of me to make them happen again. Telling myself it was wrong to think that way, I start to rinse my hair, forcing myself to push the thoughts away. As I'm rinsing the conditioner from my hair with my eyes closed, I hear the shower curtain move aside, frightening me.

My eyes pop open up in surprise as Joseph steps in the shower. "Is it okay if I get in?" he asks, not waiting for my permission as he pulls the curtain closed.

I stand there frozen in place, unable to move or say anything. The only thing moving are my eyes as they make their way down his naked body, taking him in. My eyes reach the V leading down to his semi-erect penis, making my eyes go wide in shock. No matter how many times I take in Joseph's naked body, I'm still left amazed. He is beautiful. His body perfectly sculpted, muscles covering every inch of his body.

I look over to Joseph, our eyes locking, but his look hooded and dark with hunger, making my body awaken with excitement. I feel the sparks igniting inside me, traveling straight down to the sweet spot between my thighs, making me weak with desire. Turning my body, hoping it will help bring the sensation under control, I allow the water to help cool me down.

Suddenly I feel Joseph's body closely behind me, making me go rigid as his arms wrap around my waist. "Have you washed your body yet?" he huskily asks into my ear. When I shake my head, he answers with a simple, "Good."

The hand containing a bar of soap begins to slowly run down the front of my body, his fingertips slowly trailing along with the soap, purposely teasing me. Closing my eyes, I let out a moan, unable to contain it. It's the reaction I want to give every time he touches me; a touch my body always craves.

Holding me tightly to his chest, my back leaning against him for support, I can feel his hardened erection pushing up to the curve of my butt. Gently pushing up to it, wanting to feel more of him against my skin, I imagine what it'd feel like to have him inside of me again.

Unexpectedly I hear Joseph groan, the grumble vibrating against my back as it makes its way up his chest. "I wouldn't test me if I were you," he growls into my ear, taking the lobe into his mouth, sucking it, making me groan.

Already weak from his touch, I lean my head back, it lands on his shoulder as he continues to nip his way down my collarbone and then slowly trailing kisses back up my neck. His warm tongue glides on my skin, sending a chill down my spine, hitting me like a jolt of electricity at my core.

The hand containing the bar of soap is slowly making its way up in between the valley of my breast, teasing its way over each one, while his other hand makes its way down my stomach. Down in between my legs.

My eyes are still closed, intensifying my senses, while his hands roam freely over my skin. His palms are creating a trail of fire as they move about my body, heating my blood, pushing my body to demand more.

With his head making its way up my neck, his lips continue their journey up my chin. Turning my body, to better touch him, my hands graze up his arms, over his large biceps, and then back down the front of his chest. Running my fingers over every ripple that leads down the front of him down to his rib cage before they travel to his back, dragging the tips of my nails on his skin.

Without warning, I feel Joseph bend down, lifting me up against the wall. My legs instantly wrap around his waist as my arms loop around his neck, trying to hold onto him. His mouth descends upon mine, greedily kissing me, stealing every ounce of breath I have, as he plunges himself deep inside of me, making me pull my mouth away to gasp. It's soon followed by an even louder moan as he pulls out and plunges into me again, hitting me right in the center of my core as he continues to fully stretch me. My legs are tightening around his body as I rock my hips forward to meet his thrust. My head now thrown back, his head is bent forward as his mouth attacks my breast, fiercely sucking the nipple to send my body into overdrive with pleasure.

My moaning is increasing with the speed of his thrusting.

I'm practically screaming at this point. His mouth quickly releases my breast before I hear him say, "Baby, you have to quiet down, or else you're going to wake Josephina." He quietly growls into my ear, his voice sounding strained, as if he's trying to control himself as well.

Bringing my head down to his shoulder, I bury my mouth into the crook of his neck, attempting to muffle my panted moans. It's hard to do as the pleasure builds with every thrust he gives me. I know I'm close to my peak when my body begins to tense, preparing to let go, but I'm selfishly holding myself back, not wanting it to end. When I feel Joseph's hands tightly grip my ass, I'm unable to wait any longer as I'm pushed over the edge, my insides exploding with pleasure. I'm catapulted into another world as I hear Joseph groan against my neck, still fiercely pumping into me. Within seconds he throws his head back, body growing stiff, as he lets out a loud groan with his final thrust. He stands there, still holding me up, as we both struggle to catch our breath, my body limp and sated against him.

I can feel us both vigorously panting as we hold each other tightly, as if we both refuse to let go. Opening my eyes, he's staring at me, before he comes down to give me another kiss, his lips lingering on mine. "That felt so…fucking…good," he breathlessly says onto my lips, trying to catch his breath between each word. I nod in agreement since I still can't speak yet myself.

Unwrapping my legs from around him, I let them fall to the floor, but I struggle to keep upright, causing me to sway. Joseph quickly catches me, holding me against his body as I merely stand there holding onto his arms, my head slumping forward onto his chest. He starts running his hands up and down my back, causing my body to awaken. If I wasn't still so weak I think I'd be demanding he make love to me again, but I'm still too weak to ask.

A moment later I see him reach down to pick up the bar of soap that had fallen to the floor, quickly cleaning us up before we exit the shower to dry, heading into the bedroom when done. I begin to quietly get dressed, trying to avoid waking up Josephina. Looking over at Joseph, who is standing behind me, I already hate the thought of him not being next to me tonight, but I'm not looking forward to sharing the couch with him.

Without hesitation, Joseph reaches for my hand, pulling me towards the bed as he lays down, tugging me to lie down on top of him. I don't protest, but instead make myself comfortable in the space between Josephina and Joseph, my body half draped over his. His arms wrap around my body as I lay my head on his shoulder, wrapping my arm across his chest, entwining my legs with his. As my body relaxes, I feel him kiss my temple as his arms tighten around me, making me close by eyes. I know walking away from Joseph now is going to be the hardest thing I've ever done, but I know that it's for the best, even if it breaks my heart.

Chapter 20

Joseph

I'M LYING IN bed with Kasey draped across my body, Josephina off to the other side. Kasey has her legs entangled with mine. Our bodies are closely connected side by side, her arm tightly wrapped around my waist, as if afraid I was going to escape. I wasn't going to go anywhere. I love the feeling of her warm body next to mine. It's the reason why I wasn't moving.

I can already see the sun peeking in through the window. Josephina will be waking up soon, which is why I should be getting up to move to the couch like I did yesterday, before she had woken, but I don't want to leave. I had moved so as not to confuse her. She already had enough going through her head with Elizabeth showing up.

Remembering her questions when she came sleepy eyed into the living room yesterday morning makes me smile. Kasey wasn't lying when she'd said Josephina had an inquiring mind, I hadn't wanted to have to lie to her, but a with little influencing I was able to convince Josephina that Elizabeth was only an old friend I wouldn't be seeing anymore. Which was true.

Kasey begins to stir on top of me, making me tighten my arms around her to keep her from getting up. I don't want her to leave just yet. When she lifts her head up looking straight at me, blinking her eyes as if she's trying to focus, she smiles. Her eyes are half closed in a slit with her chin on my chest, struggling to keep them open. It's clear she's still trying to wake. She looks so cute and sexy right now, I can't resist giving her a kiss on her nose.

"Hey there, sleepy head," I whisper down to her, not wanting to wake Josephina up.

Tilting her head to one side, resting it back down on my shoulder, her lips go into a wide smile. Tightening her arm that is wrapped around my chest, while trying to pull me closer with the leg draped across my body, I have to bite back a groan as my cock starts twitching against her thigh. "Baby, as much as I'm dying to make love to you right now, I don't think it's right to do it while our daughter is in the same bed as us," I say, nuzzling her ear and suckling her neck.

Her body tenses up, head whipping over in Josephina's direction as her eyes go wide. "Joseph, I have to get up before she does," she tells me, already trying to push herself off my body. I instantly regret saying anything at all.

Releasing my hold on her, she pushes herself off me, climbing off the bed, leaving me feeling cold from the loss of her body. I briefly stare up at the ceiling, frustrated with myself. Seeing that she's still on the side of the bed, I swing my body up just as fast and catch her by the wrist, pulling her to sit on my lap. She lets out a small yelp as she lands on my legs, but doesn't fight getting up. She looks back at Josephina, probably making sure she's still asleep before she faces me. I can already see the confliction on her face. "Kasey, please tell me you're not regretting last night," I say, hoping she doesn't tell me she does.

Taking her lip in her mouth she deeply sighs. "Joseph, I don't regret it," she tells me, making me smile, but just as quickly she makes it fade when she adds, "I'm just confused about what to think. Everything is only happening because you're barely coming off of a breakup with Elizabeth. I can't help but continue believing I'm simply a replacement for her," she says, her eyes turning glassy with impending tears.

Her words are a stab to my heart. "Is that what you really believe?"

She frowns down at me, her torn expression already answering my question as a tear escapes her eye. Reaching up to wipe it away, she answers. "I don't know what to think, Joseph. I've never been in a relationship before and I never asked for all this to happen. I'm already feeling guilty, I'm the reason you broke up with her, and I'm going to have to live with that guilt for the rest of my life," she ends with a whisper.

From the strain in her voice, I can tell it hurt to say the words. It hurt hearing them, but I'm angry with myself for allowing her to carry the weight of feeling guilty. She burrows her face in her hands and from the way her body is lightly convulsing, I can tell she's crying. I can't handle knowing she's crying and I want her to understand it isn't her fault.

Picking her up in my arms, I walk us to the living room, sitting us down on the couch. She tries to stand up, but I keep her tightly against my body as I wrap her in my arms. Pulling her hands down from her face, I force her to look at me. "Kasey, I already told you my reasons for breaking up with Elizabeth. I can't lie and tell you that you weren't one of the reasons," I say to her, earning me another whimper, but I quickly continue. "Although, you were the perfect reason I needed to realize she wasn't meant for me. When I got back from Afghanistan she was pressuring me to propose and I did, but my heart wasn't in it. I was blind. I was only doing what she asked. I should've seen she wasn't right for me and I should've broken up with her instead of proposing. It wasn't until you came back into my life and the fact I had a daughter, that I opened up my eyes to the real person she was. I couldn't be with someone who didn't want a family with me. Even though Josephina came into my life late, *she is my family*, and so are you because you're her mother," I finish telling her.

Instead of calming her, it only makes her sob. *Fuck*. This was not what I was expecting from my declaration.

"I was the reason you broke up with her. I'm a home-wrecker before you even had a home with her," she wails through her convulsing cries.

Dammit, was she even listening to a word I said?

"Kasey, you saved me from a life of misery. And, technically we weren't married yet, so you're not a home-wrecker," I say, chuckling at her allegation.

She angrily glares at me. "You think this is all funny?" Her reaction makes me laugh once more, which angers her more. She swats me on the chest with her palm, making me catch her wrist. When I pull it away, I kiss the inside of her hand, trying to calm her pain. I know from the burning on my chest it had to hurt her more than it did me.

Letting go of her hand to reach up for her face, I pull her to me, kissing her in hopes that it will stop her from crying. Her lips taste salty from her tears, but the kiss only fires up the earlier hunger I had for her. Wanting to start what I didn't get to do in the bedroom, I'm about to lay her down on the couch when I hear a giggle from the edge of the couch. Kasey shoves me up, breaking our kiss, so we can both sit up. She tries to stand, but my arm is still wrapped around her body, keeping her trapped in my lap. Looking over in Josephina's direction, she's staring at us with a shy smile as she hides behind her teddy bear.

"Good morning, princess. Did you sleep well?" I ask her, ignoring Kasey's wiggling body as she struggles to get up. Pushing my hip up to her ass so she can feel the reason why I don't want her to get up, I hear her gasp, her body going stiff as she stays seated on my lap.

I don't know what's funnier, hearing Kasey's tiny gasp when she feels my erection, or a giddy looking Josephina staring back at us.

With a smile still on my face, I continue staring at Josephina, hoping she doesn't catch on to what is happening between Kasey and I. "Hey, princess, hurry up and get ready. I have another surprise for you today," I say to her.

She squeals with excitement, running over to the couch to take a seat next to us. "What is it daddy? Tell me please..." she pleads, her eyes begging just as badly.

I hear Kasey groan in front of me as her body slumps forward in defeat. "It wouldn't be a surprise if I told you, would it? Now hurry up and go get ready," I tell Josephina, lightly shoving her in the direction of the room, wanting another minute of privacy with Kasey.

Once Josephina is safely in the room, I pull Kasey's face towards mine, giving her one final deep kiss. When I pull away, her eyes are still closed with her mouth half hanging open. Slowly she opens her eyes while I wait for her to look at me. "I'm going to prove to you, Kasey Wilson, that you were the perfect reason to breakup up with Elizabeth," I tell her before standing up, leaving her sitting on the couch gawking at me.

I hear a grumble behind me, making me smile. I meant the words and I planned on making sure to prove to her, she was worth keeping. Maybe then she'll have a reason to stay.

Chapter 21

Kasey

WHAT DID HE mean? Trying to catch my breath as I sit here, alone on the couch dumbfounded by his words, I slowly bring my fingers up to my lips. They're still tingling. He has that effect on me; always leaving them feeling like they're on fire. The tingling doesn't immediately disappear. Not that I want it too. I like the reminder of knowing his lips were on mine.

Every time he kisses me, or touches me, my body ignites like a flame.

Seeing him come back into the living room, eyeing me with a mischievous grin, reminds me he wants to go somewhere. Finding the strength to stand up, I head to the bedroom so I can get ready. Half an hour later, with the help of Joseph nagging every five minutes that I'm too slow getting ready, we're in his truck headed to our surprise destination. Where, I still don't know, because like yesterday, he doesn't say. We don't have to wait too long before we pull up to the parking lot of our destination. Taking in the location, I'm as amazed as Josephina.

It's Sea World.

The look on Josephina's face is priceless. Her squeals of excitement making me smile along with Joseph. The expression on her face when she took in the beach was no comparison to knowing she was going to be able to actually see members of the sea up close.

I soon discovered the reason why Joseph was in such a rush to leave when I took in the schedule and everything there was to do. It was because he wanted to arrive early so we can get a head start on the day, taking advantage of every minute for Josephina.

Without hesitation, our first destination is the dolphin show, Josephina's favorite mammal. The rest of the day goes fairly quickly as we take in every sight and show possible, leaving us exhausted when we return to Joseph's apartment at the end of the evening. Done tucking Josephina into bed, I make my way to the kitchen area, seeing Joseph getting a glass of water.

"I wanted to thank you for today," I say, as we both lean against the kitchen counter. "It really meant a lot to Josephina and I appreciate you taking us to Sea World. You didn't have to do that."

He shrugs his shoulder. "It's nothing," he casually replies.

"How can you act as if it's no big deal, Joseph? You've been spending too much money on us, especially the plane tickets to fly us out here. I can't imagine how much you spent rushing to my side. You don't have to spend more money by taking us to these extravagant places."

He places his glass on the counter behind him, turning to face me, grabbing onto my waist when he looks down at me.

"Kasey, most of the money I have came from when I sold my parents house five years ago. It's been growing interest in the bank since then. The rest came from me being overseas. They pay Marines very well to be in a war zone. I didn't have anything to spend it on until I got back, so it sat in the bank growing interest," he tells me as he gazes at me.

"You still shouldn't be spending all this money, Joseph," I reply, guiltily dropping my head, unable to face him.

He lifts my chin up, forcing me to look at him. "Kasey, I would give it all up in a heartbeat if it meant I can have you and Josephina with me again."

"You don't really mean that. You only need Josephina in your life. Not me."

"I meant every word of what I said. The *both* of you."

Before he gives me the chance to answer, his lips are on mine, my arms reaching up to wrap around his neck, pulling him to me, needing to have him closer. Wrapping his arms around my waist he picks me up off the ground. My legs dangling off the ground as he pulls me up tightly to his body. My body feeling as if it's floating in the air with every step he takes.

Reaching the couch, I feel him lower our bodies down, unwrapping his arms from around my waist to grab onto my legs, his hands guiding my legs to wrap around his waist as pushes his hips between my thighs, awakening my desire.

He's already hard as he grinds his hips up against me, teasing me, making me moan into his mouth as our tongues duel with each other. My tongue explores every inch of his mouth, wanting to taste more of him. Slowly his hands start to glide into my shirt to unhook my bra and then moving onto my breast to palm it within his hand.

He removes my shirt and bra, tossing them to the ground,

reaching for the button of my jeans next, and hastily removes them. Lying underneath him, naked as he gazes down at me, his eyes looking dark and hungry, as his hands slowly glide up my legs from the bottom of my ankles all the way up to my thighs. With his eyes locked onto mine, his lips slowly turn up to one side as I feel his finger slowly tracing the lips of my sex, building my desire.

Slowly, as if enticing me, his finger enters me, deliberately teasing me as I close my eyes, letting out a soft moan. I gasp when I feel his mouth on the center of my core. The unexpected feeling of his mouth vigorously sucking on me makes me arch my body to meet his mouth. His tongue gliding up to clamp down on my clit, taking it into his mouth before he tightly suckles around it. My hands go straight to the cushions as they grip them for dear life, needing to hold onto something as he continues to move his mouth against the heart of me. With his hands he lifts my hips, sucking harder, making me bite down on my lip to keep myself from moaning too loud; this time remembering our daughter is in the next room.

Within minutes I'm coming into his mouth. My restrained moans vibrating through my throat as he sends me over the edge, sending me into a world filled with stars and fireworks exploding behind my closed eyes.

My body is limp, my breathing labored, and my heart beating uncontrollably. I could only lie there sated and unable to move as I open my eyes to see Joseph already removing his clothing. I watch him remove each piece of clothing in front of me, memorized by his body. He's down to the last stitch of clothing, his boxers, when his phone starts to ring. At first he ignores it, grabbing for the waistband of his boxers already pushing them down, exposing his long and hard erection, but the phone immediately starts ringing again, this time with a different ring tone, making Joseph curse.

Confused, I watch as Joseph starts searching his pants looking for his phone.

Without looking at the screen he answers. "Staff Sergeant Mitchell speaking," still gazing down at me, his eyes now growing aggravated.

He listens into the phone, his expression growing angry as his lips go flat. Without saying another word he heads to the kitchen counter, still naked, searching for something. When he finds a pen and paper he begins to quickly write, his eyes focused on the paper.

"Yeah, I'll be there in thirty minutes. Give or take," he clips into the phone, hanging it up soon after. Walking back over in my direction, I see him sigh as he starts getting dressed.

I'm lying on the couch. Naked. Watching him with disappointment.

"I'm sorry, Kasey. I've got to go. One of my Marines is drunk at a bar that we usually go to and the owner is holding him there until I pick him up."

"Can't he just call a cab or something?" I ask him.

"Normally I would, but he got into a fight, which is why the owner called me instead of the cops. I'm his get out of jail card," he explains as he puts on his shirt.

Knowing there is nothing more I can say or do, I stay silent.

Joseph leans down to give me a kiss. Unable to resist, my hands make their way to his neck, pulling his body to deepen the kiss. I can taste myself in his mouth as I feel him groan against my lips, making me smile.

"He might not be going to jail, but I'll make sure he pays for it," he mumbles against my mouth, making me chuckle.

As he pulls himself away from me, looking restrained, he quickly leans back down to me, giving me another quick kiss on the corner of my mouth. Letting him go, knowing he needs to leave, I watch him walk out the door. Leaving me there on the couch, I listen as he locks the door, and his footsteps retreat down the steps. I stand up to head straight for the room. There is no need for me to stay on the couch. Getting dressed in my pajamas, I go to brush my teeth and wash my face for bed. I soon climb into bed next to Josephina and let my dreams take me away into the night.

Later, I feel Joseph climb into bed next to me, my body already recognizing him as he pulls my body tightly to his. I don't fight him, or push him away. Instead, I turn so I can wrap my arms around his chest and entwine our legs to get more comfortable. Still in my sleepy state, I feel him kiss me in the hollow of my neck, his warm face nuzzled against my skin, sending me back to sleep.

Chapter 22

Joseph

THE FEELING OF waking up with Kasey in my arms will never get old. It's been a week now since they arrived. Every night she's protesting, telling me we were sending the wrong message to Josephina, but against her protest, I still climbed into bed with them. The minute Kasey fell asleep she'd seek out my body, grabbing onto it, and refusing to let go.

The only damper on the situation was having Josephina sleeping next to us. I loved my little girl, but because she was in the bed with us, we refused to do anything else but sleep next to her. It still didn't stop us completely, though. There were a couple of times I'd lost my willpower and literally carried Kasey off to the couch. That couch was proving to be a much-overused piece of furniture in my apartment. I made a mental note to myself to never throw it out. Eventually we would end up back in the bed for the comfort.

Smiling to myself, I remember last night as I feel Kasey begin to stir against my body, awaking my yearning to be inside of her again. As I grab for her leg to wrap around my waist, her face nuzzles deeper into my neck, making me groan into her ear. She tightens her hold on my body as I feel her giggle. Unable to take her teasing me anymore, I pick her up as I stand up from the bed, already carrying her off to the couch. Kasey wraps her legs around my waist, holding on tight for the ride, as she continues to tease me by kissing on my neck.

"Mommy you look funny when daddy carries you," Josephina says, making me stop in my tracks in the middle of the room.

Letting out a groan, Kasey buries her face into the crook of my neck, her body slumping onto mine. Unwrapping her legs from my waist, she lets them drop to the floor, forcing me to put her down. I keep my arms wrapped around her waist, pulling her against my body, using it to shield my erection from Josephina as we both face her.

"Daddy was just playing with me, sweetheart. You know how he plays with you?" Kasey tells Josephina as we watch her make her way to the bathroom, closing the door behind her.

Leaning down to whisper into Kasey's ear. "Do you think if we ask nicely, she'll let us keep playing?" I ask, nibbling at her neck, placing a kiss right below her ear.

I feel her body tremble, but just as quickly she smacks my arm, trying to pull herself away. I keep her in place, rubbing my erection against her ass to prove my point of how badly I want to play. She groans, which means I've convinced her as I continue trailing kisses down her throat.

"Joseph, we really need to stop," she demands, as if she's upset about something.

Hearing the anger in her voice makes me turn Kasey to face me. "Kasey, is something wrong?"

She doesn't answer, but shoves me away, walking straight for the bathroom without a backwards glance, to check on Josephina. I'm left there dazed and confused over the situation. What the hell did I do?

Within seconds I see Josephina exit the bathroom, but the door closes with Kasey still in it. "Daddy, can we make pancakes again?" Josephina eagerly asks, before I hear the water to the shower turn on.

"Of course, princess," I tell her, still staring at the closed bathroom door.

Still wondering what has upset Kasey, I push the thought aside as I walk over to Josephina to scoop her up into my arms and I carry her away. Her tiny body doesn't feel like Kasey's, but having her in my arms makes me just as happy.

Kasey

STANDING UNDER THE warm water as it runs down my body, I allow the heat from the stream take the built up tension in my body. My mind keeps returning to what happened with Joseph in the room. It's been happening more often than I wish, but my appetite to have him again keeps taking over. I really need to stop letting my body betray me by giving in so easily to Joseph.

No matter how many times I kept repeating to Joseph what we were doing was wrong, he simply wouldn't listen, ignoring my plea for us to stop. We weren't technically in a relationship, which is the reason why it's wrong. But I really had no one to blame but myself. No matter how upset I was about the situation, my body would make me cave into my desire and have sex with him. Although it felt amazing each time it happened, I was always left with the shame, and guilt, soon after. Joseph relentlessly claimed he was going to prove his words to me, but wasn't putting much effort in at all, since the day he said those words. Unless you called consistently wanting sex from me an effort. I promised myself I would give him the week to prove his words to be true, if he didn't, then I was leaving.

During the day he would spend time with Josephina and I, taking us somewhere new to discover. However, come night when Josephina was finally asleep, the only thought on his mind was sex and my traitorous body always gave in to his demand. No matter how hard I tried to tell myself I wasn't going to have sex with him again, we still did.

My time to leave was soon approaching. I hadn't told Joseph of my decision, allowing him the time he needed without having to put any pressure on him, but his time was now up. The week was over and I was scheduled to leave. I was afraid of having to break both their hearts when I tell them my decision. I've seen how attached Joseph and Josephina have become to each other. That alone was making having to leave so much harder, but I'd already purchased the tickets back to Madison, and I was leaving regardless of what he said.

Turning off the shower, I dry myself and quickly get dressed, making my way into the kitchen. I see Joseph already placing breakfast on the table as I take a seat.

"Daddy, can we go to the zoo again?" Josephina asks around a mouthful of pancakes.

Joseph finishes chewing the piece of bacon in his mouth

before he says, "We just went the day before yesterday, princess. We can go next week."

My heart drops into the pit of my stomach as I hear his answer, bracing myself to speak. "Actually, we won't be here next week," I tell him, staring down at my plate as I shove my food around with my fork.

"What do you mean you won't be here next week?"

When I look up at him, he's staring back at me with narrowed eyes. I've never seen that look on his face before. I know he must be mad, but he doesn't scare me.

Being that I still haven't answered him, he asks again, "Kasey, what do you mean you won't be here?"

"Josephina and I are leaving tomorrow," I state.

"Why?" They both ask at the same time. Josephina's question sounding more of a whine compared to Joseph's angry growl between his clenched teeth.

"Joseph, I need to get back to Madison. I have a business to run," I reply. "I had a client call me at the beginning of the week needing more products and I wasn't there to give it to her. It's money I'm losing if I can't provide her with more to sell," I declare, watching as his lips go flat, but I continue on. "This business is what provides my income. I won't get an income if I'm not there to run my business," I stress to him, refusing to feel intimidated. "We leave tomorrow morning at eight a.m., so we have to be at the airport by six-thirty," I inform him.

"No," he clips out.

His answer doesn't surprise me. I was actually expecting it. "Regardless of what you say, Joseph, Josephina and I *are* leaving tomorrow."

"Kasey, I already told you I would provide for you and Josephina. So you really don't need to work. I don't understand why you can't get that through your head?" he scowls.

"Joseph, I refuse to let you *provide* for us. I've been doing fine on my own since before Josephina was born and I'm pretty sure I will continue to do so without *your* help. I don't have a reason to stay, Joseph. My business, *my home*, is back in Madison. That's where Josephina and I belong." It pains me to say the words, but I need Joseph to understand my reasons.

"So you plan on keeping me from seeing her? Because that's exactly what you'd be doing if you left, Kasey," he throws back at me.

His words hit me like a ton of bricks, making me feel guilty about my decision. "Joseph, how can you say that? You knew we would have to go back. I still don't understand why you didn't purchase round trip tickets for Josephina and I."

"I didn't purchase them for a reason, Kasey."

"We've already gone through the separation once when you came back after your first vacation. I'm pretty sure we'll learn to live with the distance between us again," I tell him, already feeling the pain it will cause. "Please, don't make this anymore difficult than it already has to be," I say, the words coming out more of a whisper, stinging as I say them.

"Mommy, can we please stay a little longer? Please..." Josephina whines, but I simply shake my head to answer as I brush a loose strand away from her face. "No, sweetheart. I've already bought the tickets. They were very expensive and I can't change the flights. We have to leave tomorrow," I say to her.

She bows her head as she lets out a sniffle.

My eyes find Joseph's and the disappointment on his face crushes me. "You can always come see her anytime you want, Joseph, or maybe we can work something out so that she can come visit you," I convey before narrowing my eyes back at him. "I'd never keep her from seeing you, Joseph. So don't *ever* accuse me of it again," the anger radiates off of me as I state the words.

Continuing to sit across from me with his body rigid, his eyes turn dark with anger as he stays silent. Eventually he stands up to walk away, making his way towards the bedroom; leaving Josephina and I alone at the table.

Taking in a deep breath, I sit there, wondering if I'm making a mistake.

Chapter 23

Joseph

THE DRIVE TO the airport is made in utter silence. You can feel the tension between us. I hated waking up this morning knowing they were leaving today. I didn't want it to happen. I wanted them to stay, but no matter how many times I asked Kasey… begged her… she wouldn't change her mind.

I was so angry by her decision to leave, but regardless of how mad I am, I knew I had to keep my anger under control, for both of them.

After parking my truck and pulling Josephina out, we make our way to the terminal as I dread every footstep along the way. I had wanted more time with both of them, so I delayed waking them this morning, wanting to keep them next to me longer than I should have. Of course, it now meant Kasey and Josephina only had time for a quick goodbye before she had to make her way through security. Kasey had printed her tickets online last night, so she didn't have to check in at the counter this morning, which meant I was now going to have to say goodbye the minute we walked into the airport.

Kneeling down to come eye level with Josephina, I already see the tears in her eyes, making me reach up to wipe them away as they fall. "We aren't saying goodbye forever, princess. I'll see you soon," I tell her, pulling her into my arms to hold her.

"I'm going to find a way so we can all be together again, okay," I whisper to her as I kiss her soft head.

She hugs me tight, her tiny body shaking as she asks, "You promise?"

"I promise," I tell her, knowing I will, somehow, someway.

I can hear her sniffle into my ear as I hug her body tighter in my arms; taking advantage of the last couple of seconds I have with her. I finally let her go, turning to face Kasey who is silently crying, the tears are streaming down her face.

Standing up, I tug her body towards mine, taking her face in my palms. "You don't have to leave, Kasey. You can still change your mind and stay," I beg her, the words barely making it around the lump in my throat.

She shakes her head, her hands holding on tight to my wrists. "Don't do this, Joseph. Don't make me feel guilty for leaving. You know I have to leave. My life is in Wisconsin. I have everything there, I *have* to go back."

"No you don't, Kasey. You can have your life here, with me," I argue, pulling her head up to look me directly in the eyes. "Marry me, Kasey. Stay here and marry me. You wouldn't have to live in Wisconsin. You and Josephina can have your life here with me," I plead, the tears now building up in my eyes.

She tightens the hold on my wrists to pull my hands away from her face. I watch as she takes a step back, slowly shaking her head, her blank eyes staring back at me. "No. I'm not going to marry you simply because you want me to stay. You're not asking me to marry you because you love me; you're asking for your own selfish reasons, it's not good enough," she declares.

Reaching down, she grabs a hold of Josephina's hand. "Good bye, Joseph. Thank you for everything," she blankly says without any emotion to the words, and turns to walk towards the security gates, forcing me to watch her walk away. I'm shocked by her words; my body numb as I take in her denial, my heart shattering into a million pieces.

Josephina glances back one last time, tears still streaming down her face, as she slowly disappears with Kasey into the crowd. My heart feels like it's completely stopped, refusing to beat anymore. It's broken. I stand there feeling empty…I've got nothing left.

Kasey

MY HEART IS aching, worse since I know my little girl feels the same way. Knowing I'm the cause of her pain, the reason why we had to walk away this time, it was a stab at the heart. A knife I plunged with my own hands into both our hearts. But it was for the best. I couldn't stay knowing Joseph only wanted me to marry him so I'd stay. Had he asked me because he loved me, as much as I loved him, I would have said yes, without any hesitation at all. However, I knew he didn't love me. He would've told me so. For that reason, I left.

The trip back to Wisconsin felt so much longer than it was. Every minute, every hour, felt as it was slowly dragging by. It felt as if we'd never get home, but when we finally did arrive, it no longer felt like home; not like before I went to San Diego with Joseph.

Joseph's absence from my side was already affecting me, especially on the way home with my fear of flying. It took every ounce of strength and energy to keep my composure and hide my fear from Josephina while we were on the plane. I kept returning to the memory of Joseph's kiss to help push the fear away. I would simply close my eyes, imagining his lips on my own, remembering how he calmed me the last time. I imagined him there next to me to help keep me calm, but when we finally landed, I was forced to face the reality of knowing he was no longer at my side. It tore at my heart all over again.

Josephina was very quiet on the way home, and I knew why. It was the same reason why my heart was weeping. We were both terribly missing Joseph. I wish I knew how to fix it.

Chapter 24

Kasey

JOSEPHINA IS SITTING on the couch playing with her iPad, a gloom of unhappiness on her face, which hasn't disappeared since the day we left San Diego. The glee I was used to seeing on my little girl's face was completely gone.

With every day that passed, it grew worse. No matter how hard I tried to cheer her up, it was hopeless. Her heart was broken, and to be honest, so was mine. I was doing a poor job at trying to conceal my sadness. It showed on my face every time I looked at her. It was a battle I was losing with myself every morning I awoke. I was mourning the loss of waking up in his arms. Some days I didn't want to get up, but I forced myself to do so, for my Josephina's sake.

The two weeks that have gone by have been hard on both of us. As much as I tried to occupy myself with work, Joseph was always on my mind, regardless of how hard I tried to push him away. If it wasn't for the success of my website needing me to work harder and longer to fulfill the orders, I would have gone insane always thinking about him.

Ashley had kept her word in helping me create the website for my business and now I had to practically work around the clock to keep up with the demand I had on my hands. I couldn't complain though, it kept me busy, but it didn't help with Josephina. Ashley was a godsend in that department, though. She started coming by to pick her up every couple of days to spend the day with her, knowing Josephina needed the distraction to take her mind off of Joseph as well. Although it worked for those couple of hours, it didn't take her heartache away.

Her continuous conversations via *FaceTime* with Joseph were helping, but not to completely take the sorrow away. Ironically, I was starting to look forward to his conversations as well. Hearing his voice in the background as they conversed was comforting, it helped sooth both our saddened state for those couple of hours, but I still wasn't strong enough to face seeing him. The one and only time I found the courage to sit down with Josephina while she was having a conversation with him, I had to excuse myself to the bathroom to cry. Seeing his face, hearing his deep voice, was a reminder of what I had walked away from.

Tonight during their usual conversation, Joseph mentioned a surprise he hoped to have ready for her soon. Upon hearing the remark, my eyebrows go up in curiosity, my body slowly gravitating in the direction where she was sitting on the couch.

Making sure to keep out of sight from Joseph, I listen as he speaks with her, explaining how his new surprise will allow her to see him again. Although I grow skeptical from his intentions, her eyes instantly light up with excitement. I know it's from the thought of seeing him. Even I grew excited with the idea of seeing him, but I'm soon disappointed when Josephina asks him if he was coming to visit soon, and he replies with a simple, "No," making my heart drop to the pit of my stomach, the tears already forming in my eyes. Getting up from the couch I head back to my workstation to help distract myself, the disappointment lingering with me for the remainder of the night.

It's when I'm attempting to fall asleep that night that the disappointment takes over. The tears I was desperately trying to keep within myself uncontrollably stream down my face, releasing themselves against my will.

Losing the fight, I let them fall as I cry into my pillow, masking my sobs from Josephina to not wake her. The pain of wishing I was wrapped in Joseph's arms courses all over my body as I lie in bed crying. It's then I finally realize I've made the biggest mistake of my life and I have no one to blame but myself.

I'M CLEANING UP my pots after making another big batch, yet again, when I hear a knock at my door. I already know it's Mark and Ashley. They said they were coming over tonight. I welcome their visits. They keep me distracted when they come over, which have been several times in the last couple weeks. They've been nothing but kind and helpful since I got back from San Diego. I no longer had a car and it was proving quite difficult at times. I often found myself depending on both of them when I either needed a ride somewhere far, or when I had a huge delivery to make. I don't know what I would've done without them.

I needed a car and I needed one soon, but I was dreading having a car payment, which is the reason why I hadn't bought one yet. Plus, it would be another bill I would have to add, and I can't afford much at this time.

Opening the door, I let Mark and Ashley in. "Hi Kasey," Mark says, giving me a quick hug as he enters.

Josephina sees him from the living area, already running to him, making him scoop her up in his arms as he smiles back at her. The memory of all the times Joseph would do it with her tugs at my heart, making me briefly close my eyes to fight back the tears.

Bringing them under control, I watch Mark head straight to the area with my TV with Josephina, while Ashley goes to my workbench to take a seat. Before long Mark is entertaining himself and Josephina by starting up the X-box, making me chuckle. I seriously believe he misses the thing more than he misses Josephina. The last couple of times they've come over it's the first place he heads with her.

Going over to Ashley, I offer her something to drink before we spend the next hour going over the sales of the website, adding the new products I've created in the last month. It's a routine we've been doing once a week since I returned and something I look forward to. It gives Ashley and I a chance to catch up at the same time. I take in the amount of orders I already have since my last shipment I sent out, which was only two days ago, and I'm already feeling a little overwhelmed.

"How is it I keep getting all these orders when I've only had the website up for less than a month?" I skeptically ask her, my eyes still wide as I look at the request on the screen. "I wouldn't have thought I'd be doing this good right away."

"What can you expect? They only have to read the reviews to know how good your soaps are," she explains to me with a smile.

Confused, I look at her. "What reviews? I don't remember getting any reviews?" I question, wondering what she meant.

Her lips go up into a mischievous smile, which tell me she had something to do with the reviews. "Okay. I might have had my sister and mom write a review each," she tells me already bringing up the proof. "Plus, I had their friends write some as well. I posted them on the main page when you first open up the website, see?" she says, pointing to the side of the page, where sure enough, there were currently six written reviews, all in italics. "That way potential customers will read them and *want* to buy the product. It's working, isn't it? You already have more orders than you thought you would to process," she says, making me smile.

"True," I tell her, already remembering the last large load I had to take to the UPS store.

"It's the first time I've seen you smile since you've been back," she tells me, making my frown return. She's right, I haven't smiled at all until now and I hadn't realized it until she mentioned it.

Glancing over to where Josephina is dancing away with Mark, their laughter radiates throughout the room, as I take in how silly they both look. "Yeah, it's kind of hard to smile when you're sad most of the time," I sadly tell her.

She reaches over to grab my hand, gently giving me a reassuring squeeze. "You miss him, don't you?" The question a reminder of how I fell asleep last night, making me nod as I fight back the tears which are now clouding my vision.

"He called Mark last night," she quietly states, quickly

glancing over in Mark's direction. "By the conversation I heard from our end, he's up to something. I just don't know what it is because Mark wouldn't tell me," she says smiling. "I think it's because he knows I'll tell you anyway, but by the sounds of it, it has something to do with you. Have you spoken with him?" she curiously asks.

I have to swallow the lump in my throat before I answer. "No, he only speaks to Josephina." With the words said, the tears start to fall from my eyes when I make my confession. "Oh, Ashley. I think I made the biggest mistake of my life by walking away. But, I couldn't stay and keep thinking I was his back up plan. I just couldn't," I finish saying as she embraces me in her arms, crying onto her shoulder, letting it all out. "He asked me to marry him at the airport," I say in between my sobbing cries, making Ashley yank her body back with her eyes wide in shock.

"What?"

Wiping my nose with the back of my hand before telling her. "I know he was only asked because he wanted us to stay. He wasn't asking because he loves me," I explain, sniffling again.

"Oh, Kasey. Of course you would've thought that, but let me tell you something, you might not think Joseph loves you, but deep down inside I *know* he does."

I'm about to argue her point, but she continues, "I know because of the way he is with you and by the way he looks at you. Kasey, a while ago when Joseph came home on leave, he brought Elizabeth to visit us. The difference of how he acted with you, compared to how he was around her, was completely night and day," she says, with a heavy sigh, her eyebrows going up. "Yes, he might have given his attention to her, but when he looks at you...it's with admiration and desire. He never did that with her. Never. So to me, it shows me he *does* love you."

I sit there, taking in her words as I listen to her, shocked by her declaration. It's the words I needed to hear to help make the decision I'd been contemplating lately. One I hope I wouldn't regret making.

Chapter 25

Joseph

"HERE ARE YOUR keys, Mr. Mitchell. Congratulations on your purchase. If you have any questions please don't hesitate to call me, but I believe you'll be extremely happy here," the real estate agent tells me as he hands me my keys, walking over to the door before he leaves.

I take one final turn around the empty living room, beaming from ear to ear. It's the first time I've really smiled since Kasey left, it's only because I don't have her by my side.

It kills me to know she doesn't want to speak to me. I hadn't pushed for it, but only because I couldn't stand the thought of seeing her saddened face, the same one I already see when I talk to Josephina on *FaceTime* every night. It would've only made me run back to get her. Even against her protesting, I wouldn't have given her a choice, but I didn't go after her because I wanted to make sure I had secured buying the house before I did so.

Although I had wanted to tell Kasey about the house the

day she left, I didn't, already knowing she'd say it wasn't meant for her. Plus, I had wanted it to be a surprise, which it was going to be, just like I kept telling Josephina.

The night Kasey left I kept going over all the words she said during her visit and it finally hit me, it was my fault she'd left. If I'd just told her I loved her from the beginning, maybe she would have stayed.

Taking in the house once more, I think of why I didn't tell Kasey about it. She would've easily figured out I had put an offer on it while I was engaged to Elizabeth. Yes, it was supposed to be the one I was going to live in after we got married, but I was no longer marrying Elizabeth because I found Kasey again. Life has a way of showing you what is really meant to be.

With the smile still on my face, I know the house was really meant to have Kasey and Josephina living in it with me. I remember when I had first seen the house. I had fallen in love with it instantly. Elizabeth may not have liked it, being she wanted a brand new house, something by the beach, but that wasn't me. Against her protest, I still put an offer on it, regardless of what she said. At the time I had a gut feeling this was the house I *needed*. Now I know why. It was never meant to have Elizabeth in it, but Kasey instead. The problem I was now facing was trying to convince Kasey of that point.

Somehow I was going to convince her, though. This house was perfect for her. It came with a large garage that had been used as a workshop for cars. Originally I had planned on working on my own cars in here, but that was something I was willing to sacrifice for Kasey. It could easily be converted into a studio for Kasey. It was the perfect size for Kasey to work. I already knew when I showed her she would be sold on moving here. Shit, I would get down on my knees and beg if I had to.

When I had told Mark about my plan, he said I was taking a big risk, but one that may just work, which made me happy knowing I had a chance. With his help of keeping me up to date with Kasey's business, I already knew it was taking off online, and she would need a bigger space. Mark's updates were the only thing keeping me sane nowadays since she didn't really want to talk to me. I know she was pretty pissed about the way we left things. I couldn't blame her, but I was planning on making it up to her.

I'm locking up the house when my phone starts to ring. Digging it out of my pocket, I look at the phone, and see Kasey's name on the screen. It's strange to see it, especially knowing she doesn't call me at all anymore. I'm usually the one who has to call them via *FaceTime* and even then, it's only to speak to Josephina.

"Kasey, is everything okay?" I ask, worried something might have happened to Josephina.

"Well, I do seem to have a little problem," she says, a hint of laughter in her voice, confusing me, but the words alone make the panic build up inside of me. I hate knowing she's still clear across the country and I wouldn't be able to get to them fast enough if something was wrong. I need to get them both back on the west coast fast because I can't take this shit any longer. "Kasey, what's wrong? I can call Mark or Ashley. They can get to you in a couple of minutes," I frantically say in a panic. My heart is racing, my mind building with the scenarios of what could've happened. It's driving me insane.

I hear her chuckle, confusing me, as she says, "I really doubt Mark or Ashley can help me today. Actually, I'd really hate to have them fly to San Diego just to help me this time."

I hear the rustling of the phone, as if it's being passed to someone else before I hear Josephina say, "Daddy, when are you coming home? Because I really need to pee, and your door is locked," she whines.

My eyes go wide, my heart feeling as if it's stopped. I stand rooted to the spot in shock from the words, wondering if I heard her wrong. I don't want to get excited thinking they are here in San Diego again.

I hear the rattle return, most likely Kasey taking the phone back from Josephina, because I hear her voice say clearly into the phone, "What time are you coming home?"

"Kasey, where are you guys at?" I force myself to ask, trying to calm my excited state of mind.

"We're actually sitting on the steps outside your door at this moment. I wanted to surprise you, but it back fired on me being that you're not home," she declares, sounding disappointed.

I quickly start walking to my truck as fast as I can. Practically jogging to it. "Kasey, you see the box with the fire extinguisher inside it, in between the two apartment doors? There is a key above it to my apartment. I'll be home in fifteen minutes, baby," I tell her, smiling from ear to ear as I'm jumping into my truck.

"Okay. We'll be inside waiting for you," she calmly says before hanging up the phone, leaving me listening to dead silence.

Taking every back street that would allow me to break all the traffic laws possible, I can only think about getting to them. I California rolled through more stop signs than I should have, but I didn't care. I couldn't get to my girls fast enough.

I'm finally back at my apartment, my heart racing with excitement to see them. I'm barely able to get the truck in park before jumping out and taking the stairs two at a time to get to my apartment. Rushing through the door I see them, going straight towards Kasey to pick her up, eagerly kissing her lips.

Her arms wrap around my neck, pulling me tighter to her body as she laughs against my mouth. I take advantage of her laughter to push my tongue forward, deepening the kiss. She has never tasted so good. When I hear her moan into my mouth it makes me close my eyes and thank my lucky stars she's here.

"Daddy," I hear Josephina say as she tugs at my pants.

Opening my eyes, I pull my lips away from Kasey's, and look down at Josephina. Slowly I lower Kasey down to the ground. Just as quickly I lean down to pick Josephina up, hugging her tightly in my arms to place a kiss on her head, inhaling her sweet smell.

"Were you surprised, daddy?" she enthusiastically asks, as she pushes herself away to look at me, "We wanted to surprise you by knocking on your door, but you weren't home," she says with a frown.

I smile at her. "Of course I'm surprised. It's the best surprise in the world," I say to her, telling her the truth.

Looking over at Kasey, the doubt hits me in the pit of my stomach. "Please tell me you're not just visiting?" I beg her, already dreading the fear of watching her leave.

She smiles up at me, shaking her head. "Nope," she says before taking her bottom lip as she shyly smiles at me. "We're here for good, but Joseph, there's something I want to talk to you about first," she says, making me frown. The expression on her face is worrying me. It's the same one she had the day she left. I don't want to see it again.

Placing Josephina back down on the ground, I go to turn on the TV. "Princess, your mommy and I are going to the room to talk. Will you be a good girl and watch TV for a while?" I tell her, as she is already lying down on the couch.

The yawn she gives me as she nods her head indicates she's going to fall asleep soon, which is good. It will give Kasey and I time to talk.

"I think she's going to take a nap," Kasey whispers up to me. "We had to get up pretty early this morning and the excitement of coming here has kept her awake. I think it's finally catching up to her."

Grabbing the blanket at the end of the couch, I cover Josephina up with it, giving her a kiss on her head as I watch her drift off into sleep.

Reaching out to pull Kasey's hand into mine, I lead her to the bedroom as she follows closely behind. I already fear what she'll say, but regardless, it's my chance to finally tell her how I feel. Once inside, I shut the door behind us, turning to face her before I take her in as she's standing in front of me. It's clear she's lost weight since she left. Her eyes are darkened with shadows, as if she hasn't slept, making her look exhausted. I hate seeing her like this. Stepping up to her I grab onto her waist, pulling her towards me, close enough that I'm looking directly down into her eyes. She places her hands on my arms as she begins to speak. "Joseph, the reason why I left the first time was because I felt like there wasn't any reason for me to be here. I felt like there was no *real* future between us," she says to me. "I'm not going to demand you make any promises, but I need to know if I've wasted my time by coming back."

"Is that really why you left?"

She stays silent, but I can see the hurt in her eyes; the guilt in the pit of my stomach growing with each passing second.

"Kasey, when you left, it tore me apart. I haven't been the same since. Letting you leave was the biggest mistake I ever made."

"It hurt me too, Joseph, but I couldn't stay here any longer feeling the way I did. I couldn't take it anymore," she says, her voice cracking with every word.

"How is it you really felt, Kasey?"

"I've already told you. I felt as if I was a replacement for your fiancée and *I hated it*."

Her declaration is a reminder of the night I realized how she truly felt. I'd finally understood all the times she was constantly trying to push me away, when I managed to get her close enough, as if she was protecting her heart from me. It was my fault for never telling her I loved her from the beginning.

Shaking my head at her, I reach for her face. Cradling her in my hands. "Kasey, I never saw you as a replacement, ever. Since the night I left for boot camp, you're all I've ever thought about. *She was your replacement,* one that could never live up to you. When I found you again, I realized that. I never *really* loved her. Not the way I've loved you. There will never be anyone else I could possibly love more than you," I confess.

"Not even Josephina?" she questions with a smile, making me laugh, knowing she's trying to tease me.

Bringing my head down, resting my forehead against hers, I answer. "I love my daughter with all my heart, but my love for her will *never* compare to the love I have for you. I love both of you more than life itself, but you, Kasey Wilson, own my heart."

She starts to cry, her lips trembling as she smiles. "Oh Joseph. I love you too. I loved you even though I got on that plane and left."

Realizing if we both hadn't been so stubborn that day and really told each other how we felt, she would've stayed. Seeing her crying hurts, it makes me want to take her pain away. Leaning down I pull her head up to kiss her, needing to show her how much I love her. I can taste the saltiness of her tears on her lips, as I demand she give me more. It isn't long before we're both naked and in bed making love. Our bodies demanding to give each other what we've both been missing for the last month. Over and over again I tell her I love her, staring down into her eyes as she repeats it back to me.

Before long we're both laying next to each other in bed, sated and panting for breath as I hold her body, refusing to let her go yet. As I rub her back I remember her words before she demanded we speak. "Kasey, what did you mean by being here for good?" I hesitantly ask, my heart already racing with excitement as I wait for her answer.

She nods her head against my chest, muffling her response so I don't understand it. I can already feel her body beginning to relax against mine. I know she's most likely falling asleep, but I want more details. "Kasey, not that I'm complaining you're here, but what is going to happen to your business?" I skeptically ask her, hoping she's found a solution besides giving it up.

As much as I wanted her to stop working, I've finally come to the realization of how happy her business makes her, and I want her to be happy here with me.

When she doesn't answer, I know she's falling asleep already, her body exhausted from both the travel and our lovemaking. Giving her a little shake, I hear a rumble from her throat, causing me to laugh as I shake her again, only to amuse me. She sits up, glaring straight at me. I sit up with her, pulling her to lean onto my chest, so I can hold her.

She makes herself comfortable and she quietly starts to speak. "I'll figure something out, Joseph. I *have* to keep running my business now that Ashley has set up my website," she tells me before she continues, "I packed up all my supplies and left all my unsold inventory until I can figure out what to do."

She continues to explain. "I left everything needed to makes my soaps, and any leftover inventory, with Mark and Ashley. I've been working non-stop for the last week to surpass what I would normally make in a month. When I told them my decision to move out here, they came up with the idea. They agreed to help fill my orders until I can find a shop out here to start up again. I'm praying it doesn't take me more than a week to find a place, though. I left them with a lot, but at the rate I'm receiving orders, I don't think they'll have enough to last long."

Remembering where I was before Kasey called, I jump up from the bed scrambling to look for our clothes. "I actually have the perfect place for your shop." I say, already getting dressed.

She looks at me confused, but I insist that she quickly get dressed. The excitement on my face spurs her along as she gets up off the bed without hesitation. Within minutes we're heading back out into the living room to see a sleepy eyed Josephina rubbing her eyes.

"Hey princess, remember that surprise I kept telling you about?" I ask her, earning me an excited nod of her head with a smile. "Well, how about I go show it to you and mommy? How does that sound?" I ask her, making her eyes light up.

Scooping her up, I look over to Kasey as I grab for my keys. I don't give her a chance to say anything further as I inform her to grab Josephina's booster seat. The both of them are demanding I tell them what my surprise is, but my only response is to shake my head and start toward my truck, forcing Kasey to follow. I simply tell them they will have to wait to find out. Fifteen minutes later, I'm pulling into the driveway I just left not long ago, unable to keep from smiling as I see Kasey's confused expression when she takes in the house.

Entering the house, I send Josephina off to explore as I look over at Kasey, seeing her eyes grow wide in amazement, unable to resist admiring her expression.

"Joseph, whose house is this?" she asks.

"Ours."

"What do you mean, *ours?*" she asks, her eyes wide, most likely disbelieving my answer. I take her into my arms to kiss her below the ear, feeling her shiver against me.

"I actually got the keys right before you called. It's our home, Kasey," I whisper into her ear as her jaw drops.

"I don't understand. Are you renting it? How did you even know we were coming? she asks. "Mark and Ashley promised they wouldn't tell you."

Unable to resist laughing at her eyes narrowed at me, I answer her, "No. I was already in the process of buying it when you came to visit the first time."

Her eyes grow excited, but just as quickly, her lips go into a frown as her shoulders slump forward. I already know what she's thinking.

"I'm not going to deny it, Kasey. Yes, it *was* supposed to be the house I was going to move into with Elizabeth after the wedding," I truthfully tell her. "However, even after I ended things with her, I continued with the sale because I still wanted you and Josephina to live here in the house with me, but I didn't get the keys until today. It's why I never said anything. I didn't want to upset you if I fell through on the house. I believe it was you who was the one meant to live here with me the entire time, not her," I tell her, making sure I clarify my words.

"Now I'm glad I never backed out on buying the house. I had a feeling I was going to need this over here and I was right," I tell her, already pulling her over to the door leading to the large open workshop. When I open the door, I reached over to turn on the light, allowing her to see the huge open space. Her jaw drops once more. "You see? It's like it was meant to be. You can continue your business here, Kasey. It's double the size of the old one you had, so you'll be able to comfortably make as much soap as you want."

I watch her slowly walk into the empty space, her eyes wide in awe as she spins around to take in every wall surrounding us. Walking over to her side, I force her to face me. "If you still don't feel comfortable living here because of the reason why I originally bought it, then we don't have to. I don't want you ever thinking you're a replacement. All I want is to live with you. No matter where that is."

She takes in the room one more time, before looking back at me. Her eyes are filled with tears before she answers, "It's perfect, Joseph. Thank you," making my heart swell up. She reaches up to wrap her arms around my neck, pulling me down to kiss her. Our kiss leaves me both breathless and satisfied that she loves the house. Wrapping my arms around her waist to pick her up off the ground, I spin her around in the room, happier than I've ever been.

Chapter 26

Joseph

KASEY WALKS OUT of her studio as I walk in the front door after work, stifling a yawn behind the back of her hand. Making sure the door is properly shut, she walks over in my direction with a smile. She's gotten really good about cutting back her hours spent in there at my request; she'd be in there 24/7 if I let her because she loves her new studio. It didn't take long to convert it, but I did recruit a bunch of Marines to help me. We had it done in two weekends. There's a lot those guys will do if you offer them free food and beer as payment. We designed it with everything she needed and painted it in every color she wanted, making it her new peaceful escape.

Throwing my keys and hat on the counter, our eyes meet, and I return her smile. It's been six months since she moved to San Diego and I don't think I will ever get tired of the idea of coming home to her. Especially when I know I'm coming home to both my girls. It's truly the best feeling in the world.

Kasey eyes are lit up with a radiating glow I love coming

home to. Casually, she walks to me, patting her bare feet against the hardwood floor. She reaches up on her toes, wrapping her arms around my neck to pull me down to her, demanding a kiss I'm always willing to give. Her soft lips linger on mine while I savor them, loving how her lips tastes like her favorite chap stick.

"Hmmm, I missed you today," she mumbles into my mouth.

Wrapping my arms around her waist, I draw her up against my body, walking her towards the living room. As her arms tighten around my neck, she leaves her feet dangling off the floor, making me carry her limp body the entire way. It's something she's already used to me doing. I do it pretty much every time I get home.

In the corner of my eye, I see Josephina doing something on her iPad while sitting on the couch, her little legs curled under her body as she smiles up at us. When I reach the couch I place Kasey on the floor, pulling her to sit on my lap.

She automatically curls her body into me, wrapping her arms around my neck as her face finds the crook. She starts nuzzling her nose into my neck, making me chuckle, as I feel the warmth of her breath as she inhales my scent, making me smile. She does this often and although I smell sweaty from work, she swears she could never get enough of my scent. I blame it on the soap she makes for me. She claims it's her weakness.

Holding her tight against my body, she relaxes as I rub her back and look over at Josephina. "Hey princess, how was school today?"

She looks up at me with a smile as she excitedly informs me, "I got two gold stars today for my excellent work, daddy."

"Oh really? That's great, princess."

"Mommy took me to get some frozen yogurt right after school to celebrate, but we had to bring it home cause mommy said she really wanted some pickles instead," she says, scrunching her nose, my expression matching hers.

Why the hell would Kasey want pickles? She hates pickles...

Pulling my head back to ask her, I feel her body is motionless and I'm pretty sure from the way she's softly breathing into my neck she's asleep. Since I can't see her face from the way she's sitting, I ask Josephina, "Princess, did mommy fall asleep again?"

She cranes her neck to the side go get a better view before nods her head, letting out a giggle. "Yes. She's been doing that a lot lately, daddy," she claims, followed by an actual laugh.

Now that I think about it, she's right, there's been a couple of times I've managed to come home for lunch to find her asleep on my old couch. It's the same couch I had in my apartment. She insisted we put in her studio, needing somewhere to take a nap in there. I wasn't going to argue with her, especially with all the fond memories I have of it. I wanted to keep the couch.

"She fell asleep yesterday at her work station too, right at the table," Josephina informs me. "She was even drooling," she adds, laughing again, making me smile as I imagining the scene in my mind.

I don't have to imagine too long because Josephina holds up her iPad to show me a picture. Sure enough, there on the screen is a sleeping Kasey, head to the side resting on her worktable, mouth slightly open as she sleeps.

Wanting her to be more comfortable, I scoop Kasey up in my arms to walk her to our bedroom. When I reach our bed I lay her gently down, pulling the light blanket she keeps at the end of the bed over her to cover her up, giving her a kiss on her temple while she curls her legs up, snuggling into the bed.

Standing above her to take her completely in, I start to wonder why she's been so tired. She's been getting enough rest lately, coming to bed early every night, so that can't be the reason. Still pondering the thought, it suddenly occurs to me: my eyes going wide in shock when I take in the thought. She hasn't said anything to me, though. Looking over her body, I take her in one more time, from head to toe, observing how she doesn't look any different. I quickly shake my head trying hard not to get my hopes up. The last thing I want is to get excited for nothing.

WANTING TO SPEND the evening alone with Kasey, I asked Michael if he and his wife would watch Josephina for the night. They didn't hesitate to say yes, especially when I told them my plans. As much as I love my little girl, I needed to be alone with Kasey tonight if I was going to make this work. I didn't want to take any chances of screwing this up a second time.

Being that Michael's wife, Missy, and Kasey have become close friends over the last several months, I knew Kasey wouldn't mind Josephina staying the night with them. Missy now works with Kasey in her studio, so she feels more part of the family with all the time she spends here. Missy had also been helpful in helping Kasey's transition to San Diego, which I was grateful for. I was scared Kasey would regret leaving Wisconsin behind.

Tonight Kasey was at Yoga, something she'd discovered upon moving here; she needed it to help her relax. It gave me time to prepare everything I needed, making it as perfect as I had hoped it would be in my mind. I made sure to cook her favorite dinner, set up the room perfectly, and double-checked everything was in place because I wanted tonight to be special. I wasn't holding anything back.

When I hear the rattling of the keys being inserted into the door announcing Kasey is finally home, I grow excited, quickly shutting the double doors to our bedroom. Walking to the foyer where she'll be coming in, I see her walk in, and I instantly smile seeing her beautiful face. Meeting her halfway, I scoop her up in my arms, giving her a big kiss on the lips.

Pulling away, she looks at me with a puzzled expression. "What was that for?" she asks, a wide smile across her face.

"Just because I love you," I tell her, giving her another quick kiss.

"I love you too," she answers back before looking around the room, probably searching for Josephina, who would normally already be meeting her as she walks in the door. She grows confused as she takes in the dining room set up with an elegant dinner, candlelight included.

"What's going on?" she asks with a shy smile. "I'm pretty sure it's not my birthday," she adds, with her eyebrow raised. "And, being that we haven't been together too long, it's definitely not our anniversary." Her response makes me laugh, because she knows I would be the one expected to remember something that important, not Kasey.

"I know it's not your birthday, silly, but I can't wait to celebrate our anniversary when it comes. I wanted to cook a special dinner for you tonight," I tell her, shrugging my shoulder as she suspiciously looks at me. "What? I can't cook my girlfriend dinner?" I ask her, trying not to sound too suspicious.

Her eyes turn down, the sadness taking over. "I'm really hoping you're not going to break some really bad news to me," she says, her lips going flat as her expression matches her eyes.

Since Kasey moved here, one of her biggest worries has been that I'm going to get shipped back overseas. I tried reassuring her it most likely wouldn't be for a while since I recently got back, but she hated knowing it's possible. It's part of my job after all, but I kept reminding her we have to enjoy the days we had together in case it *ever* happened.

Deeply sighing, I lead her over to the dining area, carrying her limp body as I usually do. "Kasey, please, just let me feed you. I cooked dinner for you. For the both of us," I tell her.

Nodding her head, she looks around the room, this time most likely still looking for Josephina. "Josephina is staying the night with Michael and Missy. I wanted the house just to ourselves," I tell her, placing a kiss on her temple before I put her down to pull out her chair, allowing her to take a seat.

She sits down without any further protest, allowing me to push her chair against the table. I jog back over to the kitchen to pull out the plates I have warming in the oven, bringing the plates back to the table. She takes one look at them, her eyes growing wide with excitement.

"You cooked my favorite," she says, in a whisper of amazement.

Giving her a simple nod I take a seat across from her, immediately saying grace, something I now do for Kasey. An hour later we're both completely stuffed and when I look over at Kasey's plate I can't help but smile. It's completely empty, not a crumb left on the plate, another point that hadn't crossed my mind until now. She's had quiet an appetite lately, too.

I'm about to get up and start clearing the table when she offers to clear the dishes and load them in the dishwasher. I was hoping she'd do so, allowing me to escape to make the finishing touches needed in the bedroom.

Excusing myself, telling her I need to use the bathroom, I'm already rushing to our room to prepare the last of the details. When done, I take in one last view of the room, thinking it looks perfect. She's going to love it.

Walking back to the kitchen, I see her loading the last of the dishes, allowing me to come up behind her, wrapping my arms tightly around her body to pull her back against my chest. I nuzzle at her neck as she leans her head back to rest on my shoulder, allowing me to kiss her below her ear. My favorite spot, it makes her body shiver every single time. She moans as she pushes the curve of her ass to tease me, awakening my cock. I have to force myself to breathe and get myself under control or else I might take her right here on the kitchen counter, which is not what I have planned for tonight. Pushing her body from mine, she turns to face me, a scowl on her face. I can only chuckle down at her. I know what she wants and I plan on giving it to her, just not yet.

Taking her arms to wrap them around my neck, I kiss her, making her disappointment disappear as I carry her towards our bedroom. I reach our double doors, turning to push them with my back, allowing her to see the room as I walk backwards into it. I shut both the doors, blocking out the light from the rest of the house, allowing the glow of the candles I have lit around the room to be the only light. Kasey's eyes go wide when we enter the room, a small gasp of surprise escaping her O shaped lips.

"Joseph, what's going on?" she asks as I allow her body to slowly slide down to the ground.

Taking her face in my palms I kiss her; I kiss her like the hungry man I am for her, as if it were the first time I've ever kissed her.

I lose my earlier control, stripping her of her clothing, wanting to feel her soft skin against my bare hands. Just as quickly, she does the same with mine, leaving us both naked. I scoop up her naked body, taking her to the bed, pulling back the covers to gently lie her down like the precious item she is to me.

Climbing into bed with her, I cover her body with mine, still fiercely kissing her. She opens her legs wide for me, allowing my body to sink down into hers, her moan vibrating in our mouths as I enter her. Lifting her hips with my hand, I pull back, plunging into her body again, knowing she likes it this way. Her moans become louder, her hips lifting, wanting more, but I force myself to stop, remembering what I *really* meant to do tonight.

She grumbles as I've stopped, lifting her hips, demanding I keep going, but I ignore her request as I look down into her. "Kasey, I love you," I whisper down at her. "I think I fell in love with you the first night you gave yourself to me. That night I didn't know I would be giving my heart to the one person I'd want to spend the rest of my life with, *but I did*. You gave yourself to me knowing I was the one, but I didn't listen to my heart, or say anything in return, a mistake I've regretted since that night. Instead I walked away, living with that regret until the day I found you again," I admit, placing a kiss on her lips. "Kasey, I love you more than life itself and I can't imagine living the rest of my life without you. I want to raise our children together. I want to spend the rest of my life...with you.

I want to grow old with you; until the very last breathe I take. Kasey Wilson, will you do me the honor of being my wife?" I nervously whisper the last words down to her, holding my breath for her answer.

With the candlelight from around the room, I watch for her reaction, her eyes going wide, and I fear she's going to reject me again. A single tear slowly slides down the side of her face. I catch it with my thumb, still holding my breath, waiting for her answer.

Slowly she nods her head, letting out a sniffle, giving a wide smile. "Yes Joseph, I'll marry you," she exclaims, pulling me down to kiss her. The breath I was holding escapes me as I kiss her back.

I slowly start to rock my body inside of her again, thrusting into her, robbing a pleasured moan from her lips. I make sure to take my time bringing her to her peak before I finish. Running my hand up the silky smooth skin of her body, I need to feel as much of her as I can before I have her screaming my name, but when I'm granted my wish, I quickly follow her over the edge.

I'm still above her, both of us trying to catch our breath as I continue trailing kisses down her skin. Looking down at her as I push her hair from her face, I tell her again, "I love you, Kasey. I will always love you."

Her hand comes up to my cheek to caress it as she smiles back at me. "I love you too, Joseph," she replies, her eyes already starting to flutter shut as they usually do when we finish.

Rolling off her, I pull her body with mine to drape her across me, needing to have her close. I run my hand across her skin, feeling every curve of her body with my hand.

"Kasey, is there something that you've been meaning to tell me?"

She snuggles her body up to mine, entangling her limbs with my legs, getting herself comfortable, but I shake her body to keep her attention, something she hates that I do.

"No," her sleepy answer making me chuckle.

She's already answered every suspicion why she hasn't told me. She doesn't even know herself. She can be so clueless sometimes. I already feel her starting to drift off to sleep, but I'm persistent.

"Are you sure?"

Grumbling, she opens her eyes, her eyebrows drawn down in irritation. "Joseph, if there's something I'm supposed to be telling you, then please enlighten me," she snaps, clearly irritated because I'm not letting her sleep.

I run my hand down across her hip, my hand stopping on her stomach, spanning my opened palm on it. "When was the last time you had your period, Kasey?" I ask her.

She looks at me confused, sighing in irritation as she considers my question. I see her thinking as her eyes go up and then suddenly go wide, taking in a gasp as her hand comes to rest over mine. "Joseph," she merely says, making me smile. "You don't think I'm finally pregnant do you?"

We haven't been using protection since the time we made love in the shower. At first I blamed the rush of wanting to be inside of her as my excuse, but all the other times I didn't think about it. I knew we were taking a huge risk of her getting pregnant, but deep down inside I had hoped she would. It just didn't happen until now.

This time I let out a loud laugh, throwing my head back. "Baby, if the signs are not clues enough, then I bought a test just in case," I say to her, rolling my body above hers. "But I'm pretty sure even without you taking the test, I could tell you're pregnant. You've been tired all the time and eating more than usual," I tell her, giving her a kiss as I trail my lips down her chin.

She mumbles, lifting her head further back so I can continue kissing my way down her neck. My lips continue kissing a trail down her collarbone. Her hands shove me up off her body, allowing me to look at her. She looks irritated now. "Is that the *only* reason why you asked me to marry you? Because you think I'm pregnant?"

N*ow I'm irritated* as I shake my head at her. "No, it's not the reason I asked you to marry me. If I recall, I asked you once before and you flat out denied me. I loved you the first time I asked you and I still love you, so it's why I asked you again," I inform her, placing a kiss below her ear to distract her, trailing my lips across her neck, nipping on her skin along the way. When I reach her lips, I make sure to distract her completely.

My cock is already starting to stir from wanting to be inside her, needing her again. I enter slowly this time, briefly stopping to look down at her. "I know the first time I asked you to marry me was for the wrong reason, but this time I meant every word I said. Even if you aren't pregnant, I'm still going to marry you, Kasey, because I love you," I tell her as I begin to make love to her.

Epilogue

Kasey

"MOMMY, MOMMY, LOOK what I've brought you," Josephina shouts as she runs up to me, shoving a candy apple into my hand, making me smile as I take her gift. Without hesitation I dig my teeth into it to take a bite, moaning to myself as I savor the sweet stickiness of the caramel mixed with the tanginess of the green apple below. I close my eyes enjoying my sweet treat when I feel Joseph's body push up against my back, wrapping his arms around me, engulfing me with his body as he softly places a kiss on my neck.

"I thought you'd like that," his deep husky voice whispers into my ear making me shiver, as it always does.

His hands come down to my large round belly, automatically starting to rub my stomach with his hands as I lay my head back to rest against his shoulder. My mind drifts back to the memory of the night he proposed. It happens when his hands caress our baby, making me remember that night. Alt-

255

hough I still had doubts I was pregnant, the next morning Joseph made me take the pregnancy test to prove me wrong. Of course it was positive, leaving me dumbfounded. Being that we weren't preventing a pregnancy, I shouldn't have been surprised it happened.

Soon after that night, we got married. I didn't want to wait any longer to marry Joseph. I may have had doubts about being his wife the first time he proposed, but I didn't have them the second time. I'd come to fear he wouldn't ever ask again. Especially after knowing I had made the mistake of saying no the first time.

Our marriage was simple and sweet, taking place at city hall. I didn't want big or fancy. The only thing I needed on that day was my daughter and Joseph. Everyone else who attended was a bonus, including Mark and Ashley, and their new bundle of joy as our witnesses.

As I stand there thinking of that day, I feel my back tense up, followed by a sharp pain in my stomach. I force myself to breathe through it like I learned in Lamaze class, knowing it's another contraction. I've been having them most of the night, but since I'd been having Braxton Hicks for the last couple of weeks, I didn't think anything of these during the night. I simply brushed them off as another false alarm. The last thing I wanted to do was tell Joseph about them again. After the fourth time of him rushing me to the hospital at his paranoid insistence and being sent home, I learned my lesson. I awoke this morning telling myself they were another false alarm since my due date was still another two weeks away. They were probably from me being immobile for the last week, another demand of Joseph's.

I wanted to get out of the house, needing some fresh air this morning from being cooped up in the house all week, so I insisted we come to the local Farmers Market to walk around. It wasn't until an hour ago, when my backache started increasing, that I knew they were real. I just didn't want to be rushed to the hospital to have to sit there for a whole day. My labor with Josephina lasted eighteen hours and I still remember every minute as if it were yesterday.

Leaning my weight against Joseph as he holds me, I close my eyes as I take deep breaths, feeling another contraction hit me almost immediately. This one makes my stomach tense up, causing Joseph's hands to tighten on my stomach, as his body grows rigid behind me. "Kasey, what's wrong?" he asks, the worry evident in his voice. I'm pretty sure if I were able to see his face right now, he'd look frantic.

"I'm fine," I tell him.

Needing to concentrate on my breathing, I simply ignore him and breathe deeply. I don't want to alarm Joseph. He's been really over protective of me during my pregnancy. It's almost as if he's trying to make up for not being with me the first time, but it was driving me insane at this point. He was treating me like a crystal vase that was going to break at any moment.

Some days I loved it, others not so much. At one point he'd suggested I stop working during the course of my pregnancy, claiming he didn't like the fact it required me to be on my feet for more than an hour. At that point I drew the line. My business was relaxing to me. It was a way for my mind to escape, as I got lost in my creations. If he took it away, I knew for sure I was going to grow stressed, especially now that my sales were increasing every month.

As another contraction hits me, breaking my thoughts, I have to hunch over, causing me to grab onto my stomach as I groan. When I'm finally able to stand upright again, Joseph is

GABBIE S. DURAN

already standing in front of me, the strain in his expression making me feel guilty. "I think I'm having contractions," I confess, preparing myself for the lecture to come.

"What?" he shouts, his eyes going wide as saucers, which is the reaction I was expecting. "How long have you been having contractions?" he asks looking as if he's now stopped breathing, making me laugh.

"You think this is funny?" His panicky voice makes my laughter stop and I'm feeling guilty once more.

I reach up to cup his cheek to pull his face to look directly into my eyes. "Honey, I'm fine. I've done this before and I'm pretty sure if it is up to you, it won't be the last time," I say laughing at myself. "We have enough time. Why don't you go and find Josephina, she's probably off with Missy at the booth bugging her."

He gives me a look as if I've lost my mind before he scoops me up, his head whipping back and forth as he searches for Josephina. Normally I would protest him carrying me, but right now I don't feel like walking anyway, so I let him carry me off straight for the booth.

Missy is now one of my employees, along with another two wives of the Marines that worked with Joseph. Ashley wasn't lying when she said the website was going to bring me more business than ever. Because of the increase in business, I had to hire them to help with production.

The booth at the Farmers Market was another thing I had to put my foot down with Joseph. He hadn't liked the idea of me having a booth, thinking I would work the weekends again, but when I mentioned that the girls wanted to do it, and that I would allow them to keep the profits of the sales from that day, he couldn't argue. Military families didn't make a lot of money, especially being that both their husbands were lower ranking Marines compared to Joseph, so every extra penny they can earn really helped.

Soon we find Josephina, of course at the booth with Missy, but at Missy's insistence we leave her behind. I couldn't argue, I agreed with Missy, Josephina would be best with her instead of having to endure watching her mother giving birth. An hour later I'm at the hospital with Joseph at my side, another strong contraction hitting me, making me squeeze his hand tightly, and hunch forward in my bed. Grabbing onto my stomach as I groan out loud, I hear Joseph yelling at the nurses again.

"Will someone get the fucking *doctor,* my wife is in pain here!" His growls echo in the room as he shouts at the top of his lungs at the nurse who is currently checking my cervix.

Looking down at her in fear she might call security on him for shouting at her, she simply smiles at him when she says, "Mr. Mitchell, it's too late for your wife to get an epidural. She's already dilated to ten and the baby is starting to crown. I'll page the doctor so he can come deliver your baby," she calmly states as she removes her gloves and tosses them into the trash, walking out of the door.

I'm instantly hit with another contraction, bracing myself as I breathe through it. Once it's over, I lean my body against Joseph's as he pushes my loose hair off my forehead, placing a kiss against it. My body already feels exhausted and I haven't even started pushing, yet.

When I look up at him, I see tears falling down his face. "Honey, why are you crying?" I ask him.

A tear drops onto my hand when I reach up to cup his face, forcing him to face me. It saddens me to see him this way.

"Baby, I'm so sorry I wasn't there when you had Josephina. I should've searched the ends of the earth for you. I don't know how the fuck you're able to go through this pain again for me. I don't deserve it and I don't deserve you," he says, making me cry now.

"Joseph, we can't change the past, all that matters is we found each other again. What's important is you're here with me *this time*," I whisper up to him.

Another contraction comes and this is the one that tells me the baby is coming, I can feel it. I'm about to panic thinking the baby is going to come without the doctor, but he is walking in as the thought crosses my mind. Three painful pushes later our baby is delivered into the world. When they hand me my son I see this little bundle of joy in my arms, I know all the pain I endured was worth every second for this little person. Just like the first time. Looking up at Joseph, he's still crying, but this time with a smile of his face as he cradles my body against his chest, holding our son's head in his large hand as he leans down to give me a kiss. I hold him there for several seconds, wanting him to understand how much I love him. He brings his forehead to mine as he says, "Thank you, Kasey. Thank you so much for my children. They are the best gift you've ever given me."

I smile back at him. "I love you, Joseph."

"I love you more, Kasey Mitchell, and I will love you until the day I take my last breath."

Joseph gives me one more kiss before looking down at our son. "So what should we name him?"

We hadn't chosen any names because we didn't know the sex of the baby. I'd wanted it to be a surprise, like the first time, and although I didn't know what I was having, I secretly had a name chosen since the day I found out I was pregnant.

I look down at him to say. "Edward. Edward Joseph

Mitchell."

Joseph chuckles above me as he rakes his finger across our son's forehead. "You really like my name don't you?" he asks, trying to keep his deep voice to a whisper to not awaken our now sleeping son.

The only answer I can give him is, "It's the name of the first person I fell in love with. So I think it's only fair I name my child after that person," I say, looking down at our son.

Joseph places a kiss on my head, pulling me tighter against his chest as I close my eyes, letting the exhaustion take over me. As I slowly drift off into sleep, I can only think of how lucky I am to have found Joseph again.

The End

Read on to enjoy a sample chapter of
Gabbie S. Duran's debut novel,

Unspoken Memories

Available now!

Chapter 1

I CAN HEAR voices, two to be exact, a man and a woman. They're speaking quietly, but loudly enough that I can clearly make out their conversation. I can't open my eyes, no matter how hard I try, and they feel heavy, so I keep them closed.

"I can't leave her, she's our money ticket!" he says in a very stressed tone.

"How much good is she to you now? She's in a coma! We don't know if she's ever going to wake up." This comes from the woman, and from the way she says it, I know she isn't happy.

"Well, it doesn't matter, I need a little more time to try to figure out how to access the rest of the funds. The longer she's in this coma, the more time is on my side, and the more money we get."

Okay, this is where the conversation is getting really interesting to me. At this point I'm trying hard to open my eyes, but I keep getting pulled somewhere else, back into the darkness. My gut feeling is telling me keep my eyes closed and keep listening, so that's what I'm trying to do, I'm fighting the pull that wants to take me away.

"Well, I'm tired of being your fuck buddy, I want more!" she demands of him in a very loud whisper.

Fuck buddy? Why is she being a fuck buddy, and whose? But by the way she tells him this, I have a feeling that she's been his fuck buddy for a while.

"Look, when we started this you knew to never expect more, but if she's going to be a vegetable for a while, I'm thinking things are going to change very soon."

This doesn't sound good. I start to freak out, especially since I feel like a vegetable right now. No matter how hard I'm trying, I can't move a muscle. I wonder, are they speaking about me?

The room suddenly grows quiet, and I start to hear footsteps fading in the distance. I believe they're leaving, because I hear the opening and closing of a door.

I give it a couple of seconds, but the room is still silent. I can finally relax. Then all of a sudden, the darkness begins to take over again.

I FEEL MYSELF slowly waking up again and I let out a light moan. I can feel the grumble of it traveling down my chest, and it aches. I feel so groggy and weak. I don't want to wake up, but my body is not allowing me to fall back asleep and I try to slowly open my eyes. It's hard at first, but after a couple of blinks, I'm successful at bringing them to a slit. My body is aching as I try to lift my arm. It feels like weights are holding it down, but I'm able to move my hand, I think.

What is that sound? It's a constant beeping, coming from the side of my head, and it's speeding up as I move in that direction. I try to lift my arm to get to it, with little success because there's something tugging at it. When I look down, I see an I.V. attached to my arm, why would I have an I.V.? I attempt to completely open my eyes. I see an older lady who is wearing nurse's scrubs walking towards me. She must have done something, because the loud beeping is finally gone. It was making my head hurt, so I'm grateful she finally made the thing shut up.

"Good, you're awake," I hear her say next to me.

I feel her warm hand grab onto my wrist while she looks down at a watch she is wearing. I'm still confused. I have no idea where I am.

I manage to move my head a little and take in my surroundings. It looks like I'm in a hospital room. It's white, and almost empty, with only a couple of chairs in each corner. There's a flat screen on the wall directly in front of me, with a clock to its side, stating it's almost six. Underneath the clock there's a white board with writing on it. I guess my nurse's name is Karen, since that's the name on the board.

"How are you feeling Ms. Adams?" Karen says, still focusing on her watch.

I lie there wondering why I'm even here, and how did I get here? Wait, what did she call me? Is it my name? It doesn't sound familiar.

I have no clue where in the world I am and I don't like it.

"Where am I?" I ask Karen, wondering why I would be in a hospital room.

She looks up from her watch, with a blank face. "You're at Washington Memorial Hospital, Ms. Adams." Then she goes back to looking at her watch.

I'm still confused, why is she calling *me* that name? "Who's Ms. Adams?" I ask her, confused.

She lightly snaps her head up again to look down at me, and draws in her eyebrows. Her smile has disappeared and goes directly to a frown. "Why, you are, of course," she informs me.

She places my wrist down back on the bed, patting it lightly. "I'll just page your neurologist and we'll go from there, okay?" she says as she turns and walks out of the room, leaving me there still baffled by the whole situation.

A couple of minutes later, another lady walks into the room. I'm assuming she is my doctor because she's wearing a white coat. She looks Indian and young. But as she's walking in she has a smile on her face and it gives me a bit of hope.

A bit.

"Ms. Adams, I'm Dr. Kumar, your neurologist. How are you feeling, dear?" she enthusiastically asks me, while swiftly grabbing my chart, opening it, and beginning to review it.

Knowing the truth will never hurt, I say bluntly, "I feel like shit and I really have to pee."

This makes her laugh, as she pulls out what looks like a pen from her coat pocket, walks to the side of my bed and leans above me. I realize it's a flashlight as she starts flashing it back and forth between my eyes, making me flinch. It burns my eyes and if my arms didn't feel so weak, I would have swatted that darn thing out of her hand.

Trust me, I try, but I quickly give up the notion. Once she's done shining the death light at me she replaces it in her coat pocket and walks to the end of my bed to pick the chart back up and starts scribbling notes into it. I lay here staring at her.

As she's still scribbling, the nurse walks in again with a

new I.V. bag and busies herself with changing it while the doctor asks me, "Ms. Adams, would you be more comfortable if I have Karen here remove your catheter so you can go to the bathroom yourself?" She is still staring down at the chart making notes.

I nod my head in agreement, but can't help asking again, "Who is Ms. Adams? You both keep calling me that name?"

The doctor quickly snaps her head up, while the nurse stops fiddling with the bag and they both stare at me in shock.

The doctor immediately looks at the nurse. "Call her fiancé, and order a CAT scan STAT." Then she looks down at me and says, "We'll just order some more tests to make sure there isn't any swelling remaining and go from there, okay?" She finishes with a smile.

Still very confused about what is going on, I nod my head in acceptance and hope that I'll remember something in a couple of minutes. Right now the only thing I keep thinking about is the conversation I heard earlier. Or I think it was earlier. I really have no idea when it took place. It almost feels like it only happened a couple of minutes ago and I'm really anxious to find out who was in my room. But more than anything I still have to pee.

My thoughts must have taken me away for a couple of minutes because the nurse has managed to remove my catheter and with a lot of assistance, I'm able to sit up on the bed. At first my body is wobbly and unbalanced, but after a few minutes I find the strength I am searching for and make my merry way along, holding onto the nurse for dear life. The metal stand holding the I.V. bag follows me the whole way.

It's hard to walk when you have something attached to your arm following you around. After the first tug at my arm, I want to yank the thing out myself. However, the nurse keeps saying I have to leave it in, since it is providing me with the fluids to increase my health.

That is the only reason it stays in.

After some major maneuvering, again with the nurse's help, I'm finally able to relieve myself in the attached bathroom. I can't go at first, knowing she is standing there staring at me. But even after asking her for some privacy, she only moves to the doorframe of the bathroom.

Finishing up what I needed to do, and washing my hands, I take a moment to stand in front of the mirror and stare at my reflection. Other than needing to take a brush to my hair, I look perfectly fine.

Or at least I think I do for someone who is in the hospital.

Actually, I don't recognize myself at all. You would think that I would at least recognize my reflection, but it doesn't come to me. So I stand there staring at myself and take in my features.

My hair is blonde, very long, and my eyes are a very bright green. I'm also tall. I remember being at least half a foot taller than the nurse, towering over her a bit. Another noticeable thing is that I'm very skinny. Don't I ever eat?

When I hear the nurse knock on the bathroom door making sure that I'm still okay, it distracts me from my thoughts, also reminding me that we have to go get my CAT scan done right away. I exit the bathroom and allow her to lead me to the bed, laying me back down.

An hour later, after being put through a cocoon-like machine, as I'm being wheeled toward my room, I see a man rushing in my direction. He's practically running when he walks and he looks exhausted. I don't know who this man is, but by the way he's looking straight at me and still walking in my direction, he knows me.

He looks to be in his mid-thirties and he's wearing an expensive looking suit. He's lean, and tall, but not too tall. He has disheveled black hair, as if he's been running his hands through it. He has stress lines around his face, but at this moment his face is lit up and he's happy to see me.

"Oh honey, you're finally awake, I've been so worried about you," he says as he reaches me, giving me a kiss on my forehead. I'm really confused about who he is because I don't recognize him. But when my mind takes in his voice, realizing that it sounds very familiar, I panic.

If I were still hooked up to the monitor at this moment I'm pretty sure it would be making the crazy noises from earlier, because my heart rate is going crazy. First it feels like it had stopped, and now it's accelerating because I'm freaking out.

This is the voice, the male voice I heard the last time I heard anything, but he's alone this time. I immediately start looking around, thinking about the other mystery voice, the one that belongs to the woman, expecting to hear it any minute. But I don't.

He follows, as the nurse continues to push me back into my room and once we're all in the room, he starts attacking the doctor and nurse with different questions. There are so many, it's even confusing to me. Although the most important one is how much longer I'm going to be here now that I've woken up. That particular question is the one I care about the most, because I'm pretty sure when I leave here I don't want it to be with this guy. The uncomfortable feeling I'm getting from him is not making me feel good.

I keep staring at the guy, hoping that I would recognize him somehow, but I can't. He seems worried about me, so obviously he must be someone important. However, I think about the ominous conversation that took place that included his voice.

Wanting to know who he is, I demand, "Who are you?" I say out loud, looking directly at him.

He snaps his head to look at me and he's disoriented, like I just asked the stupidest question in the world. At this point it sounds pretty stupid to me too, but I really need to know who this stranger is.

He frowns, bringing his lips into a flat line, and finally he says, "I'm Bill, your fiancé."

Now I'm screwed, I think. I'm pretty sure that this was the voice I heard with the woman the last time I tried waking up. But, why would my fiancé be someone else's fuck buddy? I don't understand. Right now my life is starting to feel like some kind of soap opera and I'm obviously the starring actress.

They're all still looking at me, as if they're waiting for me to say something.

"Abigail, are you sure you're feeling okay?"

If my throat weren't hurting so much, I would be saying right now: *No you dumb ass, I just woke up, my body feels like shit, and you guys keep calling me a name I don't recognize.*

Another thing to add to the list is that I don't trust them! But I keep my mouth shut knowing this is the best thing to do. However, I ask again, knowing that I still need an answer. "Who's Abigail?"

Ignoring my question, Bill turns to the doctor. "What's wrong with her, why doesn't she know who she is?" he demands, pointing his hand in my direction.

Looking perplexed over the whole situation herself, she answers him, "She seems to have had a bit of a memory loss." The doctor gives him a calming look like this is normal. "She may just need time to recover properly; it can happen with patients in her situation."

Shaking his head, Bill grabs the bridge of his nose with his thumb and forefinger, sighing to himself. He's still quiet, like he's concentrating on what he's going to say next. I think he's still shocked.

I hate that they won't give me any detailed answers.

"What happened to me?" I ask, looking between Bill and the doctor.

Everybody is looking at me, still very uncertain whether to tell me or not.

Bill walks up to my bedside, taking one of my hands into his, and drops his head, looking gently at my face.

He takes a breath and begins, "A friend of ours was having a party at a hotel downtown, and as usual we had a room there so you could get ready. As we were waiting for the elevator to go down to the party, you became impatient, and decided to take the stairs instead. You were wearing some really high heels and lost your footing on one of the steps and hit your head pretty badly on the way down." He pauses like he's concentrating on what to say next, then carries on, "When you arrived at the hospital you had some really bad swelling in your brain, so the doctor here suggested that we put you in an induced coma."

I'm trying to absorb all the information he's just given me, then I look over to the doctor, still really confused about the whole situation.

"How long have I been in a coma?" I whisper, staring at the wall ahead of me, holding back the tears that are fighting to come out.

She looks to Bill first, then directly back at me answering, "It's been a little over four months since the swelling in your brain reduced and we reversed the medication. You didn't wake up right away," she calmly states, as if reassuring me everything is fine.

I look over in Bill's direction and ask again, "Who are you?" I want confirmation.

He's now starting to look irritated by my question, but he responds again. "I'm Bill, your fiancé, baby."

His answer still throws me for loop and I panic a little.

Why would my fiancé want me to stay in a coma? He had looked relieved to see me awake, but I keep replaying the conversation in my head, wanting to doubt it. I know what I heard. It was loud and clear, even if my eyes weren't open.

Another thing that comes to mind, is why does he have someone else as a fuck buddy?

My panic is obvious to Bill, so he says, "We've been together for over a year now. We met at one of your shows over two years ago when I became your agent and we started dating a little while later. It was love at first sight for me." He tries to reassure me with a smile. But I'm not buying it.

I look over at the doctor with a look like, "Please tell me he's kidding." From the way she's looking at me, I know she believes his story. Bill looks up to the doctor and begins asking how soon I'll be able to go home.

While she goes over the lecture about needing my rest before leaving, I block out their bickering at each other.

This is when I start reciting a number in my head, 951-555-2945. It comes to me naturally, like I've called it regularly.

That's weird, why would I be thinking of a phone number at this moment? I'm happy that at least something is coming back to me.

"Bill, what's your number?" I ask, loud enough so they both can hear me.

They both snap their heads in my direction in confusion for asking such a question, but Bill automatically answers. "555-6213, why?"

Mmm, not the answer I was expecting, so I try again, "Is there any other number I would call you at?"

I must have excited the doctor because her face is beaming. "Are you remembering something Abigail? Whatever it is, it might help. What is it you remember?"

Bill looks excited as well, but knowing that it isn't his number, I just fib. "I thought I remembered, but it was only a glimpse of an area code, then it disappeared." I lie to both of them, keeping the number to myself.

"By the way, what is the area code here?"

The doctor is the first to speak up, "206."

That is definitely not the area code I'm remembering. They're both still patiently waiting for me to say something, so I answer with the only excuse that I can think of at the moment. "That's why I asked Bill to recite his number hoping it would spark something, but I was wrong... I'm sorry." I look at them, disappointed.

Seeming just as irritated about the whole situation, Bill turns to the doctor, barks at her to order more tests, wanting to know why I've lost my memory.

The neurologist decides to steer the conversation by saying, "Although she has a bit of a memory loss, she might get it back in time, especially once she goes home and begins to see things more familiar to her. Give her time; she's just woken up," she says before her lips go into a frown of disappointment as well.

"Then how soon can she go home so she can start remembering?" he barks at her, making me flinch from the anger in his tone.

He turns to me and with a nicer voice says, "Baby, your name is Abigail Adams. You're a famous model. Is it ringing a bell?" he questions with desperation.

I shake my head and pick at the imaginary lint on my blankets. The name doesn't ring a bell at all. I want it to, but it doesn't.

Bill notices my lack of response and begins fumbling with his phone like he's looking for something and once he's found it he brings the phone close to my face for me to look into the screen. On it is a photo of myself with a whole bunch of make-up, and I'm half-naked.

"See, that's you at your last photo shoot, it's for *Vogue*!" he says with enthusiasm. "Of course you know who you are, you're legendary since this cover came out." The phone is still in front of my face as if he expects the light bulb to turn on in my head.

When I shake my head at him he only sighs again, clearly disappointed. I think I'm really beginning to irritate him.

He moves to the corner of the room dragging the doctor with him, by the arm, and in hushed tones he begins speaking with her. The nurse walks in at this moment saving me from having to look at both of them, knowing that they are discussing me and leaving me out of the conversation. The nurse entertains herself by fluffing my pillows, in an effort to make me more comfortable, but I know she's really just trying to be nice about the whole situation.

They both stop talking and look over in my direction and he smiles. The only trouble is that his smile is worrying me and I want it to go away. It's the type of smile meant to reassure me that everything is okay, when in reality it's not.

Knowing the situation is not going to get any better until my memory comes back, I bring up the excuse that I'm tired so they will leave me alone. Right now I want to be alone and sleep. My body feels drained, even though I just woke up a couple of hours ago. What I really want is for Bill to leave, so whatever excuse I can give them to make him leave works for me.

They all leave me to get my rest and as I'm left alone with my thoughts. I wonder again if I'm wrong about Bill. I keep trying to convince myself that maybe it was someone else, or maybe I had dreamt the whole conversation. I begin to get drowsy and my eyelids start to feel heavy, dragging me into sleep once again.

In my dream, I feel happy, and I see this guy who's laughing with me.

He's young, early twenties, good looking, and really fit. He's taller than me, enough so that I have to look up at him. He has a narrow looking face, his hair is a dark color, with dark chocolate brown eyes, and thick lashes that are long, curl, and make you jealous that he has them. But what really catches my attention is his smile. He has a smile that just makes you melt inside and it makes you smile with him. He's all sweaty and I note that he looks like he just finished working out. Or has done something that has made him breathe really fast and heavy. His shirt is soaked and he's chugging water from a water bottle like he's dying of thirst. I look at my surroundings and notice that we are in a park, at the end of what I think is a trail, and in the background there are a lot of tall trees. He then throws his arm around my shoulders and says, "Keep up that pace and we're definitely going to PR this race."

What race and what PR event is he talking about? My dream begins to fade away, and I'm trying really hard to ask him what's going on, or who he is?

Unfortunately, I can't get the words out of my mouth. I want to know his name, but he quickly fades away.

As I open my eyes, I notice it's morning again, with the light coming in through my hospital room window and a new nurse is taking my blood pressure, which is what must have woken me up.

Now that I'm awake, I take the time to focus on trying to bring back some type of memory. When the nurse sees that I'm awake, she informs me that Bill came by early this morning while I was still sleeping and dropped off my stuff.

I turn my head and notice an iPad on the side table and I reach over and grab it. Wanting answers fast, I start to Google my name, "Abigail Adams." Right away all kinds of articles and images come up.

According to the Internet, I'm not a world famous model, but I am in high demand in the states. Thanks to my current fiancé, slash agent and manager, I was on the way to becoming the most highly sought after model in recent history. Before my accident, I had wrapped up an interview and photo shoot with *Vogue* that was going to get me those international shoots I was working towards.

I was born in Seattle, but raised in the foster system. My mother died when I was twelve, leaving me to be raised by the state in different foster homes until I was discovered at the age of eighteen. I had begun with small photo shoots for a local agency that kept me financially above water for a couple of years, until I met Bill, making him my current agent and manager.

On the Internet there were a ton of pictures of me, some from different interviews, photo shoots, or pictures that must have been taken by paparazzi when I was out and about. There were so many, it's almost like I wanted to be constantly photographed or spoken to, which feels a bit disturbing.

After reading a couple of articles and flipping through what seems like thousands of photos, I feel even more confused than when I started. The only thing it's proven to me is that I was a shallow and conceited person who only cared about herself. For some reason this makes me feel like crap.

After sitting in my room for most of the day, I notice that I start to feel jittery and stressed. Eventually, I start twitching my leg, swinging my foot back and forth and feeling trapped like I want to get out and do something. It is driving me crazy.

I blame it on being immobile for so long.

On this second day since I've woken up, the doctor is in my room giving me my routine daily check-up. Bill showed up this morning, but most of the time he's on the phone barking commands at someone about a deal that he's trying to close. He's been coming to visit me as often as he can, but I have a feeling that he'd rather be at his office than with me.

He claims that he is really busy at work, but that he misses me badly and wished that he could spend every waking hour with me, but I doubt it. It takes all of my willpower not to roll my eyes at his response. Even when he kissed me that first day, it didn't feel right. There was no emotion in it on my part. As if to confirm that my body didn't really know him. It had worried me, but I had made it a point to Bill that I just needed time and space, giving him an excuse to stay at a distance.

Before I could even allow him to think things were back to normal, I had to figure out what normal was.

Acknowledgments

To my husband and children for putting up with my grouchy attitude during this journey, it was a tough one, but I wouldn't change it for the world. You stood by me during my frustration and I love you so much for that.

To my blue box girl's aka BBG, who are all in the same box with me:

Juliana Cabrera, who puts up with my crazy demands, my never ending change of decisions, and plea to let me do things. You're always there on the other end of a phone call to listen and give reason. Thank you so much for everything you do and continue to do for me. I'll take the curse words with a smile, because at the end of the day I know you really meant to say, I love you.

Cezanne Dilbert, you are my right hand girl who does everything that needs to be done without me having to ask. I'm so glad you won. It'll be a crazy ride from here on out, but I know you'll be at my side, no matter what.

Yamara Martinez, it started with a simple postcard, which turned into helping C take over my world. Without you, I wouldn't know where to go. Thank you for directing me in the right direction.

Lisa Ravenscroft, aka my Lisa, you're my grammar Nazi, always there to remind me why I do this, why it's worth it, and who I will one day be. Without your lectures, I would have probably given up a long time ago. Thank you.

I wake up saying good morning to these ladies and can't fall asleep without saying goodnight to them every... single... day. Without them, my day wouldn't be complete. They are my voice of reasons, my free therapy, and my bitches that support me, no matter what I decide. I can't imagine my life without them and hope I never have to.

To Edee Fallon, it would take me forever to explain in words why you're *my heroine*, so I won't, but know that you are. Thank you for salvaging *With Me.*

A huge, thank you to my fresh pair of eyes: Lisa Ravencroft, Cezanne Dilbert, Yamara Martinez, Janett Gomez, Rebecca Marie, and Colette Noak. You helped "With Me" sound perfect.

Julie Titus, who makes my words beautiful, and puts up with my never-ending delays, I swear I'll get better with time.

Last, but not least, to all the betas, readers, and bloggers who took the time to read With Me. Without you I wouldn't have a reason to write. Thank you from the bottom of my heart.

For more information about Gabbie
and her books, visit:

GOODREADS

http://www.goodreads.com/author/show/7093957.Gabbie_S_D
uran

FACEBOOK

https://www.facebook.com/authorgabbiesduran

TWITTER

https://twitter.com/gabbiesduran